LOSING LIZZY

A Pride and Prejudice Vagary

by
Regina Jeffers

Regency Solutions

Copyright ©2020 by Regina Jeffers
Cover Image "Virgin Queen" from AJ Dane Gayosa
Cover Design and Interior Design from Sarah Callaham at SKC Design
All Rights Reserved

This is a work of fiction. Names, places, characters and incidents are either the product of the author's imagination or are used fictitiously, and any resemblance to any actual persons, living or dead, businesses, organizations, events or locales is entirely coincidental. All trademarks, service marks, registered trademarks, and registered service marks are the property of their respective owners and are used herein for identification purposes only. The publisher does not have any control over or assume any responsibility for author or third-party websites or their contents.

All rights Reserved under International and Pan-American Copyright Conventions. No part of this book may be used or reproduced, transmitted, downloaded, decompiled, reverse engineered, or stored in or introduced into any information storage and retrieval system, in any form or by any means whether electronic or mechanical, including photocopying, recording, etc., now known or hereinafter invented without the written permission from the author and copyright owner except in the case of brief quotation embodied in critical articles and reviews.
WARNING: The unauthorized reproduction or distribution of this copyrighted work is illegal. Criminal copyright infringement, including infringement without monetary gain, is investigated by the FBI and is punishable by up to 5 years in federal prison and a fine of $250,000. Anyone pirating ebooks will be prosecuted to the fullest extent of the law and may be liable for each individual download resulting there from.

ABOUT THE PRINT VERSION: If you purchased a print version of this book without a cover, you should be aware that the book is stolen property. It was reported as "unsold and destroyed" to the publisher, and neither the author nor the publisher has received any payment for this "stripped book."

IF YOU FIND AN EBOOK OR PRINT VERSION OF THIS BOOK BEING SOLD OR SHARED ILLEGALLY, PLEASE REPORT IT. By payment of required fees, the purchaser has been granted the non-exclusive, non-transferable right to access and read the text of this eBook. The reverse engineering, uploading, and/or distributing of this eBook via the internet or via any other means without the permission of the copyright owner is illegal and punishable by law. Please purchase only authorized electronic editions and do not participate in or encourage electronic piracy of copyrighted materials. Your support of the author's rights is appreciated.

LOSING LIZZY

by
Regina Jeffers

Regency Solutions

CHAPTER ONE

3 August 1816

"England," Darcy whispered. "Home." He had stood along the rail of the ship most of the night, waiting for this very moment. "Elizabeth," he murmured. Was there any chance she would welcome his return? He doubted it, for whether his actions had been intentional or not, he had ruined her. Although no fault of his own, he had left her at the altar, never making an appearance on their wedding day. Society, by now, had presented her with various names: a jilt, a tease, a fallen woman, thinking he had not stood up with her for their nuptials because he had discovered her free with her attentions to other men, when he knew, without a doubt, she had been a virgin, for it was he with whom Elizabeth Bennet had lain for the first time.

"One evening," he groaned as the memory of her resting beneath him in all her exquisite glory—a look of pure wonderment marking her countenance—filled his mind. It was the one memory that had sustained him during his long ordeal upon *The Lost Sparrow*.

Three years. Eight months. Two and twenty days.

He had not known the exact count, although he had made rudimentary calculations when he had first been taken aboard *The Lost Sparrow*, but over the days and months and years of his long imprisonment, he had lost count. It was only when the ship—a British frigate—had fished him from the icy waters of the Atlantic that he had been made aware of the number of days he had lost with Elizabeth at his side.

For the years of his imprisonment, any time *The Lost Sparrow* came into port, he had been confined in the hole, chained to the inside of the ship, for the captain and the crew knew he was hell-bent upon returning to his family. "Just consider," he said in a voice barely above a whisper, "I have not set foot on dry land since long before the war with the French knew an end." He was not certain his legs would cooperate; yet, Darcy was determined to reach Darcy House as quickly as his rolling gait would carry him.

"Your family will know surprise with your return," Captain Robert Bruester said as he joined Darcy at the railing.

"I imagine so."

Bruester and Lieutenant Wilder had both spent their years at university with Darcy. Thankfully, Wilder had been on the deck of *The Resolution* when Darcy had made his swim to safety.

The Resolution had been spotted early on by those in the crow's nest of *The Lost Sparrow*, and the pirate ship and its crew had claimed the cover of an island's sheltered cove. From there, they had watched the slow progress of *The Resolution*, debating on whether to engage the ship or let it pass without notice.

For Darcy, the vigil had renewed his hope of escaping his ordeal. "Ironic," he had thought the words without saying them aloud. "Historically, an 'ordeal' was an ancient test of guilt or blamelessness brought about by subjecting the accused to severe pain. The accused's survival was taken as divine proof of his innocence. I wonder how others will judge me, for I hold my suspicions, and I know how I will judge those who acted against me."

After so long a time upon the ship, neither the crew nor *The Lost Sparrow*'s captain had considered him anything other than one of them, although they never permitted him to be a part of those who plundered other ships. Evidently, they were either ordered to keep him away from others or they had come up with the scheme themselves. In truth, he was not certain how it all came about. He was, however, assigned much of the labor on the ship from scrubbing to repairs. Because he could read and write and perform his sums, he had often been tasked with dividing up the booty confiscated from the crew's various skirmishes. Therefore, on this evening, no one noticed he had become one of those on deck to keep an eye on the British ship's maneuverings.

With each breaking of water from the frigate's approach, Darcy estimated whether he could swim out far enough to reach it without the notice of those aboard *The Lost Sparrow*. As night fell, he had hidden below the stairs leading to the hole. Everyone remained eager to learn that the frigate had moved on; so, no one had checked on his whereabouts. No alarms had been raised. No lanterns lit to allow those on watch to take notice of him in the dark shadows waiting for the perfect moment to stage his escape. Among those in charge, it had been decided that they would permit *The Resolution* to pass them by, for the British ship sported eight and thirty guns, and *The Lost Sparrow* had but twelve.

Hence, with a dark ship, the crew of *The Lost Sparrow* sat in silence as Darcy's chance at freedom slipped away. A frigate could easily cover twelve knots with a good wind, and if it kept moving away, he would never reach it in time. Finally, the British Navy brought in their sails and also settled in for the night. With a grumble of displeasure, *The Lost Sparrow*'s captain left men on deck to sound the alarm, if necessary, and sent the others to their beds. With only a handful of men remaining on deck, Darcy had shored up his courage and had sneaked from his hiding place. He had spent nearly four years of his life walking the boards of *The Lost Sparrow*. He knew every squeak and nail. Barefooted, he had eased himself over the railing and down the ladder, quietly slipping into the water. Treading to stay afloat, his heart pounded so hard he was certain someone on board would hear it, but no one on *The Lost Sparrow* had sent up a cry. Grabbing his chance at freedom, he reached out and cupped the water with one hand to pull his body forward. Then, slowly and quietly, he repeated the motion. Easy stroke after easy stroke. *Nothing frantic*, he warned himself over and over. *Slow and steady until you are away from the ship and the crew's hearing. One stroke at a time. One stroke closer to freedom and Elizabeth.*

Within minutes, he reached the island. Pulling himself from the water, he had stumbled forward. The exercise had been harder than he had expected, for it had been too many years since he had gone for a swim for his body to recall the movement without his concentration. As he suspected, when he attempted to stand and to take a step on the beach, his legs wobbled, giving him the appearance of being drunk or being a new foaled horse; yet, he made himself fight his way through the vegetation. The rocks cut his feet, and the branches slapped him across the face; however, he did not falter — refused to surrender, for this was the only opportunity he had been presented in the nearly four years he had been on *The Lost Sparrow*.

The island was only a narrow strip of land, not much wider than some of the parks in London. He kept telling himself, "If I can make it to the other side without being seen by someone aboard the ship, I can swim to where the British frigate has chosen to sleep for the night."

When he finally burst through the scraggy trees to the other side of the island, Darcy bent over long enough to recover his breath. He looked back toward where he had come. The trees were not so dense as he had first thought. He could be seen if someone on *The Lost Sparrow* turned to look his way.

"Now or never," he declared. "I cannot go back. I must either return to Georgiana and Elizabeth or die in the sea. I can wait no longer for another opportunity to show itself."

<hr />

Even after reaching England, it had taken them another two days to maneuver up the Thames and dock in London. In all, he had spent three weeks with the crew of *The Resolution*, an appropriate name for a ship that brought about an ending to his ordeal, who, once they had retrieved him from the water and had heard his tale, had altered their course to trap those on *The Lost Sparrow* in the cove before the pirates could respond. They may have made it to England sooner if they were not required to tow *The Lost Sparrow* into port, but Darcy knew satisfaction when he finally stepped down on the docks in London, where his nightmare had begun. The clothes he wore had been borrowed from various members of *The Resolution*'s crew. They were ill-fitting, but so much more than the rags he had known since being pressed into service on *The Lost Sparrow*.

Wilder had hired a hackney to return Darcy to Darcy House. Now, as he stepped down before his London home, people stared at him in distaste as he approached the door and released the knocker, but Darcy made himself not turn around, concentrating all his energies on surviving the next few minutes. He knew his appearance was less than pristine, for he wore mismatched clothes several sizes too large for him. *One step at a time*—the advice from Bruester, who had heard from his parents in a letter how Lord Matlock had moved to declare Darcy as dead after the authorities had found his cane and the ring he had purchased for Elizabeth somewhere upon the docks, rattled about in Darcy's head. Therefore, he did not know what to expect when the door opened, but any preparations he had made mentally had not been enough.

"Yes, sir?" A man he did not recognize swung the door open.

"Where is Mr. Thacker?" he asked before he could stop himself.

"Mr. Thacker has taken another position, sir. That was nearly four years past." The man pulled himself up stiffly. "I am Mr. Jones. Do you have business with the master?" The man eyed Darcy's mishmash of clothing up and down and edged the door partially closed.

"The master?" Darcy asked. He knew his voice held surprise, but there was no way to control his reaction to this new reality.

"Mr. Fitzwilliam." Again, the door moved another inch closer to being slammed in Darcy's face.

Darcy employed his best Master of Pemberley voice. "Yes, I would like to speak to Mr. Fitzwilliam." The idea the Matlocks had taken over his house did not sit well with him. If he were dead, it should be Samuel Darcy residing in this house, not the colonel. His father's cousin, Samuel, was the heir to the Darcy fortune, not those in the Fitzwilliam family.

"Who is it, Jones?" a familiar voice called out from the second storey landing.

"I am not certain, sir." Jones narrowed the opening.

Darcy caught the edge of the door and gave it a good shove, sending the butler stumbling backward. "Fitzwilliam!" he called, using his shoulder to barrel his way into the foyer.

From above, he heard his cousin cry out, "What the—?"

Darcy paused from his exertion to look up. "Why are you acting as master of my house?" he demanded.

His cousin caught hard at the railing. "My God, Darcy. It is you."

"Most assuredly, it is I." He started for the stairs, but two unfamiliar footmen stepped before him. "Have you removed all who once served me?" he questioned, a scowl of disapproval forming on his features.

Fitzwilliam gestured the servants from his way. "Permit Mr. Darcy admittance," his cousin instructed. "After all, as he says, this is his house."

As Darcy climbed the stairs, never removing his eyes from his cousin, he ordered, "Mr. Jones, if you expect to retain your position, bring me a small meal and a proper cup of tea, and do so quickly."

"Yes, sir," the man called as he scrambled away.

Fitzwilliam appeared as stunned as was Darcy. There was no embrace of emotions. Only something that appeared like regret upon the colonel's features showed. "Lead on, Cousin," Darcy said through tight lips, a feeling of betrayal settling in his chest. "I am most eager to hear your explanations."

Without uttering a word, Fitzwilliam turned crisply upon his heels and preceded Darcy into the study. In anger, Darcy purposely closed the door behind them.

His cousin crossed to the tray holding a decanter of brandy. "May I pour you a drink?"

Darcy eyed the room. Subtle changes had been made in the furnishings of the room. At least all he held dear had not been set aside. "I will pass. I fear I will require a clear head to understand what has gone on in my absence."

Fitzwilliam turned toward him, his features grim. His cousin was a man Darcy had always trusted, but, now, he wondered if he had made a serious mistake in judgment. "It is not as this must first appear," his cousin pleaded. "What I have done, I did so to protect your interests and your sister."

Darcy thought to assume the chair behind the desk, but, rather, he chose the two wing chairs before the hearth. "I am willing to listen, but know, I have recently been in the company of Captain Robert Bruester, who had heard from his family that Matlock has attempted to have me declared dead."

"Bruester? I thought him at sea," Fitzwilliam remarked as he joined Darcy before the empty hearth. The colonel studied Darcy carefully.

"He was. As was I until I managed to escape the pirate ship upon which I have been held for nearly four years." He nodded to his cousin. "Was my uncle successful? Must I begin my return to the world by proving I am truly alive?"

"A pirate ship? My God, Darcy! I would never have thought you had been caught by a press gang. We assumed you had been robbed and tossed into the Thames."

Darcy held himself very stiff. "It is not that I object to making an explanation regarding my capture and my escape, but I require some answers from you first."

Fitzwilliam nodded his agreement. With a heavy sigh, he began, "We were all at sixes and sevens when you did not show at your wedding."

Darcy wished to ask of Elizabeth, but his first task was to learn where his father's legacy stood before he could inquire of Elizabeth Bennet's fate.

"What did you do?"

If Fitzwilliam had expected Darcy to ask of Elizabeth, the colonel quickly hid his curiosity. He permitted Darcy to dictate their conversation. "Georgiana and I returned to London, and I began to trace your steps. The day your sister and I departed for Netherfield, you were to retrieve Miss Elizabeth's ring from the jeweler. That is where I began."

"And you discovered?" Darcy questioned.

"Very much what I shared a moment ago. I employed the services of my friend Thomas Cowan, who you might recall was a former Bow Street Runner. He and I called upon the jeweler, whose assistant told us two men were seen following you when you exited the shop."

Darcy wished he had paid more attention on that particular day, but his head was full of memories of Elizabeth Bennet, and he belatedly realized he had not practiced caution. "Why was not an alarm raised?"

"A series of excuses, but none worth pursuing," his cousin said with a frown. "The jeweler and his assistant each blamed the other for not performing as they should have. When we departed the jeweler, Cowan suggested we search the docks and question those who were employed there. One of your tasks that day was to see to a shipment in which you and father had invested."

"That was my destination," Darcy admitted, but he listened carefully to hear what the colonel left out of his tale.

"We learned of two ships that departed the night you left the jewelers. I spoke to everyone who would share information; yet, there were no substantial leads as to your whereabouts."

Darcy remembered how the men who had caught him had struck him repeatedly until he had gone unconscious. When he finally woke up, *The Lost Sparrow* was departing the docks, but not those in London. He had been transported further down the Thames to somewhere in Kent.

Fitzwilliam continued, "Cowan located the ring and the cane in a pawn shop, and we traced the items back to the man who pawned them. He swore he found them behind some crates near the docks."

Darcy recalled throwing the ring away, hoping against hope the men only meant to rob him. He thought they might leave him be long enough for him to make an escape, but they ignored the box. They had ripped the cane from his hands as he had used it as a weapon against them and had tossed it aside also.

"There was nothing to connect him to your disappearance. If you say he was involved, I will have Cowan locate him and bring him in for questioning."

Darcy shook off the idea. "I know the identities of those involved. There were five all together. Two were killed in a skirmish with another pirate ship and the other three are presently in the custody of the British navy, along with their captain and crew mates."

"Were you never permitted on land in all those years?" Fitzwilliam asked in bewilderment.

"Not once," Darcy said in deep sorrow. "I thought, especially in the beginning, I would go mad. Only the memories of Elizabeth and Georgiana kept me alive."

"You wish to know of Miss Elizabeth's fate?" Fitzwilliam asked in sympathetic tones, which made Darcy's heart ache. How would he survive if she had married another?

"Not yet," he said solemnly. "You still have not spoken to me of the earl's efforts to declare me dead nor why you are at Darcy House rather than my father's cousin, Samuel Darcy?"

Fitzwilliam shifted his weight uncomfortably. "In truth, I do not know what Matlock hoped to achieve. I suppose Aunt Catherine managed to harangue him into action. Initially, Lady Catherine appeared pleased you had not married Miss Elizabeth, declaring for one and all that you had come to your senses and meant to marry Anne after a proper period — time for the gossip to die away. However, when we could discover no evidence of your purposeful absence, her ladyship scolded the earl into securing the Darcy fortune before someone swept in and married Georgiana, essentially taking hold of all your holdings. It was determined my brother Lindale would be Georgiana's groom."

"Lindale?" Darcy knew he frowned, but this conversation could bring no other emotions beyond pure anger. "Why would

Matlock think to turn over my father's holdings? Has not Matlock always feared that Roland Fitzwilliam would ruin the earldom with his profligate ways?"

"Aye," Fitzwilliam confirmed. "The plan was for me to marry Anne and Lindale to marry Georgiana, solidifying both family fortunes."

Darcy did not approve of how his relations had worked against him. "And declaring me dead would make the transition easier?" Darcy thought, *"And make the Fitzwilliams richer, for what my father left me was nearly five times what the Fitzwilliam factions know, and that does not take into account what I have added since assuming Pemberley's realm."*

His cousin nodded his affirmation of Darcy's assumption.

"I pray you put a stop to this madness. You are, after all, also Georgiana's guardian. You would know my thoughts upon such a joining."

Again, Fitzwilliam appeared uncomfortable with Darcy's words. "I fought the good fight, making certain the law would not turn over the Darcy assets to my father or Roland. Not being able to locate Samuel Darcy was both a blessing and a curse in this matter. Thankfully, your father's will is very specific on the inheritance."

Darcy's high dudgeon eased somewhat. "I thank you for your care of Georgiana and my father's legacy. I realize standing against your family placed you in a tenuous situation."

Fitzwilliam took a large swallow of the brandy before setting the glass aside. "You may not wish to offer your gratitude so quickly."

Darcy scowled, but before he could ask the question rushing to his lips, the door swung wide to bang against the wainscoting along the wall. "Tell me it is true!"

Darcy scrambled to his feet as quickly as his sea legs would permit to turn to face his sister standing in the open door. She was pale and swayed in place when her eyes landed upon his countenance. Immediately, Fitzwilliam was across the room to steady her.

"William?" her lips moved, but no sound could be heard.

"I have returned, my girl," he said as he made his way to her.

Then, she launched herself into his arms, nearly sending them both to the ground. However, Darcy locked his knees in place and absorbed the impact. Tears of what he assumed were joy dampened the coarse fabric of his borrowed shirt.

"All is well, Georgie," he whispered close to her ear. "I am home, and I will see all is set right. I am grieved you suffered in my absence. Just know you were never far from my thoughts, and if I could have returned to you quicker than I did, I would have claimed that opportunity. It was not my choice to leave you."

"Where?" she managed to ask on a hiccup.

"It is a long tale," he said softly. "The short of it: a press gang removed me from London."

"Come, my dear," Fitzwilliam said from somewhere off Darcy's shoulder. "There is more than enough time for Darcy to explain it all. I do not want you to become upset. Think of the child."

It was only then that Darcy realized his svelte sister was pleasingly plump. He leaned back to look upon her more fully. "You are with child," he stated in awe. Looking to his cousin, he said, "I thought you indicated you had thwarted Matlock's plans to marry Georgiana off to Lindale."

His cousin led Georgiana to a nearby settee and supported her to the seat. Standing tall again, he settled a steady gaze upon Darcy. "I did thwart the earl's plans by marrying Georgiana myself. We married a little over a year ago, and our first child will be born sometime in the next month. If the child is a male, he will be your heir presumptive, replacing Samuel Darcy, until you choose to marry and produce an heir of your own."

CHAPTER TWO

To say his cousin's announcement had left Darcy momentarily thunderstruck would have been an understatement. At length, he moved a chair closer to Georgiana and sat. "Tell me this was your wish," he said, ignoring his cousin's very large presence in the room.

Then his sister did what he had never thought to see her do: She comforted him. "I am excessively happy with Edward. And you should know how much our cousin gave up to protect me. His career. His family. How could you ask for more in a husband for me? For more than two years, the colonel staved off each maneuver Lord Matlock and Lady Catherine placed in my path, while still serving our country. We discussed what to do: He and I decided this was best for both of us. We thought you would want both of us to be happy, and we are. Papa would have approved, William. You know he would."

Tears had filled his eyes and hers. "You are correct. The deed is done, and I could have come home to find a complete stranger installed in my house as your husband." He reached across the space to pat the back of her hand in reassurance. "It will simply take me a bit of time to adjust my thinking. In my mind, you were still to be my sixteen-year-old younger sister. However, now that I think upon it, you will celebrate your twentieth birthday soon. It grieves me I lost those years where you blossomed into an extraordinary young woman. I am assuming you were not permitted a Come Out."

Georgiana shook off the idea. "I was never expected to take well anyway. You know how shy I am around new people, and, although Lady Matlock offered to bring me out, I kept telling everyone I could not think of marriage until I knew something of your fate." Darcy had hoped his marriage to Elizabeth would have aided Georgiana's Come Out. Elizabeth would have been more than his wife: She would have been Georgiana's elder sister, a woman who could have guided his sister through the intricacies of Society's many whims and provided Georgiana the confidence to shine.

Darcy looked again upon his cousin. "I have much to learn of what has occurred in my absence, but it appears I am deeper in your debt, sir."

Georgiana motioned the colonel to sit beside her. Then she asked what Darcy knew she would. "Please. I must know what happened to you."

Darcy provided them an accounting of his abduction and his life upon *The Lost Sparrow* and his escape nearly a month removed. He, naturally, omitted the parts of what he had endured, attempting to spare her the worst of his condition when he was pulled from the icy waters of the Atlantic; however, from the look upon Fitzwilliam's countenance and the manner in which his cousin studied Darcy, he suspected the colonel had read between the lines to hold a better understanding of what occurred. Darcy did not tell either of them how his back was riddled with scars from the captain's cat-o'-nine-tails before he gave up fighting his kidnappers and waited for his opportunity to escape. For his insolence, for a long time, he thoroughly expected his captors to kill him, but, then, he had taken a different approach. Realizing he would never be permitted on the deck until he quit "fighting" his abductors, Darcy had settled into ship life. As he had often traveled on his yacht, he knew something of sailing and maneuvering a vessel upon the open sea. Using that knowledge, he had slowly won the respect and the acceptance of many in the crew, but never that of the captain and his first mate.

That is when he came to the conclusion that his being taken had been purposeful.

He was just about to ask Georgiana what she knew of Elizabeth, when Mr. Jones announced the Earl of Matlock. His lordship quickly crossed the room to catch Darcy up in a very masculine embrace, which Darcy did not return. Behind him, he heard Fitzwilliam and Georgiana rise to their feet.

"I could not believe my ears when I heard the news of your return," the earl declared. "Permit me to look at you." Darcy presented his uncle a look of contempt, but Matlock evidently ignored the warning by design. "You do not appear worse for the wear."

Darcy said blandly. "I suppose are you correct if one considers I am, at least, fifty pounds lighter, my skin is so tanned from the sun, it will likely remain so for the remainder of my days, and there is not an inch of skin on my back not raised with scars."

Georgiana gasped, and Darcy instantly regretted he had spoken so plainly before her.

"There is no reason to speak so cruelly," the earl warned.

"I have lost nearly four years of my life," Darcy hissed. "I returned home to learn how your and Lady Catherine's plans for my sister overrode those of my own. You knew I would never have tolerated an alliance with the like of Lindale for Georgiana."

Matlock shot a look of contempt to his youngest son. "My sister and I only wished to protect the Fitzwilliam family — your family."

"Do not think I believe your motives based in genuine concern," Darcy countered. "Your protest has problems with its reasoning: You willfully ignored what George Darcy designed for his son and daughter. Georgiana and I are Darcys," he declared in anger.

Matlock pulled himself up to his full height. "You and Georgiana are Lady Anne Fitzwilliam's children. You are part of my family. I take those responsibilities seriously."

"You fool only yourself with your declarations." Darcy

was not intimidated by his uncle because Darcy's anger and his stubbornness were natural complements derived from both his parents. "Lady Anne agreed with her husband's estimation of the Fitzwilliam family. I was in her bedroom, at her side while she was dying. My mother begged my father to see that Georgiana and I were protected from the earldom." He glanced to his sister for permission to continue, and she lifted her chin in a beautiful act of defiance, one he had missed while away at sea. He continued, "Although I have always been grateful for your patronage, I have spent twenty years of my life without my mother's influence, and Georgiana does not recall one day with Lady Anne. Her memories of our mother are all borrowed from those who knew your younger sister. Therefore, we are Darcys, and my father had distinct plans for both of us."

"Such as your marrying that woman from Hertfordshire?" the earl accused. "You cannot tell me George Darcy would have approved of that woman or her family."

Darcy growled, "*That woman* would have been the greatest gift I could ever have known. My parents would have adored her, for the lady made me happy. I would advise you to keep your opinion of Miss Elizabeth Bennet to yourself."

"Well, I see I am no longer welcomed in my sister's house." Matlock glanced about the room as if waiting for someone to deny his assumption, but no one did. Therefore, the earl turned his disapprobation on Fitzwilliam. "I pray you will not deny your mother the pleasure of knowing her first grandchild."

"The countess will be made aware of when Mrs. Fitzwilliam is to deliver," Fitzwilliam said evenly. "My wife and I have discussed it. We would wish the countess present."

"But not the rest of the family?" the earl accused.

"Although my mother would never wish another bride upon me, for she has always adored Georgiana, the countess has readily admitted she had hoped for a different outcome for both of us." Fitzwilliam reached for Georgiana's hand, which Darcy's sister readily provided, a telling sign of Georgiana's tender feelings for her husband. Darcy's acceptance of their marriage took root. "I love my wife, but I am grieved that she never had a Season—never knew the time when the world could look upon her and discover her brilliant talents and her kind spirit, and all because of the manipulations of my family."

Georgiana looked lovingly on her husband and spoke with equal clarity. "From the time I was fifteen, my greatest wish was to be the colonel's wife," she said softly, a slight blush marking her cheeks. "Yet, it grieves me he had to abandon his military career to save me in my brother's absence from those who professed to love me. To save me from the people who should have thought to protect me. From those who should have consulted me on how I viewed my future. My father chose wisely when he named Fitzwilliam, along with Darcy, as my guardians, Perhaps, he suspected what was to come. And although I doubt he thought we would become husband and wife, I like to think he would have approved if we had had the opportunity to ask his permission. Unfortunately, we will never know George Darcy's thoughts on the matter. I pray he would not know disappointment in his daughter's choice."

Darcy smiled at the pair. Though he had not been happy to learn that Georgiana had lost so much while he had been imprisoned on *The Lost Sparrow*, he said, "In my humble opinion, it was as if George Darcy had anticipated what others would plan for his daughter's future and chose a man of honor to protect her when I could not."

Matlock scowled at them all. "Then I will take my leave. I know when I am not welcome in a household. Inform me when you come to your senses, Darcy, and understand I acted to protect the family." With that, he was gone.

Darcy, his cousin, and Georgiana remained silent until they heard the front door slam into place. As Georgiana turned into her husband's ready embrace, Darcy crossed to pull the bell cord. "Do you know how to reach Mr. Thacker, Jasper, and Samuels?" he asked without turning to look upon the Fitzwilliams' intimate pose. He knew it would make him sad to view Georgiana, so like a lady, instead of the young girl he had left behind, and to think it should be he and Elizabeth seeking comfort in each other's arms.

When Darcy finally turned around, Fitzwilliam appeared confused. "Jasper and Samuels traveled with us from Pemberley. They are below stairs. As to Mr. Thacker, I imagine the information is in your ledger. I understand he took another position, one of less standing. Your secretary handled many of the details in those early days of our searching for you. Why is this so important?"

Darcy did not have an opportunity to explain before Mr. Jones stepped into the room. "You rang, Mr. Darcy?"

Darcy turned his full anger upon the man. "Yes, Jones. I want you and the two new footmen out of my house within an hour. Otherwise, I will summon the magistrate and have you forcibly removed."

"Pardon?" the butler asked in flustered tones.

"I will explain once more so you are not mistaken of my intent: You and the two footmen have been dismissed with no letters of reference, that is, unless you can convince Lord Matlock to provide one, for you are, obviously, more dedicated to his patronage than you are to the Darcys' interests. I will have no one in my employ who is not loyal to me and my family. There was no means for the earl to learn so quickly of my return without someone within this household sending him word. Whether that person was you or someone you oversee, Darcy business has no place on the lips of Society. Your services are no longer required in my home."

Elizabeth Bennet took another sip of her tea. As she had always done, she had risen shortly after sunrise—only now she prepared her own cup of tea and hot rolls on a new wood-burning stove she had yet to master, rather than grabbing two rolls from the work table in Longbourn's kitchen before she headed outside for a walk about Hertfordshire's countryside. She sighed heavily: She missed her Longbourn family more than she could express in words. "However, this existence is more than I deserved. Papa." Tears stung her eyes as she recalled her most devoted parent. "Papa fought for me—stood up to all the naysayers and demanded retribution for Mr. Darcy's snub."

Her daily dose of self-pity played out before her closed eyes. She offered up her arguments from long ago on that fateful day and attempted to bolster them with her complete feeling of abandonment. However, a flicker of hope always grew in her chest as she remembered those early days after her being left at the altar.

She and Mr. Darcy were to have married early on Monday morning, and although Mr. Darcy had not returned on Saturday evening as he had promised, she had simply assumed his business had run longer than he expected. Then Sunday, for her, had been a day filled with her mother's fluttering nerves, as well as details of the wedding breakfast and final fittings of her wedding dress. Realizing Mr. Darcy would not travel on the Sabbath, she assumed he would leave London at the crack of dawn on Monday morning. Their wedding was not scheduled until half past eleven, and he would have had plenty of time to arrive and be at the church before they were to exchange their vows.

Afterwards, she had chastised herself for believing a man of Mr. Darcy's consequence could truly love a woman of simple tastes and sharp opinions. "Yet, was it necessary for the man to destroy my whole life because of my earlier rebuke?"

As quickly as Elizabeth said the words, she knew them false. Her whole life had not known destruction. In many ways, her current life was superior to anything she had ever anticipated. "Except the man who owned your heart did not love you in return," she whispered.

Images of the day that changed everything flashed before her eyes. If she were honest with herself, and, generally, she was, she knew when she woke on her wedding day that it would prove to be doomed. She had felt it in her bones; however, she had put her qualms aside, blaming her nerves for her unease, and permitted herself to be carried away by Jane's and their mother's enthusiasm, even though she was aware Mr. Darcy had not returned to Netherfield by supper on Sunday evening. Yet, how could she believe he would not come at all, especially after the evening they had spent together only five days prior? How could she believe he would abandon her? Had she not witnessed the love in his eyes when she had submitted to the desire coursing through both of them?

"Lust," she whispered in contempt, giving herself time to bolster up her pride once again—to place the blame on his shoulders, as well as her own. "Nothing more. Simply lust and deceit." She sucked in a deep breath, admitting reluctantly, if only to herself, there had been more between her and Mr. Darcy than simple desire. On her part, it had been love, and, deep down, she, despite her wish to despise him, knew he had not been unmoved by what had occurred between them. "Could it be as others have said? Could it be he truly did his best to return to me?"

In those early hours following her being left at the altar, pure chaos had taken over Longbourn and Netherfield. Although Mr. Bingley, obviously, wished a different course, the gentleman, who appeared equally incensed by his friend's actions, as was her family, performed honorably by offering Elizabeth his hand in marriage, in order to salvage Elizabeth's reputation. Most assuredly, she could not think to accept a man who adored her sister Jane, simply to save her, a person Society would assuredly reject no matter what course she chose. Even though all her instincts warned her not to make a sacrifice of her life for that of her family—a decision with which her father adamantly disagreed was spoken to Netherfield's master. She had gratefully thanked Mr. Bingley for his kind gesture, but she refused him and begged him not to turn from Jane because of what had occurred between Mr. Darcy and herself.

Unfortunately, she had been sent away before anything could be resolved regarding Bingley's proposing to Jane, for his family had known horror when they learned of Bingley's kindness to her and had whisked the gentleman back to London before he settled with Jane. A little less than three months after the disaster of her wedding, Elizabeth departed Hertfordshire, escorted, ironically, by Mr. Darcy's valet, Mr. Albert Sheffield.

"Dearest Sheffield," she murmured with a smile. "How would I ever have survived without him."

16 January 1813

Two months to the day after she and Mr. Darcy were to have exchanged their vows, Mr. Albert Sheffield had called upon her and her father at Longbourn with a plan of his own. Her father, at first, had been skeptical, but he had listened to the gentleman because, by then, Mr. Bennet had already run the gauntlet of Mr. Darcy's uncle, the Earl of Matlock, as well as Mr. Darcy's man of business and solicitor for her sake.

"I have left Mr. Darcy's employment," Mr. Sheffield announced at the beginning of their conversation.

Her father sarcastically remarked, "You have come to your senses then. You no longer wish to work for a man of no character. I am certain Mr. Darcy is pleased with how he has ruined our family."

Mr. Sheffield frowned then. "Mr. Darcy would never purposely have exacted harm on Miss Elizabeth. Whatever else you may believe of the man, Mr. Darcy loves your daughter with all his heart. I served the man from the time of his mother's passing, first as his tutor and then as his valet when he left for formal schooling, until two months prior."

Despite her continual misery, Elizabeth's bruised heart had cherished Mr. Sheffield's evaluation of the Derbyshire gentleman's true feelings for her, especially as her opinions of the man had never proved so accurate as at the moment. Even so, she had wondered why, if Mr. Sheffield still admired the man, why he left Mr. Darcy's employment. None of what occurred since that fateful day had made any sense, and she had begun again to question both her feelings for the man who had betrayed her and the reason for said betrayal.

"If Darcy loves Elizabeth," her father had accused, drawing her from her musing, "why did he not appear at the church to exchange vows with my daughter? And why has he not personally addressed the issue of what he owes to Elizabeth, instead turning my negotiations over to his uncle? If Darcy thinks the Earl of Matlock will intimidate me, the man has made a mistake. I have known plenty of men of Matlock's ilk in my life, and despite being only a country squire, I have never stepped aside nor permitted those full of self-pride a path through me."

Mr. Sheffield shifted uncomfortably and appeared pained by what her father had disclosed. "I cannot say for certain what arrangements Mr. Darcy has made with Lord Matlock regarding this matter. In truth, I have not spoken to Mr. Darcy since he sent me forward to Hertfordshire in preparation for his wedding. I traveled with the party, which included Colonel Fitzwilliam and Miss Darcy."

"Was not the man at Darcy House when you three returned to London?" her father demanded.

"No, sir."

"I believe you must provide an explanation of what occurred," her father instructed. "This is the first I have heard of this situation. I was led to believe Mr. Darcy refused to speak to me himself."

Mr. Sheffield pulled himself up stiffly, as if delivering a message to the King. "When the colonel, Miss Darcy, and I arrived at Darcy House, an absolute hue and cry reigned. Evidently, Mr. Darcy had not been seen for three days. In the master's absence, Lord Matlock had released Mr. Thacker, the Darcy butler of some twenty years, for lodging objections on how the earl had conducted a search for the master. When I, too, expressed my concerns, I was ordered to leave Darcy House without a reference. Such would have been my fate if Miss Darcy and the Countess of Matlock had not intervened. However, I knew I would pay for my impertinence; therefore, I tendered my resignation."

Unable to stifle her question, Elizabeth asked, "Do you believe Mr. Darcy met a tragic end?"

Surprisingly, Mr. Sheffield's eyes filled with tears, triggering her own quick remorse. "I know the honor with which Mr. Darcy has always operated." A slight blush marked his cheeks when he explained. "Although I was not intended to know of your rebukes of Mr. Darcy's hand in Kent, the master's many drafts of the letter he must have presented you before our departure were left to me to dispose of. I had never before thought to read any of the master's correspondence, but I did on that occasion because I viewed the pain upon his face as he left Rosings in search of you and the great sense of loss in his stance when I encountered him that morning. I feared for him, for I had only viewed that expression two times prior with the passing of each of his parents.

"I must tell you, Miss Elizabeth, in all honesty, although I am certain such was not your intent at the time, you performed a great service to Mr. Darcy that evening. You presented my master's world a good shake, one he had required for some time. He had become too comfortable with his consequence and was traveling down a road I had feared he would soon regret. You made him a better man, and I can say, without a doubt, if he had had to crawl on his hands and knees to stand between you and the world, he would have gladly done so." Elizabeth instantly thought of how Mr. Darcy had arranged for Lydia's marriage to Mr. Wickham in order to save her family's ruination. Surely, he would not have exacted his revenge later. "Mr. Darcy would not have deserted you as long as he breathed the breath of life."

A shudder of dread had raced down her spine. Despite the Derbyshire gentleman's previous rejection, Elizabeth had always thought, if Mr. Darcy could be reached and informed of her current condition, he would have acted honorably. Yet, if he were dead, as Mr. Sheffield insinuated, likely, she would be truly on her own. The bottom fell out of her world, realizing, belatedly, she had always held hope Mr. Darcy would act the gentleman and make her whole again. How could she continue on without that hope? She doubted she was strong enough to face the world she would know as her future.

Her father asked, "I return to my previous question: Why have you sought us out today?"

Mr. Sheffield smiled tenderly upon her. "If Mr. Darcy has passed, Miss Elizabeth is never likely to earn true retribution from his estate. I have experienced Lord Matlock's means of solidifying his family, and, although I realize you have done the best you can for your daughter, I am certain whatever terms you were presented are not enough to keep Miss Elizabeth from a life of penury. Mr. Darcy would not have wanted your daughter to suffer." The gentleman cleared his throat from the emotions filling his words. "I am more fortunate than many men who choose to serve fine gentlemen, for I have been privy to many conversations between Mr. Darcy and his various men of business. Therefore, when the master thought to invest in a project, so did I, but on a lesser level. When he sold his investments, so did I. Although not of his consequence, I am a wealthy man. It would be my wish, if your daughter is willing, sir, to accept Miss Elizabeth in my household in whatever capacity she feels comfortable in assuming."

"You are offering Elizabeth marriage?" her father asked in obvious suspicion.

Mr. Sheffield blushed in what only could be called surprise. However, he said, "If such is Miss Elizabeth's wish, I am willing to speak my vows and live by them."

At that point, Elizabeth had lodged her objection. "I am thankful you wish to continue your duty to Mr. Darcy by saving my reputation, but I cannot allow you to sacrifice so much. You deserve a better life than that. If you are now free to marry, it should be someone you affect."

Seizing a rare opportunity, her father ignored her posturing. "I have negotiated a contract with Darcy's man of business for two hundred pounds a year for the remainder of Elizabeth's days, which is reasonable, but not enough to live on. What do you have to offer her?"

"Father!"

"Shush, Elizabeth," Mr. Bennet had warned. "I am not speaking of marriage, if such is not your wish, but I cannot send you off to make your way into the world alone, especially if Mr. Sheffield is willing to offer you his protection. A woman on her own is too vulnerable, and our Scottish cousins have refused you under your present condition. If I cannot be there to protect you, I would wish another to do so. Your world, in its pompousness, insists I must send you away soon, so your sisters have an opportunity to someday know marriage."

The stiffness in Mr. Sheffield's shoulders lessened when the idea of marriage had been removed. He glanced about the book-filled room serving as her father's study. "Much of my free time over the years has been spent with a book in my hand. If Mr. Darcy were here, he would tell you I remained in his family's employ simply so I could have access to Pemberley's library." At this point, he chuckled. "The master likely had the right of it." He folded his hands in front of him and rested them on the edge of her father's desk. "With books and the pleasure of reading as my impetus, I have made a bid to purchase a bookshop in a seaside town of some importance. The shop does not provide a separate cottage, as I had hoped it would, but there are rooms both above the shop for sleeping and socializing with a kitchen below, as well as another room for sleeping in the rear of the building. It is not what you are accustomed to, but I am willing to offer you a home with me for as long as you require one." He paused to smile upon her. "You may do so as my wife or as a cherished daughter who is a war widow or any other tale we wish to offer the world. I would consider it my honor to provide for you."

Elizabeth's tears flowed easily then. The man had been her answer to a prayer, but she could not accept his offer until he knew the full truth of her situation. "Before I agree to your kind overture, you should be made aware, sir, I am likely breeding."

Instead of the horror she had expected upon the man's countenance with her declaration of her condition, Mr. Sheffield's gentle smile widened. "Mr. Darcy's child?"

She nodded her affirmation.

"The master would have been beside himself with happiness with this news. You and the child will have the rooms above the shop for sleeping. I am accustomed to a small private room at both Darcy House and at Pemberley, and so it would be no hardship for me to remain in the lower one. You will be safer above the shop if trouble was ever to know our doors."

It had been mid-September, 1813, before they had actually taken possession of the bookshop, for other arrangements had to be made before she could appear at Mr. Sheffield's side as his niece.

"Uncle Albert," Elizabeth whispered when she heard him stirring about in the extra room at the back of the store that they had converted into his bed chambers. He would join her for breakfast in a matter of minutes once he was dressed properly for the day, a special day for all of them. "My guardian angel. I would never have survived those first two years after what all the world declared to be Mr. Darcy's death without Albert Sheffield. To everyone in town he was "Sheff," her late mother's younger brother, and she was Mrs. Elizabeth Dartmore, the widow of Lieutenant William Dartmore, late of the British Royal Navy.

"Mornin', Mama," a still-sleepy child said as she rubbed her eyes. Elizabeth quickly wiped away her tears with the heels of her hands, to set aside her maudlin until another day, when it might have full rein.

"Good morning, Lizzy. How is my birthday girl?"

CHAPTER THREE

IF DARCY HAD HAD his choice, he would have been off to Hertfordshire the morning following his return to London to learn whether he could still claim a future with the woman he loved; however, as yesterday had progressed, he realized he must, first, secure his father's legacy, for, without it, his future and that of the Darcy family was in jeopardy.

"Pemberley is suffering," Fitzwilliam had confided when Georgiana claimed her bed for a short nap before last evening's supper.

"How so?" Darcy asked with a frown.

"As you have been at sea for so long, you cannot know the devastation that has engulfed the Continent and all of the United Kingdom following Napoleon's defeat at Waterloo."

"You refer to the devastation of war?" Darcy asked, still confused.

Fitzwilliam shook off the question. "Did you not notice how damp and dreary everything was in London?"

"London is often cloudy and damp," Darcy responded, but now that his cousin had mentioned the weather Darcy's eyes were drawn to the window. "In truth, I was so glad to be standing on English soil again, I would have welcomed a Derbyshire winter without coat and gloves for the opportunity."

"Yet, we have had months of this weather," Fitzwilliam corrected.

"Months?"

"Crops have rotted in the ground. The newsprints say, in Europe, there are places that have experienced more than one hundred consecutive days of rain. Here in England, riots broke out in the East Anglian counties this past May. Armed laborers bearing flags saying 'Bread or Blood' marched on Ely, north of our beloved Cambridge."

Darcy took a moment to digest what his cousin disclosed. "I had plans in place for such contingencies. Multiple crop rotation. Stored grain. Sheep. Dairy cows. Other means to keep Pemberley solvent. Who made the decisions for Pemberley?" His mind raced to understand what had occurred while he was fighting to survive on the sea. "Were you not in Derbyshire to support Georgiana?"

"Until June of last year, I was still in the army, Darcy. Some of the damage had been done before I could finish my service to Wellington and resign my commission. I have done my best, seeking the advice of your land steward; yet, I am not certain my efforts were enough. I fear the Pemberley fortune has taken a step backward."

"My bank accounts and investments should sustain us," Darcy insisted. "Again, I had plans for drastic times in place. Such is not ideal, but we can divide and conquer until we know better conditions."

"I pray such is so." His cousin paused in contemplation. "I never received the type of training you did in estate management. Even when we called on Lady Catherine for her annual accounting, you saw to her estate books, and I addressed the tenant quarrels and hiring and releasing of staff. I am truly concerned, Darcy, with what I have seen in the ledger books for your properties. I am convinced money has been shifted in accounts."

"Your father again?" Darcy accused.

"I cannot say who is to blame, but I am certain you will recognize the patterns with just a glance at the ledgers," Fitzwilliam confessed. "I believe tomorrow, you and I should begin a thorough accounting of the books."

Darcy nodded his agreement, but thoughts of Elizabeth still distracted him. "Would you speak to me as to what occurred at the church when I did not appear?"

Fitzwilliam shook his head in what appeared to be regret. "It was pure Bedlam." His cousin's brow wrinkled in displeasure. "It was I who delivered the announcement to those gathered at the church that you had not returned to Netherfield as we all had expected you would. Mr. Sheffield came looking for me when it was well past time for you to arrive."

"Elizabeth?" Darcy demanded. He cared not what the good citizens of Meryton thought of him. Only Elizabeth's thoughts mattered.

"I was not watching Miss Elizabeth when I spoke to the room at large, but Georgiana was. Your sister reported that the lady's expression was one of resignation, as if Miss Elizabeth had half expected it to be so."

"And afterwards?" Darcy asked. Regret filled him—for the pain Elizabeth had endured, for, although different from the physical pain he had suffered, a pain that cut deeper than the cat-o'-nine-tails used on his back. He also knew regret for what was, likely, the end of his dream to know Elizabeth as his wife.

"Georgiana and I rushed to London, only returning to Netherfield long enough to pack our belongings."

"Neither of you spoke to Elizabeth? Neither of you assured her something monumental must have occurred to prevent me from not exchanging our vows of marriage?" Darcy asked in agitation.

"I attempted to offer some sort of explanation; however, the lady's father ushered her quickly from the room, sending rebukes my way to be delivered to your door when I next encountered you."

"Then Elizabeth was offered no comfort," Darcy reasoned. "Oh, my dearest girl, how you must despise me," he murmured in despair.

Fitzwilliam argued, "It was you who knew the whip of a hard taskmaster."

"I would suffer it all again to remove the stain upon her life." Darcy swore under his breath. "A whip is never so sharp as Society's tongue." He swallowed the emotions rushing to know a release. "Finish it. Finish the tale so I know it all."

Fitzwilliam nodded his agreement. "Once we recovered your footman's, Davis, body in the Thames, we assumed you had known the same fate," his cousin explained. "Unfortunately, that was some five weeks after your disappearance. Georgiana and I had a long conversation, with your sister insisting I save Miss Elizabeth's reputation by offering her marriage."

"Did you?" Darcy held his breath. Although it would have been a brilliant marriage for Elizabeth, he was glad she would never know the Earl of Matlock's contempt.

"It was some three months after what occurred at the Meryton church that I made my way to Hertfordshire. Sometime in mid-February. I must tell you, Mr. Bennet's ire had not lessened. It took all my powers of persuasion to convince the gentleman to speak to me, for he was less than pleased to see me on his threshold." Darcy held his breath and waited for news of Elizabeth marrying another. "I was told Mr. Bennet had negotiated a living for his daughter."

"How much?" Darcy demanded.

"Two hundred pounds per year for life."

"With whom?"

"Your man of business, but I assume such means with Matlock's approval," Fitzwilliam confessed.

Darcy's mind raced to understand what exactly had occurred. "Two hundred is not ideal." He thought whoever arranged it had likely thought Mr. Bennet a fool, but they had erred. The man had accepted less than Elizabeth deserved, but she would still be receiving funds against the Darcy estate even if she chose to marry another. Her father had managed his own revenge with a yearly reminder of all Darcy had lost. "Yet, Elizabeth could survive on that amount if she is sensible. Does such mean she refused you?"

"I never had the opportunity to extend my offer. The lady

was no longer at Longbourn," Fitzwilliam explained. "I was sent away without speaking to her." His cousin settled his gaze upon Darcy. "I know what you are thinking. Your hopes are she remains unmarried."

"I must discover the truth," Darcy argued. "Please share anything you are withholding from me. I do not think I can exist another day without knowing if there is any possibility Miss Elizabeth has not married another."

Fitzwilliam nodded his agreement. "I knew your sister would demand the same truth for which you ask. Therefore, when I departed Longbourn, before leaving Hertfordshire, I called upon Colonel Forster to learn something of what had occurred after I departed Meryton. I knew the colonel would keep my questions to himself and not add to the gossip surrounding the Bennets."

"And?"

"You will not wish to hear what the colonel shared," Fitzwilliam cautioned.

"Yet, I must." Darcy resigned himself to his worst fears.

Fitzwilliam sighed heavily. "Bingley offered for Miss Elizabeth after the Bennets all returned from the church, but your lady refused him."

Darcy said with some assurance, "Elizabeth would not claim Bingley's hand and rob Miss Bennet of knowing Bingley as her husband." Darcy admired his friend's honor, but he had no doubts Elizabeth never entertained the gesture for even a moment. One of her initial dislikes of Darcy's person was his objection to her sister.

"Perhaps Miss Elizabeth should have claimed the honor of Mistress of Netherfield, for, according to Forster, Bingley's sisters insisted upon his leaving the area before he committed another error in judgment. Bingley did not renew his option on Netherfield when it came due the following Michaelmas. According to some of your shared acquaintances, he has not returned to Hertfordshire. It is assumed, with Miss Lydia's questionable marriage to Wickham and Miss Elizabeth being left at the altar—" At this point his cousin raised his hands in a sign of surrender before continuing. "Through no fault of her own, the assumption remains that the other daughters have been shunned by suitors."

"Poor Miss Bennet," Darcy whispered. "The lady deserved someone better than a mercurial shipowner." After all he did to return Bingley to Miss Bennet's side, his friend again had listened to his sisters and had proved himself unworthy of Jane Bennet. "In many ways, I wish now I had not allowed Miss Elizabeth to sway my earliest decisions on the lady. Miss Bennet would have been better off with another." He straightened his shoulders to hear the rest of his cousin's tale. "Anything else?"

"Forster says Miss Elizabeth departed the neighborhood in late February, and no one seems to know where she has gone. Even her sisters and her mother are very closed-mouthed about the situation, many thinking she has been disowned in order to save the others."

"Alone? She was sent out on her own with no one to care for her?"

"Miss Elizabeth left on her own," Fitzwilliam confirmed. "However, there was a report by Mr. Phillips, through one of Mr. Bennet's servants, of an older gentleman calling upon Mr. Bennet in mid-January. Speculation is the man offered for Miss Elizabeth and was accepted, if not by her, then by her father."

Darcy knew he sounded desperate, but he could not swallow the words. "Mr. Bennet would not accept my offer for Miss Elizabeth without her first consenting to my suit. I cannot imagine, even under such dire circumstances, he would ignore his favorite daughter's wishes. Perhaps the man was a relative willing to take her in for a portion of her settlement or perhaps he hired her as a governess for his children. There is no proof she married another."

Fitzwilliam warned, "There is no evidence she did not marry another. You know, as well as anyone, how cruel Society can be toward a woman rejected at the altar."

"She was not rejected!" Darcy declared, slamming his fist against the chair arm. "I fought to return to her!" Agony filled his heart, and his breathing became shallow. He murmured, "I never stopped fighting my oppressors." Tears filled his eyes. "Never stopped loving her."

"Then you should return to Hertfordshire to learn your own truth. Perhaps Mr. Bennet will provide you the words you wish to hear. I know you cannot go on with your life until you learn the truth, but please prepare yourself for unwanted news. I cannot imagine Mr. Bennet would allow his daughter to leave with a man who was not her husband, nor would I expect a man to hire a jilted woman as governess to his children. You must know reason, Darcy: It has been nearly four years since what would have been your wedding day."

Elizabeth contentedly looked on as Albert Sheffield read a book to Lizzy. By week's end, as was the way with children first discovering the world of books, the child would be able *to read*, rather to say, *to recite*, it back to the man, who had, quite literally, saved her and the child she had carried when Elizabeth departed Hertfordshire. Hers had been a difficult delivery, one brought on by the stress of her situation mixed with her melancholy and a touch of an unpredictable fever. She would have surely died if she had been alone. God had sent her her own personal angel in the form of Mr. Darcy's former valet, and, although "Uncle Albert" had been thoroughly embarrassed by what the midwife had asked of him, the man had never left her side, promising to care for "Little Lizzy" when Elizabeth thought she might die from the fever that did not leave her until well after Elizabeth Anne Dartmore's birth.

Sheffield had done it all—assisted in the delivery of the child, bringing in a surgeon to make the cut so Elizabeth Anne could be born, employed a wet nurse for Lizzy, and tended to Elizabeth until she knew health once more. If the man had not presented himself to her at Longbourn on that fateful day in January 1813, Elizabeth's story would likely have taken a different course and with a different outcome: Her daughter could have died, and she would have been alone in the world.

"'Nother time," Lizzy pleaded, even though it was well past the child's bedtime.

"Just the last three pages," Sheffield admonished, but the man's smile said he enjoyed Lizzy Anne cuddled upon his lap.

Elizabeth studied her daughter's features: dark hair and pale eyes, not blue—more silver, just like her father's—eyes that had once upon a time followed her about a room in what she had foolishly interpreted as contempt when the emotion, she had later learned, had been disbelief in his inability to disguise his affection for her. How often, especially since having Lizzy, had Elizabeth wished she had accepted Mr. Darcy's offer of his hand in Kent! Then Wickham would not have dared to ruin Lydia, and Mr. Bingley could have been "encouraged" by her to return to Jane's side, and, more importantly, she, her child, and Mr. Darcy would have been safe at Pemberley and together. It was not as if she was not thankful for Mr. Sheffield's protection. It was as her father had said, a cruel world for women on their own; yet, she felt, especially in moments such as this one, she had robbed this "gentle" man of a family of his own. Sheffield could have married and been holding his own daughter, at this moment, instead of devoting time to hers. Moreover, it appeared, of late, he could be considering offering for Mrs. Harris, a widow, but one well past childbearing years, and he might never know the joy of cuddling his own child as he did with Lizzy. Moreover, Elizabeth did not much think Mrs. Harris's nature was the type to share her home with another woman and a child.

She smiled upon the scene again. Most assuredly, Fitzwilliam Darcy would never have been able to deny the child as his own. Lizzy Anne was the female image of her father: There was very little of Elizabeth in the girl's features. Initially, the noted similarities had caused Elizabeth great pain—her loss of the man she had come to love was too fresh not to evoke her emotions, but, with time, she had learned to adore possessing a little piece of Fitzwilliam Darcy within her house. She now celebrated the fact her daughter was everything Darcy. High cheek bones. A crooked smile. A small dimple on one side of Lizzy's mouth.

All indications showed Lizzy would be tall and statuesque, nothing like her mother's more petite frame, and the child was as intelligent as her father. Elizabeth feared the girl would be quite exacting in her approach to the world if she and Sheffield did not keep a steady hand on the child's shoulders.

Even without Mr. Darcy's influence on the child, Lizzy would calculate every possibility before acting. "And line up her books upon the shelf from largest to smallest in a perfectly straight line," Elizabeth murmured to herself as she watched Lizzy's head nod in sleep. Although Elizabeth had viewed the library at Pemberley only once, she knew the gentleman's organization had been just as exacting, but with more of a plan to determine where to look for books on certain subjects or by certain authors, yet, as perfectly organized and stringent. The child was equally as proper at the table, often adjusting the cutlery to certain angles, and, as well as in the manner in which her toys were stored in her room.

The dark head finally fell forward to rest on Mr. Sheffield's chest, and Elizabeth left her musings to gather her child from the man's embrace. "Thank you, my friend," she whispered as she bent to kiss the gentleman's forehead.

"Always a pleasure," he said in affectionate tones.

She adjusted the child in her arms so Lizzy's head rested upon her shoulder. It would not be long before Lizzy would be too heavy for Elizabeth to carry. "Will you call upon Mrs. Harris this evening?" she asked. Elizabeth was not overly fond of the woman, but she wished Mr. Sheffield happiness if the lady was his choice.

Mr. Sheffield shook his head in the negative. "We shared our midday meal. I wanted this evening to be all about Lizzy Anne." Sheffield had presented Elizabeth Anne with her new "favorite" doll and a book for her drawings. He caressed the child's hand. "A person is only three years old one time."

Elizabeth wondered what would happen to her and Lizzy when Mr. Sheffield made an offer of his hand to the Widow Harris. The woman appeared to be as disenchanted by Elizabeth as she was with the lady.

Elizabeth nodded her head in understanding. "Good evening, then."

"I will check the locks when I go below. I shall see you in the morning, Elizabeth," he said softly. He bent to kiss her forehead. "Mr. Darcy would be so proud of you and the child you bore him."

Tears rushed to her eyes. She adjusted Lizzy to a more comfortable place upon her shoulder. "I was thinking something similar as I watched you two sharing the book. Lizzy possesses many of his mannerisms."

"Even how her laugh explodes at the most unexpected times." Mr. Sheffield straightened the cut of his coat before adding, "I miss the young master."

"As do I," Elizabeth assured.

Leaving Sheffield to his evening, she carried Lizzy into the small room serving as the child's bed chamber. Placing her daughter gently on the bed, she bent to remove the child's shoes and stockings before carefully wrestling Lizzy from her dress and placing it aside. Spreading the blanket across her, Elizabeth picked up Lizzy's small hand and kissed it, holding it to her face. "You are a small part of the great man who was your father. I so wish he could view you just once. You are my gift from him, a perfect piece of Fitzwilliam Darcy no one can ever deny me."

Darcy made his way through a dark Darcy House. Georgiana and Fitzwilliam had retired early, and he felt terribly alone, for his nightmare still held no end in sight. Earlier, after supper, he had called in below stairs to thank his staff for remaining with the family through the dark days of his absence and to learn what he could of Davis, the footman who lost his life in Darcy's defense along the streets of London leading to the docks.

"Samuels and I claimed the body and delivered it to his mother, sir," Jasper said in humble respect.

"And the funeral?" he asked.

Mrs. Guthrie, his housekeeper, explained, "Mr. Nathan and I took up a collection to aid Davis's family." His housekeeper did not need to explain that no one else took the time to learn the fact Davis had been the chief wage earner for a family of seven after his father's death.

"I do not know what difficulties I may encounter reestablishing myself at my bank and other facilities, but as quickly as it may be done, I will see to Mrs. Davis and her children, as well as to have you reimbursed for your forethought."

"There be no need, sir," Cook said. "Miss Darcy see'd to our donation to the family."

Darcy smiled weakly. "My sister possesses a kind heart. She is very much like my mother in that manner."

"She be a Darcy. None of us would expect anything less. You be the very best to employ so many of us when the world be falling apart," Cook continued. "We be blessed."

He accepted their praise of his sister and his family with a nod of his head. "Nevertheless, I shall see to Mrs. Davis until times are better. At the least, she deserves her son's pay for the foreseeable future. All I ask is you bear with me for a bit longer, and, hopefully, we will know a return to what we expect as part of the Darcy household. Until Mr. Thacker can accept his old position or I can employ a new butler, I will ask Mrs. Guthrie, Samuels, and Jasper to respond to the door and to assist with a variety of duties." He turned to his two long-standing footmen. "If I may, as Mr. Sheffield has also left my employ, I will require one of you to assist me in the morning with clothes, something other than these borrowed ones, for which I am most thankful." He gestured to what he had worn when he departed the British ship earlier in the day. "I was not granted new clothes for nearly four years, and the ones I wore on the ship were in rags when the British navy rescued me." He reminded himself to offer his servants a smile. Those gestures which had once been so natural to him had disappeared. "I am assuming nothing has been removed from my quarters. Mrs. Fitzwilliam says she and the colonel chose not to move into the master's suite."

"It is as you left it, sir," one of the maids reported.

Again, he nodded his gratitude. "I will leave you to your duties then."

Now, as he stood in the middle of what would have been Elizabeth's rooms, a great sadness filled him. The room was as he remembered it. He had had it painted and the furnishings refreshed in expectation of Elizabeth's arrival as his bride. The jeweled hairbrush and two combs rested on a silver tray on a vanity, both were to have been wedding gifts from him, along with the silk night-rail and matching wrapper hanging on a hook near the dressing room door that connected their quarters.

"Where have they sent you, my Elizabeth?" he whispered to the darkness. "Do you still think of me? There has not been a night since the Meryton assembly I have not thought of you, my love."

Tears filled his eyes. He had not shed one tear in the nearly four years of his imprisonment—prayers, certainly—curses, many—pleading, often, but no tears; however, he shed them now for what could possibly be the death of his dream.

"There is no doubt someone meant to separate us, love. Have you also come to that conclusion? Perhaps or perhaps not. If what Georgiana shared of how you appeared to think I meant to punish you for your refusal at Kent, you may not be aware of those who set themselves against us. Yet, I am praying, after your initial fit of temper, you realized I could never have walked away from the prospects of perfection in our joining. It was too tempting to know anything less."

He sat upon the bed and removed his borrowed boots, stockings, and jacket, and then crawled across the bed to rest upon the pillows meant for her. "Beginning tomorrow, I will set my world aright, and I will be coming for you, Elizabeth Bennet. I will not countenance the idea you have chosen another. I will come for you, and Heaven help anyone who thinks to cross me again. You will finally be my wife."

CHAPTER FOUR

"Good morning, Mrs. Dartmore."

Elizabeth looked up from her task of unboxing the books Mr. Sheffield had ordered from London for several of their regular customers to view Mr. Sidney Townsend. She groaned internally, but placed a smile upon her lips. Mr. Townsend for the last four months had made a point of calling upon her, despite the fact she had never encouraged the man. He would appear at the most inconvenient times and insist upon walking her back to the store.

"Good morning, sir," she said politely, as she wiped the dust from her hands on a rag she kept under the counter. "I have just unboxed the new shipment from London. Allow me an extra minute or two, and I shall have your book wrapped properly for you."

"I do not mind the wait when I have such a lovely lady to keep me company."

"I shan't keep you long," she repeated. Retrieving the book the man had ordered from the stack sitting upon the nearby table, she busied herself cutting the brown paper required to wrap the book.

"Do you enjoy poetry, Mrs. Dartmore?" Townsend asked.

Elizabeth glanced to the book in her hand and hid the frown forming upon her features. "I have yet to develop an overwhelming love for Lord Byron, but I am not opposed to reading his works upon occasion," she said diplomatically.

Mr. Townsend's eyebrow rose in disbelief. "I thought most women preferred the romantics these days."

Elizabeth had her own questions as to why a man would purchase Byron's works unless to impress some woman upon which he had set his sights. She prayed such was not Townsend's purpose. If so, he would know no purchase where she was concerned. She swallowed the retort rushing to her lips. "I fear I am not much of a 'romantic,' as many call this new movement toward 'sensibility,' rather than 'sense.'"

Mr. Townsend leaned against the counter in a casual manner. "A woman of your fine countenance should possess a protector — a man who holds you in affection."

Elizabeth immediately thought of Fitzwilliam Darcy. After his absence from their wedding, she had despised him, thinking he had betrayed her, but, since coming to live with Mr. Sheffield, she had grieved for the loss of the man who had owned her heart. She had cherished Mr. Sheffield's remembrances of his young master, tales she would share with Lizzy Anne when the child was older and began to ask of her father.

"I have been held in affection," she said in solemn tones.

"Yet, you are a young woman," he argued. "You should consider marrying again."

"I am a young woman satisfied with her life as it is. My daughter and I shall do well together," she countered.

"What happens to you if Mr. Sheffield chooses to marry Mrs. Harris?" he demanded. "All of Brighton says it will be so." Elizabeth had begun to wonder something of the connection between Mrs. Harris and Mr. Townsend. Was the gentleman also attempting to woo the widow? Or, had he and the widow joined forces to separate her and Mr. Sheffield, each with their own reasons to lodge a wedge between her and her guardian angel. "You might wish to consider my suit, Mrs. Dartmore. I would see both you and your child wanting for nothing. Your Elizabeth Anne requires a father. I could be that man in her life."

"And you wish a mother for your two young sons?" she questioned. She had yet to take the acquaintance of the gentleman's sons, so she held no opinions of the children, but the man's close presence made her want to scratch at the hives she was certain had formed along her arm.

"Naturally, Emerson and Tobias require a mother. I have observed you with your daughter. Your kindness would prove a boon for my sons, who miss their mother desperately."

As the former Mrs. Townsend supposedly passed less than a year prior, in Elizabeth's opinion, it was too soon for Townsend's children to accept another woman's touch or her rules. Because her daughter had never known her father, the child might easily connect to Mr. Townsend; however, Elizabeth was not certain she wanted Lizzy to desire the attention of any man beyond Mr. Sheffield and Lizzy's real father.

She said with as much delicacy as she could muster, "I am honored by your interest in me and my daughter, sir, but, for now, I do not expect, in the near future, to be in a place where I shall wish the protection of another. In truth, I still grieve the passing of my daughter's dear father. It would be a disservice to another gentleman to accept a man I did not affect."

"It has more than three years, Mrs. Dartmore," Townsend reminded her.

"And it may be three more years or even thirty before I am prepared to commit myself to another. I shall know when I am capable of accepting the attentions of another," she said in firm tones.

The gentleman accepted the wrapped book she handed him. "For the time being, I will abide by your denials, but I have not thrown away my hopes." He presented her a curt bow. "Until we meet again, Mrs. Dartmore."

When the door closed between her and the gentleman, Elizabeth expelled a heavy sigh of resignation. "Oh, Fitzwilliam," she whispered. "What havoc your actions have brought to my life. If you could do it all again, would you have left me in Hertfordshire to address an issue on one of Lord Matlock's ships?" She sat heavily upon the stool and rested her head on her arms upon the counter. "Again, I am the odd bird in a family of doves. I had a brief taste of perfection before it was snatched away. At least, you left a bit of yourself behind. The only fault, of which I may complain, is Elizabeth Anne will never know what having you as her father could have meant to her future."

Over the next three weeks, Darcy had systematically worked his way through the disaster that proved to be his financial situation. There had been a steady flow of bankers and investors through his door, and, with each, he had threatened to sue them for allowing others to touch his fortune. Most were visibly shaken when they had exited his home, each promising to recover what they could of the money lost at their hands. He had insisted that Fitzwilliam join him as Darcy had shifted through the chaos left behind by Matlock and Darcy's former man of business.

"I am grieved," Fitzwilliam said over and over again. "I should have realized what was going on."

"It is as much my fault as it was yours," Darcy had assured. "Considering you were Georgiana's guardian, I should have insisted you be made aware of the workings of the Darcy wealth. My only excuse is you were so involved with your military career, I did not think to add to your responsibilities."

"I have always known I would inherit Yadkin Hall when mother passes. I simply assumed I possessed the time to learn all that would be required of me." His cousin saluted Darcy with a raised glass of brandy. "I do blame you, Cousin," Fitzwilliam said, "you made it appear so easily accomplished."

Darcy smiled weakly. "I assume you mean, if you had emulated me, your charms in the ballroom would have suffered." It felt good to return to the customary banter between them. Since returning home, Darcy had recognized the strain in their relationship. It was not only his father's legacy he must rebuild: It was trusting the man who shared his house and his sister. Although the colonel had proven his worth, Darcy felt betrayed by the world on many levels.

"I am a married man," Fitzwilliam protested with an equal

fear of the world, and Darcy knew that fear would bond them in time. "If I shamed your sister, I would be forced to defend myself on Putney Heath."

"Exactly." Darcy allowed himself a smile. "And never forget I am better with a sword than you."

"Then I will choose pistols." They sat in comfortable silence for several minutes. At length, his cousin asked the question Darcy had been expecting for days. "What will you do regarding Miss Elizabeth?"

He swallowed hard against the pain that predictably filled his chest whenever he thought of what Elizabeth must have endured because of his shortsightedness. He explained, "I have contacted Bingley, who will call at Darcy House later today." Darcy had yet to go about in London, avoiding the myriad of questions that were sure to torment him until he had control of his holdings again. "I will ask what Bingley knows of the Bennets' situation and, specifically, where Elizabeth might be."

"You still mean to seek her out?" Fitzwilliam asked in cautious tones. They had exchanged more than one round of volleys regarding Darcy's wish to know of Elizabeth's whereabouts.

"If she is not pledged to another, I wish to speak to her again."

"Just speak?" Fitzwilliam questioned.

Darcy silently counted to ten before he responded: More than enough heated words had been spoken between them of late. He realized his cousin only meant to protect him, but no one understood Darcy's complete dependence upon Elizabeth's goodwill. "If the lady is not involved with another, it would be my desire to make her my wife."

"Even though it appears you were targeted upon the docks because of your pledge to Miss Elizabeth?"

They had yet to determine who had paid to have Darcy abducted, but from what they had discovered of the movement of funds from one account to another and from several upon *The Lost Sparrow*, Darcy had been specifically "chosen" to be a part of the crew.

"Whoever dared to cross me would not be so foolish again." He had his suspicions, but did not, yet, have enough proof to see the culprits to justice. "If the lady will have me after all she has suffered, I will count myself the most fortunate of men."

"Is this venture why you met with Mr. Cowan earlier today?" Fitzwilliam demanded.

"I have employed the former Bow Street Runner to learn what he might of this mysterious man who likely offered Elizabeth solace. If Mr. Cowan can discover nothing of merit, I will call upon Mr. Bennet and demand to know of Elizabeth's current situation."

Fitzwilliam warned, "Bennet was less than cordial to me. It is likely, after nearly four years, he will drive you from the estate with a whip in one hand and a gun in the other."

"Even so, I must find her. My heart will never be whole without Elizabeth Bennet in my life."

Elizabeth led her daughter across the street when she spotted Mr. Townsend approaching in the distance.

"Why are we hurrin'," Lizzy asked as her little legs pumped to keep up with Elizabeth's longer stride.

Elizabeth made herself slow down while keeping an eye on Townsend as he stopped to exchange greetings with several on the street. She had managed to avoid the man the last two times the gentleman had called at the bookstore, as well as after church services on Sunday. "We must call at the bakery before it closes," she improvised. "Uncle Albert asked if I would bring home a loaf of Mrs. Cache's berry bread."

Lizzy snarled her nose in obvious distaste. "I not like berry bread."

Elizabeth smiled down upon her daughter and bent to tug the child's coat tighter about her. It had turned unreasonably cold and damp of late. "Then I shall, instead, purchase you a berry tart, but we must be quick." She stood to catch the child's hand again. Elizabeth held no doubt her daughter would be cooperative if a sweet would be earned in the end.

Picking up her pace again, she ducked into the bakery just as Mr. Townsend reached the bookstore and stepped inside. Elizabeth prayed Mr. Sheffield would not disclose she was out shopping, for the man would likely keep searching until he discovered her.

"Good day, Mrs. Dartmore," Mrs. Cache said as she looked up from where she rearranged the display of items remaining from which the customers could choose.

"Good day. I pray I am not too late for your berry bread. My uncle dearly loves it."

The shop mistress smiled kindly on her. "I set two loaves aside for Mr. Sheffield. I know he prefers the loaves with the currants and a bit of honey."

Elizabeth chuckled easily. "Yes, both Sheffield and Miss Lizzy possess a sweet tooth."

"But you do not?" Mrs. Cache asked as she retrieved the bread.

"Upon occasion, I enjoy a good custard or a pudding," Elizabeth admitted reluctantly. Over the years, she had been very careful not to disclose too many details of her life before arriving in Brighton.

"One or two loaves?" the shopkeeper asked.

Elizabeth shook off another round of maudlin. Of late, she had been missing her family terribly. "I will take both and a berry tart."

Mrs. Cache frowned. "I have no more berry tarts. I apologize."

Elizabeth kept hold of Lizzy's hand, willing her child not to turn to a tantrum before others. "Then we shall choose something else, will we not, darling?" She knew Lizzy was not the type of child who did well when there was a change of plans, but a gentle squeeze of her child's fingers coerced the proper response.

"Yes, Mama."

She lifted the child to her so Lizzy could better choose

from the selection. She pointed to several choices before her eyes fell upon an apple concoction sprinkled with cinnamon. Without thinking upon what she did, Elizabeth sighed heavily.

"What 'miss?" her daughter asked in obvious concern. Lizzy patted Elizabeth's cheeks in imitation of how she often caressed her little girl's.

She shook off Lizzy's worried frown. "Nothing is amiss. Mama was simply considering how much your father would enjoy one of Mrs. Cache's apple tarts."

Lizzy's sweet features turned into a downward frown. "You miss Papa?"

Elizabeth had always made it a priority to speak of the child's father, providing Lizzy memories her daughter would never have on her own, while not disclosing too much information — information that could jeopardize her daughter's legitimacy. She wanted Elizabeth Anne to realize how much her father would have wanted to know her, while keeping some secrets to herself. "Yes, I miss him with all my heart," she said before swallowing the sadness that always brought tears to her eyes.

There were moments, such as this one, when she wished she could forget Fitzwilliam Darcy and accept another man's attentions — wished desperately to give her daughter a real father, not just a borrowed memory of one. Unfortunately, Elizabeth's heart still had not accepted the loss of the man, and she was not certain it ever would.

So often she had observed a stranger on the street who held himself with the same exactness as had Mr. Darcy, and her heart would characteristically stumble to a halt for a few elongated seconds. Then the pain of losing him would rush back in, as real and as completely devastating as it had been when Mr. Sheffield had pronounced his speculations as to Mr. Darcy's fate.

"Papa like apples?" Lizzy's questions drew Elizabeth from her musings.

She smiled easily upon the gentleman's features arranged upon her daughter's face. "Your father loved anything with apples and cinnamon."

"I love them, too," Lizzy declared.

Elizabeth was not certain her child knew the difference between one tart and another, but she said, "As you are definitely of your father's nature, I imagine so. Do you wish the apple tart in place of the berry one?"

"I be like Papa," Lizzy declared with a smile.

"Yes, you will be, my love. There is no doubt in my mind, for you are carved in his image."

"Darcy!" Charles Bingley crossed Darcy's study, his hand extended in greeting.

Darcy stepped from behind his desk to accept his friend's hand, although he was no longer comfortable with such niceties. Onboard ship, few extended their hands unless it was used to strike out against another. It would be necessary for him to relearn some of what was expected of him as a gentleman.

"I cannot tell you how surprised and pleased I was to receive your note upon my return to Bedlow Place. My prayers and those of many others were finally answered."

"My prayers also," Darcy said simply before gesturing to the two chairs before the fire. Although it was late August, his body had yet to adjust to the dampness prevalent in London. On the *Sparrow*, the crew had spent much of their time in the waters off the southern Americas where the temperature was often sweltering.

Once he and Bingley were settled and drinks dispensed, Darcy provided his friend the edited version of what had really occurred — the version he and Fitzwilliam had agreed upon as to what they would tell the curiosity seekers.

"Unbelievable!" Bingley repeated several times before saying, "I knew you would never purposely abandon Miss Elizabeth at the altar, no matter how often Caroline and Louisa declared it otherwise."

Darcy held himself perfectly still, attempting to appear at ease, when he would very much like to hunt down every naysayer, including Bingley's sisters, and present them the direct cut for belying Elizabeth's reputation. Deliberately, he asked, "I understand you attempted to save Elizabeth from ruination by offering her your hand in marriage."

Bingley squirmed in his seat. "It was all I could think to do. Miss Bennet made the suggestion." In other words, Bingley had not had an original idea, something that did not surprise Darcy. His friend was too easily persuadable. "The lady and I were both moved by the despair marking Miss Elizabeth's features when the colonel made his announcement."

Bingley's description of Elizabeth's state of mind after it was apparent he would not show for their wedding was like a knife to Darcy's heart. However, he managed to say, "It was magnanimous of both you and Miss Bennet to attempt to save Elizabeth."

Bingley continued to appear uncomfortable. "Now that I know the truth of your absence, I am exceedingly glad Miss Elizabeth refused me."

Darcy could not control his desire to torment Bingley for daring to aspire to Elizabeth's hand, even if the gesture had been a kind one. "I am also glad of Elizabeth's refusal. It would have been difficult for us both, to say the least, for me to return to London to discover the woman I planned to marry installed at your house as your wife."

Bingley swallowed hard. Obviously, his friend had not expected Darcy to know of his actions. "You know how impetuous I am," his friend said nervously. "I felt a responsibility for Miss Elizabeth's loss. After all, I was the one who introduced you two, even attempted to see you partner her at the Meryton assembly. Jane, I mean, Miss Bennet begged me to assist her family."

"I am not angry with you, Bingley," Darcy said in calmer tones than he felt. "You acted when others did not, but, surely, you recognized Elizabeth's answer before you made the gesture. She was determined to view you as Miss Bennet's husband, not hers."

"I suppose," Bingley said weakly.

At that moment, much of the respect he had always felt for Bingley disappeared. Darcy purposely used silence to allow Bingley to consider the choices he had made. At length, Darcy asked, "Why did you choose to leave Hertfordshire? Why not remain at Miss Bennet's side to provide comfort to her and her family?"

Bingley blushed. "My sisters insisted I could be of more use to the Bennets if I assisted your family in locating you."

"Yet, you did not return to Netherfield when it was determined I was deceased."

Bingley shifted his weight from one hip to the other. "It was always my plan to do so."

"You planned to return to Hertfordshire, but you did not. For more than three years you chose to ignore those for whom you once spoke of fondly," Darcy stated firmly. "Help me to understand, Bingley. You were willing to risk your family's reputation to save Elizabeth's, but you were not willing to save the one woman you claimed to adore. Was it because you knew before asking her to marry you that Elizabeth would refuse, and you could claim honor without acting upon the matter?"

Bingley's color returned, only this time it was touched by anger. "There is more to consider than the Bennets, Darcy."

"You offer me an imitation of your sisters' words," Darcy said coldly. "You are correct. There is more than my absence from the wedding executed against the Bennet family's future. There is bigotry. Shortsightedness. Small minds. Snobbish views of one's own self-worth. Those things have existed all around us our whole acquaintance, but you, my friend, never allowed them to change your affable nature. Even when I foolishly erred in my views of Miss Bennet, you forgave me because you knew I acted as your friend—that I meant to protect you." Darcy set his glass on the table with a heavier hand than was necessary. "I can guarantee you that if the situation had been reversed, nothing could have kept me from making Elizabeth my wife, and I would have protected Miss Bennet simply because she was my wife's sister, even if Georgiana had begged me to free myself of the commitment."

"Life is not that simple," Bingley protested.

"That is where you and I differ! Even if some day I discover Elizabeth Bennet has accepted another man to husband, I will never stop loving her, nor will I quit doing all within my power to see her to an easy life."

"I have not stopped loving Miss Bennet," Bingley protested.

"So you say, but, if I were the lady, I would prefer, at this point, to know your detestation, for your love had struck me a blow that tore my heart in two."

CHAPTER FIVE

DARCY STEPPED DOWN FROM his carriage before Longbourn. There had been frost upon the Thames when he departed London, and it was not much warmer here in the countryside. Mr. Cowan's report said, apparently, no one, other than Mr. Bennet, knew of Elizabeth's whereabouts. Therefore, Darcy braced himself for the upcoming confrontation. He had been in London a month, moving about the chess pieces of his father's legacy and reclaiming his reputation as a ruthless businessman. From what his Cousin Fitzwilliam had shared, Darcy's maneuvers had left the Earl of Matlock scrambling to set his finances aright. To the news of his uncle's failures, Darcy had replied, "Uncle Matlock has always assumed his peerage would provide him power over the rest of the world. He forgets the majority of England care not for the posturing displayed regularly upon the floor of the House of Lords; the average citizens of England are too busy earning their daily wage to give a fig about anything but feeding their families."

"Mr. Darcy for Mr. Bennet," he said when the Longbourn housekeeper answered his knock upon the door.

From the shocked look upon the woman's countenance, news of his "supposed" demise had reached Hertfordshire. "Is the master expecting you, sir?" she managed.

"Simply inform Mr. Bennet that I am prepared to sit before his house for as long as is necessary to hold a conversation with him."

The woman bobbed a curtsey and scurried away, leaving Darcy standing in the foyer. Closing his eyes, he brought forth one of his favorite images of Elizabeth Bennet. She had walked him out to say her "good evenings." It was the day she had agreed to his proposal, and they each had spoken to her father, seeking Mr. Bennet's permission.

She stood before him, so close—too close for propriety's sake, but still not close enough to sate his desires. Everything had been too recent for what could be called gaiety to mark their interactions, but the evening had passed tranquilly. They both realized, without discussing it, there was no longer anything material to be dreaded and the comfort of ease and familiarity would come in time.

"I shall speak to Mama this evening," she had whispered, never looking away from his steady gaze. "We may tell everyone tomorrow."

He had intertwined their fingers and had tugged her closer still. "It is enough to know we will spend our life together," he said softly. "I adore you, Elizabeth Bennet."

As was typical, she blushed, but she boldly rose upon her tiptoes and briefly kissed his lips. It was not the most passionate kiss they would share, nor was it the first time they had kissed, but it was the first kiss where they would share a brief moment of familiarity where she had initiated the action. "I look forward to being your wife, Fitzwilliam Darcy," she had responded as she rested her forehead against his chest. "Very soon," she had whispered, the heat of her mouth penetrating the fine lawn of his shirt. His heart had never known such happiness as at that moment.

"Mr. Darcy," Mr. Bennet's voice brought Darcy back to reality. "I understand you *insist* upon speaking to me."

Darcy nodded his agreement. "You do not appear surprised to learn I am not dead," he accused.

Mr. Bennet's frown deepened, as if the man had not considered that point previously. The man announced in contempt, "I have been unfortunate of late to have been the recipient of a bevy of callers from London." The man turned on his heels to lead the way to his study. "Come along, and I will repeat to you what I told the others."

Darcy did not like the idea that others searched for Elizabeth. He prayed she was not in danger because of him.

Once he and Bennet had closed the door behind them, Darcy said, "I wish to know where Elizabeth can be found."

Mr. Bennet said with a snarl, "And I wish for five thousand a year, a sensible wife, and an heir to whom I might pass this estate. Most assuredly, our wishes are not happening for either of us."

Darcy kept his tone even. He had expected Mr. Bennet's anger. "Unless Elizabeth has exchanged vows with another, our betrothal remains in place. I mean to claim my bride."

"You forfeited that right when you failed to appear for the exchange of vows. The license has expired by more than three years," Bennet hissed.

"A new license can be procured," Darcy stated plainly.

"Elizabeth despises you," Bennet insisted.

Darcy smiled, recalling how he had suffered when Elizabeth Bennet disdained him above all others. "It shall not be the first time your daughter found fault with me. Yet, I am willing to risk her shrewish tongue for the opportunity to plead my case. Your daughter is of age, our coming together is no longer your choice."

"It was not my choice when you appeared in this very room nearly four years ago. I permitted Elizabeth her say then, but I will advise her against another round of heartache with you if she asks."

Darcy argued, "It was never my choice to leave Elizabeth on our wedding day. I was snatched off the streets of London and held captive aboard a ship sailing the southern hemisphere for more than three years."

"So say you," Bennet accused.

"Would you care to view the scars upon my back?" Darcy

growled. "I put up a fight in my attempts to return to your daughter's side."

"I do not care to view you or your uncle or your aunt upon my threshold ever again." Bennet slammed his fist down hard upon the desk, sending papers scattering. "You and yours cost me my most precious gift. I have not known a day of peace since you stole away my darling Lizzy. My precious girl is lost to me — to her family forever. My other daughters possess no future, for they are marked by the shame you exacted upon my household."

Darcy did not respond to Bennet's accusations, for, on the whole, they were true. Instead, he persisted with his arguments. "It can all be set to right if you will simply tell me where Elizabeth has been sent. Permit your daughter to make the choice. Afterwards, I will assist you in finding well-placed husbands for the others."

Bennet leaned forward to point his finger at Darcy. Vehemently, he gritted out his insult. "Why would I provide the likes of you with Elizabeth's location? You did not honor her enough to leave her untouched for another to claim in your absence. I might have found her another husband, if not for you. She might have been able to accept Bingley or Sir William's son, but no man wants another's leavings. You ruined Elizabeth twice over."

Darcy knew great shame at having succumbed to his lust, for he knew Elizabeth had suffered because of their impetuous actions; however, he did not regret those few cherished moments. The memory of Elizabeth in his embrace had sustained him in his darkest hours. He did not respond: Bennet was in no mood for an apology. Rather, he returned to his previous argument. "Elizabeth can decide if she will forgive me. All I require is her location."

"As I told Lord Matlock when he offered me six thousand pounds to use as dowries for Jane, Mary, and Kitty, I do not know where Elizabeth has settled. When I took her into my embrace on the day she departed Longbourn, it was the last time we spoke. I do not know whether she is dead or alive," Bennet said on an angry sob.

Darcy was concerned as to why Matlock wanted to know of Elizabeth's whereabouts, but he did not speak his fears to Mr. Bennet. If Matlock expected Darcy to fall in line by issuing a threat to Elizabeth, his uncle would be sadly mistaken. Matlock would soon know Darcy's wrath. "Not even a letter?" he asked.

"It was decided it would be best if no one knew of Elizabeth's new life. Mrs. Bennet could not be trusted with the tale, and Elizabeth thought it best for her sisters if they were not placed in a position to choose between her and their futures. Every vestige of Elizabeth's existence as part of this family has been removed from Longbourn, except her name in the family Bible. The idea rips my heart out." Tears formed in Mr. Bennet's eyes.

"Elizabeth turned one and twenty in the months following what occurred after our wedding day. She can conduct her own business. The settlement I arranged for her is in her hands now."

"None of that matters," Bennet declared with a sad shake of his head. "I cannot assist you, Darcy."

"Cannot or will not?" Darcy demanded.

"Both."

Darcy swallowed the angry words rushing to his lips. If the man could not view how desperate Darcy was to find Elizabeth, this trail had ended. However, before he left, it was necessary for him to know what else the Matlocks had practiced against him. "What of the Countess of Matlock? What role does she play in this drama?"

"Not Lady Matlock," Bennet corrected. "I have not had the pleasure, or should I say, displeasure, of the countess's call upon Longbourn. No. It was that harridan to whom Collins bows and scrapes. We at Longbourn were again gifted with the less than gracious Lady Catherine de Bourgh. She assumed I required more of an enticement than her brother had delivered. Instead of six thousand pounds, her ladyship offered me seventy-five hundred. Fifteen hundred pounds more than the earl. When I refused her, with a few choice words of what I thought of both her and her brother, she breezed out of here with her customary threats to my family and another round of insults directed at my wife's low connections."

Darcy had held suspicions regarding Lady Catherine's involvement in his kidnapping, for during those years at sea, he had heard a handful of comments regarding the woman who had paid to have him removed from London. Most assuredly, none aboard the ship expected him to learn of the duplicity practiced against him. However, he knew of two times the captain of *The Lost Sparrow* had written to London to demand additional payments to keep him imprisoned. Originally, he had thought the woman could have been Miss Bingley, but after the first year, Miss Bingley would have desired his return in hopes he would marry her. On the other hand, when Lady Catherine arrived upon his doorstep to demand he do his duty to his Cousin Anne and then had confessed at having called upon Elizabeth and demanded Elizabeth release him, they had argued in emphatic tones. He denied any contract between him and Anne and pledged his love for Elizabeth, and she had made a variety of threats that he belatedly realized likely had led to the worst years of his life.

He said in more calm than he felt, "I will deal with Lady Catherine. She will not dare to cross your path again."

"I have threatened both of your relations with violence if they even think to darken my door again."

"Yet, you still refuse to tell me what you know of Elizabeth."

"My daughter wished a new life," Bennet said simply. "I promised I would guard her wishes with my life. It is all she asked of me when I sent her out into the world alone."

"You mean Elizabeth wanted a new life—one that did not include me?" Darcy asked.

"Elizabeth was told you were dead. She had few options."

Darcy stood. "I will never stop searching for her. Until I hear the words from her lips denying our relationship, Elizabeth is my betrothed. Nothing has changed except the date of our wedding."

Bennet did not rise to show Darcy out, nor did he summon a servant to do the honors. "You have erred, Darcy," he said as he leaned back into his chair, a sad smile upon his lips, "everything has changed, and you cannot turn back time."

Although he did not want to depart without a definite location for where to find Elizabeth, Darcy knew if both Matlock and Lady Catherine could not break Bennet, neither would Darcy.

Frustrated, he returned to his coach to depart Longbourn. "London," he instructed Mr. Farrin.

"Aye, sir."

Darcy climbed into the carriage and laid his head back against the squabs. "Where have you gone, Elizabeth Bennet?" The coach rolled into motion. He briefly closed his eyes and attempted to keep his memories of the woman he loved fresh, but, even so, he knew he no longer held a clear image of her. "Do not leave me, love. I do not think I can live out my days without you."

He stared out the small window of the coach, watching the trees lining the drive speed by as Mr. Farrin set the horses to their paces while Darcy decided upon what he should do next. Lost in his thoughts, it had taken him several seconds to realize Miss Bennet stood beside the open gate to Longbourn waving her arms in the air, not in farewell, but in an attempt to draw his attention. He used his cane to rap on the coach's roof to signal Mr. Farrin to stop.

When the coach rolled to a halt, Darcy disembarked and trotted back to where the lady waited for him.

"Thank you for stopping," she called as he drew near.

Darcy presented the lady a brief bow. "It is pleasant to see you again, Miss Bennet."

"And I you. I could not believe you walked through Longbourn's door again. We all had heard you had died in some sort of attack in London. Footpads or highwaymen." She blushed. "I suppose there are no highwaymen in the City. When I saw you today, I thought myself delusional for a moment, for Elizabeth has been much on my mind of late."

"There are many days since we were last together, I considered death superior to the conditions under which I resided."

The lady glanced to his waiting coach, "Would it be ungenerous of me to ask that your coachman move your carriage around the bend in the road so it cannot be seen from Longbourn's upper storeys. I would prefer those within did not observe us conversing."

Curious as to what Miss Bennet had to say, he presented Farrin the necessary orders, and then he offered the lady his arm. Nodding toward a nearby wooded path, he said, "Perhaps you would honor me with a walk together."

She tentatively placed her hand on his arm, and they stepped off the main road to the manor house. "You have come looking for Elizabeth," she said softly.

"I have, but your father claims no knowledge of Miss Elizabeth's directions," he explained.

"I am not surprised," she admitted. "Mr. Bennet has shared nothing with the family as to what has become of my sister. Whatever Elizabeth did not take with her has been given away to charity. The idea was to 'disown' her—banish Lizzy—in order to save the rest of us, but the plan was an act in futility. The neighborhood is too small for others not to consider my sister tainted and us equally so by connection."

Darcy heard the sadness in her words. "I am grieved my shortsightedness brought ruin to your door."

Miss Bennet blushed thoroughly. "I did not mean to place blame upon your shoulders, Mr. Darcy. I always believed something beyond reason kept you from Elizabeth's side."

He admitted, "I was attacked upon London's docks and pressed into service upon a ship sailing under multiple flags."

"A ship meant to rob others!" she gasped. Tears rushed to her eyes. "Even I could never have imagined such an outcome! I simply knew you loved Elizabeth too dearly to abandon her unless you suffered some great tragedy."

He confided, "Thoughts of your sister kept me alive for

nearly four years. Two months ago, I escaped when a British naval ship came near where *The Lost Sparrow* was hiding. I jumped overboard during the night and swam for my life."

"How courageous," she said in awe. "But I always recognized your strong will. You are not a man who would abandon those for whom you cared."

He knew she was thinking of Bingley, but Darcy mentioned nothing of recently seeing his former friend. He would not present Miss Bennet false hopes. Instead, he cleared his throat. "Miss Bennet, your father tells me my uncle, Lord Matlock, and my aunt, Lady Catherine, have each recently called upon him, offering to finance dowries for you and your sisters if your father would tell them where Elizabeth is now living. As my uncle conducted questionable business dealings in my name during in my absence, I fear Matlock and others in my family mean to implore Miss Elizabeth to deny me again. Matlock and his sister will make a similar offer to Elizabeth, and, God bless her, you know her nature. She will agree to shoulder the punishment for something she has not done in order to save you and your sisters. She will slip from sight, and I might never find her. I am willing to fight the Devil himself to win her back, but I require assistance in locating her."

Miss Bennet frowned, "Elizabeth has already suffered enough for our sake."

"Yet, we both know she would agree to much worse to protect each of you."

Miss Bennet remained silent for several minutes as they strolled along the path together. At length, she said, "If you are asking if I know of Elizabeth's whereabouts, I do not. She and Papa were very secretive after she refused both Mr. Bingley and Sir William's son, John Lucas."

"Other relatives?" Darcy speculated.

"Early on, Papa's relations in Scotland refused to take Elizabeth in," she explained.

"Your mother's relations?"

"There are only the Phillipses and the Gardiners," she

confided. "Aunt and Uncle Phillips are too close to escape the gossips, and, although the Gardiners volunteered to take Elizabeth in, my sister refused."

Darcy knew he frowned, but her explanation was almost too perfect. "Why would she not seek assistance from the Gardiners? From my limited observations, they always proved to be most supportive of you both."

Miss Bennet paused and looked away. "I do not know the reason Elizabeth refused, but I suspect—"

When the lady blushed again, he prompted, "You may speak honestly with me, Miss Bennet. I will not judge you. I know, like me, you desire Elizabeth's best interests."

She nodded her understanding, but did not look at him. "I ... I saw you ... you and Lizzy leave—"

"The library at Netherfield," he finished for her when she looked off to the path before them.

"Yes," she said so softly he could barely hear her.

He cleared his throat in discomfort. "Your sister and I should not have anticipated our vows," he confessed. "I have no excuse except I love Elizabeth Bennet to distraction."

"Not *loved*?" she asked. Again, he thought the lady might be thinking of Bingley's promises of cherish her forever.

"If I must search every village and town in England, I mean to find her again and profess my undying love and pray she has not chosen another."

"I am glad of it," she said. "Elizabeth deserves happiness." She looked to where they had walked. "I should return to the house. I am certain your visit has set Mama worrying again, and it is not fair to leave Mama's 'nerves' to Mary's care each time."

He turned with her. Although he was not certain he wanted to know the answer, he asked, nevertheless. "Miss Bennet, my cousin, Colonel Fitzwilliam, reports when he called upon your father several months after my disappearance, Colonel Forster told him a tale of how an older gentleman called upon Mr. Bennet regarding Elizabeth. Is it possible your sister departed with this man?"

It was the lady's turn to appear confused. "The only gentleman of whom I am aware of calling on Papa during that trying time, and I would certainly not name him as 'old,' was your valet."

Darcy took a step away from her to digest her words. "Mr. Sheffield, are you certain?" His valet was ten years Darcy's senior, in his early forties now. Older than Darcy, but, most assuredly, not as old as the man Darcy had been imagining.

"My rooms overlook Longbourn's drive. Just as I saw you disembark today, I viewed your valet step down from a small coach one afternoon some two months after your wedding date. I assumed he was delivering a message from your family to Mr. Bennet. He only remained at Longbourn a few hours. He did not even stay for supper or to take tea with us."

"How long after Sheffield's visit did Miss Elizabeth depart Longbourn?"

"Perhaps three weeks. Papa placed her in the family coach, and we all said our farewells. The coach was gone most of the day, but not overnight, returning shortly after dark. Surely, Elizabeth did not leave with your valet."

"Miss Bennet," Darcy said, "I do not want to speculate." Although he did not wish to hope Sheffield had done the honorable thing and assisted Elizabeth, the action would have been quite typical of the man. Albert Sheffield had always been his compass when Darcy lost his way. "My Cousin Fitzwilliam says it was chaotic in those early weeks of my going missing. Yet, I would ask that you not mention Mr. Sheffield's presence to another until after I clarify if this information is significant or not."

The lady reached out to stay his departure. "I fear it may be too late. Mama, in a fit of anger, at Lady Catherine's most recent snubs told her ladyship your servant had possessed more empathy than did your aunt."

CHAPTER SIX

ALTHOUGH MR. FARRIN HAD made the journey from Hertfordshire to London with all good speed, Darcy was not able to locate the directions for where Mr. Sheffield's pension was delivered and be on his way again, for his household was at sixes and sevens when he arrived.

He let himself into the house with his key when no one answered his knock. He would be glad when Michaelmas arrived and Mr. Thacker could return to his position at Darcy House. Thacker's present employer refused to release the man until the quarter day.

Darcy caught a maid by the arm to ask, "What is amiss?"

"It be Mrs. Fitzwilliam, sir. Her time for lying-in has come."

Immediately, Darcy was storming the steps, attempting to reach Georgiana. He would have entered her quarters if Lady Matlock had not exited the room just as he reached for the latch.

Her ladyship shoved him backwards. "You cannot go in. This is woman's work."

He glared at the offending door keeping him from his sister's side. "I just want Georgiana to know I am here."

"Such is Fitzwilliam's right, not yours," she declared.

"Georgiana is still my sister," he insisted. "I will still protect her."

"And she is my son's wife. The mother of my first

grandchild."

All Darcy's frustrations of late could not be set aside any longer. "I do not appreciate how the Fitzwilliam family seems to think this house is theirs and my word means nothing," he accused.

His aunt pulled herself up stiffly. "Georgiana is now a Fitzwilliam."

"She would not have been so if not for the interference of your husband and his sister. Moreover, you know, as well as I, I do not speak of my sister when I speak of the ills the Fitzwilliams have brought to my door. My sister is equal Fitzwilliam and Darcy, as was her mother."

"And the colonel?"

"Another exception," he growled. "At least, your younger son did not set himself against me and mine. He did all he could to keep Georgiana safe, and for that, I will always be in his debt."

His aunt did not respond to his declarations. Instead, she charged, "I understand you banished Matlock from this house and your life; yet, you still call foul when it comes to my family."

"I pray you are ignorant of your husband's maneuverings of late. I pray you were not part of those who set themselves as judge and jury for my life. If so, please know, after this day, you, too, will no longer be welcomed in my homes."

"What has Matlock executed to set himself against you?" Her ladyship's frown lines deepened.

"You should know, if you do not already have knowledge of the act, over the last four years I have attempted to determine who had me kidnapped. I know someone did, for I often heard those of the crew of *The Lost Sparrow* speak of my abduction and the money paid to remove me from London. Since my return to England, I have begun to wonder how my uncle, your husband, was so quick to London to take over the running of my household and my business interests when he was supposedly in Derbyshire, such was the reason I was asked to look in upon the shipment from India only two days before my wedding. According to the note I received in Hertfordshire, you and he had been called home for some sort of emergency and could not attend the wedding. His lordship begged me to oversee the shipment. Explain to me how the day I went missing, Lord Matlock was sitting behind my desk at Darcy House and ruling my household. How did word reach him so quickly?"

"None of what you say makes sense. I took ill with a heavy cough and fever before your wedding. Such was to be the note Matlock sent to you at Netherfield—a note to offer our excuses," she said in what appeared to be true disbelief, but, Darcy's frustrations would not abate long enough to allow her any innocence in this matter.

"Even now, after four years, the earl and his sister mean to keep me from reuniting with Miss Elizabeth, and I will not tolerate their interference," he stated in no-nonsense tones.

"I do not understand," Lady Matlock declared. "Although Matlock thought you could have made a more advantageous choice of brides, he was willing to accept Miss Elizabeth into the family."

"On the subject of advantageous marriages, did you truly approve of Fitzwilliam taking Anne to wife? How could Anne de Bourgh have advanced his career? Even if we had all agreed to an alliance of the families, how could my Cousin Anne have served any of us: Fitzwilliam, me, or Lindale? She has been kept tethered to her mother's side to the point she is incapable of making the slightest decision for herself. Anne would never be able to serve as mistress of an estate, and, God only knows, whether she could bear her husband an heir and survive or whether she could tend the child afterwards. Yet, as best as I can determine, you made no move to prevent the manipulations Matlock and Lady Catherine practiced in that matter. Fitzwilliam married Georgiana to prevent your husband from forcing my sister to marry Lindale. You know, perfectly well, if I had been here, I would not have entertained the slightest possibility of such an arrangement. Moreover, I would have executed all within my power to prevent Fitzwilliam from being coerced into marrying Anne. Your younger son deserved a better life than to be bullied by Lady Catherine for another twenty years."

Her ladyship appeared quite shaken by Darcy's accusations; however, he had not finished his tirade. "I just returned from Hertfordshire where I learned both your husband and his elder sister have called upon Mr. Bennet and offered the man a great deal of money if the gentleman would share with them the location of where they might discover Miss Elizabeth Bennet. I ask myself why they have chosen to assist the Bennets, when neither, as you say, thought my proposal to the lady would provide an 'advantageous match.'" He shook his head to clear his thinking. "Nor do I comprehend what they hope to achieve when they discovered her whereabouts. Do they plan to gloat at her reduced circumstances? Be certain she continues to suffer for the mistakes I made in trusting your family? However, there is one thing I do know for certain, if either of them places himself again between me and the lady, I will march over, not around them, to reach her."

His aunt blanched white in obvious distress. "I shall speak to Matlock."

"Warn him, not just speak to him," he said in sad tones. "His lordship's supposed 'guidance' has cost me a large portion of the Darcy fortune, but I will not permit him also to steal away my greatest treasure. Warn him I am George Darcy's son, and I will come for his blood, if necessary, to protect those I love."

It was another two days before his coach arrived in Brighton. "Ironic," he whispered as anticipation rolled through him. It had been Lydia Bennet's stay in Brighton that had precipitated his winning Elizabeth's agreement to marry him. "Silly chit," he murmured as he thought how he had tracked Elizabeth's youngest sister and his former school chum, George Wickham, down in a seedy inn in London and forced Wickham to marry the girl, thus, earning Elizabeth's undying affection.

"I pray her love is undying" he whispered.

When he had departed Darcy House, he had kissed his sister and his new nephew. As Fitzwilliam had predicted,

Pemberley was safe. Georgiana's son could inherit Pemberley and the Darcy fortune if Darcy chose not to marry; yet, he wanted his own son—a child whose surname was Darcy, not Fitzwilliam to inherit what his grandfather and his father had spent their lifetimes crafting so he might present it to his own son one day.

His coach eased to the curb, and Jasper opened the door to set down the steps so Darcy could exit the coach. It was late in the afternoon and the streets were thin of people. He turned in the direction to which Jasper gestured to read the bookseller's sign hanging above the establishment's door. In the bottom corner were the words: "Albert Sheffield, Proprietor."

"Excellent," he murmured as he set his steps to cross the street. "Wait for me," he instructed his driver and footman. He still was not certain whether there was a true connection between his former valet and Elizabeth Bennet, but he would soon know the answer.

Elizabeth swallowed the words rushing to her lips. For the third time in as many minutes, Mr. Townsend had asked her to join him for supper. "I am sorry, sir," she enunciated each word clearly, "as I have said previously, I could not consider leaving my uncle alone. Mr. Sheffield has been ill for several days now, and the brunt of his care, as well as the operation of the store has fallen to me, as is only appropriate considering how my uncle's generosity has always been directed at me." She glanced to the clock on the shelf beyond Townsend's shoulder. "In fact, I must close the shop and retrieve my daughter from Mrs. Harris's house so I might return before my uncle wakes and requires my assistance."

She started around the man to open the door to usher him out. Unfortunately, he caught her arm to pull her into his body. Instinctively, she stiffened. She had not been near a man since she had lain with Fitzwilliam Darcy, and Elizabeth had no desire to think upon allowing another man such privileges.

"I would thank you to remove your hands from my person, Mr. Townsend. These actions are highly reprehensible to me," she hissed, "and not likely ever to win my favor."

"You require a man, Mrs. Dartmore, and I require a woman of merit in my bed." He bent his head as if he meant to kiss her.

Elizabeth turned her head to the side to prevent his lips from claiming hers and prepared to strike him; however, such was not necessary. Townsend was sent flying backward to land sprawled upon the floor. In her struggles, she had not heard the bell over the door signal someone had entered the shop. Quickly adjusting the cut of the dress she wore, she turned to express her gratitude only to feel the air rush from her lungs and her knees go weak. Her vision blurred as her rescuer turned to reach for her. "William!" she called as everything went black.

Darcy had seen her through the window coming toward him, and his heart had leapt with joy. Yet, things changed quickly. She had been brought up short. For a few brief seconds, a man in a gig had blocked Darcy's view as he jumped out of the way of the careless driver. Finally reaching the door, he opened it to discover the horror of another man holding Elizabeth in his embrace.

Unable to control the instant anger coursing through him, he rushed forward to grab the man by the nape of his neck to spin him around, landing a solid punch to the tip of the scoundrel's chin. The dastard went flying backwards. Sharp breaths rushed in and out of Darcy's lungs as his stance dared the man to rise from the floor.

Sensing her behind him, he swiveled around just as the light in her eyes turned dark, and she swooned. His name was upon her lips.

Darcy moved without thinking, catching her under the arms to drag her up against him. "Come, love," he coaxed as she sagged, a dead weight, nearly knocking him over until he locked his knees in place and dragged her deeper into his embrace. He tapped her cheeks lightly. "Wake, Elizabeth."

The man he knocked to the floor demanded, "Who in blazes do you think you are?"

"The lady's husband." Darcy raised his eyes to view a blanket-draped man, a man who had served him for more than sixteen years.

"Good day, Sheffield," he said with more calm than he felt. Darcy bent to lift Elizabeth into his arms to carry her to a nearby chair, where he sat first and cradled her on his lap.

"You are Lieutenant Dartmore?" the stranger questioned.

Darcy glanced to Sheffield who held himself perfectly still. Obviously, Darcy's former valet had provided approval for the charade Elizabeth practiced. With a lift of his eyebrow, indicating his disdain, Sheffield said, "Did I not just say the gentleman is my niece's husband?"

"I thought you dead," the man accused.

"Hardly," Darcy responded pointedly, evoking his best Master of Pemberley voice. "Now, I mean to tend my wife." He liked the sound of the word "wife" on his lips. "And as she and I are long overdue for a reunion and do not require an audience, if I were you, I would make myself scarce, before I recall how poorly you treated her and challenge you to a duel."

The man frowned deeply, but presented Darcy a nod of agreement, turning crisply on his heels to exit the store.

"Thank you, Sheffield," Darcy said in dismissal. "Thank you for seeing to Elizabeth when others turned their backs on her. I am forever in your debt."

The man he had known since Darcy was twelve years of age bowed as would any good servant in addressing his master, but Darcy and this man had always held a relationship that had gone beyond the hierarchy of those positions. Likely, it was because Darcy had required someone's advice — an older brother of sorts — after his mother's passing and during his father's deep grief. Perhaps it was because Sheffield had been born a gentleman's son, as was Darcy. The only difference was George Darcy was worth more than five times that of Sheffield's father, and the late Artemis Sheffield had had four sons to provide for. The eldest would receive the small estate the family owned. The second entered the military, as was expected of second sons, such as his Cousin Fitzwilliam. The third took up law. Albert Sheffield was to join the clergy. Yet, the young Albert knew himself not the type to deliver sermons, and so he sought to become a teacher at one of the universities. He had come to George Darcy's employment as a tutor for the elder Darcy's son while he waited his turn to claim a professorship. After being with the Darcy family for several years, Sheffield transitioned into the role of a gentleman's gentleman.

Sheffield pulled the blanket tighter about his person. "I ... I am most gratified ... to view you ... safe, sir," he said with emotion filling his voice. "And to be accurate ... about my care ... of Miss Elizabeth, it is I ... who has been blessed ... to be of service ... to her. Enjoy your reunion."

Then, Sheffield disappeared toward the rear of the store, leaving Darcy alone with Elizabeth. He shook her gently and cooed, "Come, love. Wake for me." Darcy studied her features as she made her return to consciousness. How often over the last four years had he imagined waking up beside her? More than he could properly recall.

Her eyes fluttered open and closed several times before she smiled at him. Shards of his broken heart fell into place once more. She whispered, "William."

For several elongated seconds everything was perfection. Then, reality arrived. Elizabeth bolted upright, fighting to scramble from his hold on her. Literally, she fell backwards upon her rear, having tripped over her hem.

"Away!" she cautioned, holding out her hand to ward off his advance. "Who are you?" she demanded.

Darcy rose to extend his hand to assist her to her feet. "You know who I am," he said with a small smile of understanding.

"You cannot be Fitzwilliam Darcy. They told me Fitzwilliam Darcy was dead."

He extended his hand a second time. "Trust me. I am very much alive, although there were many attempts to end my life."

"William?" Her mouth formed the word, but no sound escaped her lips. A thousand different emotions darted across her features: Confusion. Fear. Anger. Defeat. Denial. Hope.

Darcy knelt before her to gather her to him. "Yes, love. William. Your William."

Her hands searched his face—his shoulders—and his hair. "How can it be you?" She leaned into him then, nearly knocking him over. She kissed his jaw—his throat—the corner of his mouth. Her tears wet his cravat. Wet his face. Her softness. Her scent. Filled him. Returning all the pieces of his heart to where they belonged.

At length, their mouths met. Urgency. Joining. Parting. Rejoining. A reacquaintance. He ran a string of kisses over her cheeks and nose before returning to her mouth. Their tongues intertwined. Testing. Offering proof of what existed between them, while comparing this moment to all those they had known previously. For the first time since that fateful day on the docks, Darcy felt whole again.

"You have no idea how frightened I was without you. The pain on my father's face when we parted was unbearable."

"I did not wish to frighten you," he said softly. His fingers renewed the memory of her as he spoke. "In truth, I was not certain you were with Sheffield." He kissed her cheeks and forehead. "Since my first day back in England, I set my mind to finding you. I constantly prayed you had not claimed another." He lifted her chin with his fingertips. "Pray, say it is not too late for us."

For the briefest of moments, she swayed as if she meant to fall deeper into his embrace, and then she was shoving against his chest, demanding her release. "Late!" She scrambled to her feet. "I am late!" She rushed to lock the shop door. "I must go!"

"Go where?" he asked as he trailed her through the shelving area toward the back of the store.

She turned to him, walking backward. "I must call upon Mrs. Harris, Mr. Sheffield's particular friend."

Darcy was thankful she was not hurrying off to meet another man, but he wondered how this Mrs. Harris superseded their need to speak of a future together. Was not their relationship more important than a social call? Could she not send her regrets?

She slid her hands into the sleeves of her pelisse before reaching for the door. She stopped quite suddenly, never turning around, but she said, "I would be pleased if you would accompany me. We have much to say to each other, but I am required at Mrs. Harris's home immediately."

For some reason her shoulders stiffened, but she smiled up at him when he joined her in the opened passageway behind the bookstore. "Would you prefer the use of my carriage?" he said when he fell in step with her. "The weather is quite cold for early September." Darcy wished to reach for her hand to place it on his arm as a symbol of possession, but Elizabeth tightly clasped her reticule before her, evidently not wishing his touch at the moment. At least, she had not sent him away.

"It is only a few streets over," she explained. "And you know I am an excellent walker." Her eyebrow lifted in a natural challenge, and he breathed a bit easier. They were still on common ground.

"I recall your walking to Netherfield through the mud," he said with a return of the easiness between them. There was so much he wished to say to her, but she bit her bottom lip as she walked, indicating her nervousness. He understood. His heart was pounding out a fast tattoo. It had been so long since he had even looked upon her, the whole situation unreal. Therefore, he chose a subject not centered on their future, thinking she must be as overwhelmed as he. He did not wish to push her too quickly. Certainly, his reappearance had to be a shock to her. "Mr. Sheffield possesses a 'particular friend'?" he asked.

"Mrs. Harris," she explained, although she did not look at him, a fact which perplexed Darcy, "set her sights on Sheffield when we arrived in Brighton. He has been slow to respond: I fear he worries what is to become of me if he takes up with the lady."

Darcy thought if she would again accept the offer of his hand in marriage, Mr. Sheffield could choose whether to pursue the lady or not. He wished to voice those thoughts, but there would be time to reconnect with her later. Darcy had no other plans for the time being, other than to win Elizabeth's approval of their joining.

"The man in the shop," he began, attempting to learn whether she wanted the gentleman's attentions or not.

"Mr. Townsend," she supplied the man's name. "Mr. Sidney Townsend."

"Mr. Townsend," he repeated, all along thinking he would be soon learning all he could of the man, perhaps another job for Mr. Cowan. Seeing Townsend apparently forcing his attentions on Elizabeth reminded Darcy of the scene he had walked in on between Georgiana and George Wickham. "The man in the shop called me 'Lieutenant Dartmore.'"

She blushed thoroughly. "Mr. Sheffield had told several in the area he had been previously in the employ of Mr. Darcy of Pemberley. Before arriving in Brighton, he and I had decided I would be posing as his niece."

She led the way along a narrow path on the outskirts of the thriving port city. When he came abreast of her again, he asked, "I appreciate Mr. Sheffield moving to protect you, but when you fainted, Sheffield told Mr. Townsend I was your husband, Lieutenant Dartmore."

"Of His Majesty's Royal Navy," she confirmed. Another blush flooded her cheeks.

"I do not mind assuming the role of your husband," he said, "but why was it necessary for you to be a married lady? Being Sheffield's niece should have been sufficient for those about town who had a desire to know more of you."

She ignored his question, crossing through the yard of a nicely situated cottage. "Mrs. Harris?" Elizabeth called as she rapped on the door. "It is Elizabeth." She knocked louder. "I am grieved to be late."

When no one answered, she moved to the window to peer inside. Tapping on the glass she called, "Mrs. Harris!" Her voice began to display her alarm. "Mrs. Harris!"

He tried the door, but it was latched. "I will go around to the back."

"I shall go with you," she said as he led the way.

They found the back door wide open. "Mrs. Harris?" she called again.

Darcy placed her behind him. "Allow me to go first."

"She would never leave the door open," Elizabeth said, her voice trembling. "The lady lives alone, and, of late, there has been an influx of men searching for food and goods to either sell or pawn for money."

Darcy edged around the corner of a large china chest to note a middle-aged woman sprawled out on the floor, a trickle of blood marking her forehead. He knelt to examine the lady's condition, but Elizabeth sprinted around him, calling out as she opened doors along the hall.

"Lizzy! Lizzy Anne!" She slammed another door and rushed the stairs. "Lizzy! Come out! Do not be frightened! Lizzy!" she screamed, turning in circles.

He caught her then, holding her in place. "Who is Lizzy?" he demanded. She sucked in a quick breath, but he knew her beyond recovery because of the wild look in her eyes. He presented her a good shake, his own anxiety rising quickly. "Who is Lizzy?" he repeated.

"Our daughter," she murmured, collapsing against him.

CHAPTER SEVEN

"DAUGHTER?" HE QUESTIONED. SHE felt him sway in place, but he held her to him.

Elizabeth's mind attempted to understand what had occurred. "There must be—" her mind repeated. Needing to continue her search, she broke free of him.

She looked at him as if seeing him for the first time. Her head felt foggy, and she gave it a good shake to clear it, but to no relief. Her mind kept repeating two words: Lizzy. William. Lizzy. William.

Elizabeth stumbled away from him. Although she knew her thoughts irrational, she had to act immediately. Racing up the stairs, she continued to call her daughter's name, going so far as to look inside wardrobes, behind drapes and under beds. "Elizabeth Anne Dartmore, show yourself!" she ordered in her best mother's voice, but nothing in the house stirred.

She rushed back to the top of the stairs to stare down at him. He had not moved. "Did you take her?" she demanded. "Please do not take her from me, William. I cannot live without her. I nearly died giving birth to her!" Again, a sense of urgency filled her. What were the chances that her wayward betrothed returned on the very same day as her daughter had gone missing?

"I did not know I had a daughter," he declared in a voice that spoke of dismay, but Elizabeth could not be certain of his honesty. It was all too convenient. Moreover, she knew Mr.

Darcy a powerful man, who would do all possible to have what he wanted.

Her announcement of the existence of their daughter had shaken Darcy's world as nothing ever had. Immediately, he understood why Elizabeth had made use of the tale of a deceased husband. Even before she broke away from him, Darcy knew what she was thinking: He would have thought it also if the situation had been reversed. Such did not mean when she accused him of stealing away their child that it did not rip away part of his soul.

He had stood his ground as she frantically searched for the child. "Elizabeth Anne," he had whispered, learning his daughter's name. Named for the girl's mother and his. Even though he had not been present in her life, Elizabeth had presented the child his mother's Christian name: Anne.

"I did not know I had a daughter," he had responded to her accusation. He found breathing difficult, as she stared down at him: Vehemence marked her features.

"You have yet to explain where you have been for four years," she hissed. She rushed down the steps to strike him. "How could you? I loved you!" She hit him again, her fist pounding against his chest. Her anger had not come simply from her fears for their daughter, but, also, for all she had endured because he had trusted the wrong people. He stood very still and permitted her finally to express her rage at the world. At least, one of them should be free of guilt.

He braced himself for each blow. For four years he had stood strong when the Devil himself used his whip against him, but nothing had ever executed the kind of damage her small fists did.

Eventually, she wrapped her hands about the lapels of his coat and tugged hard, as if she wished to rip out his heart. She had no idea she had accomplished exactly that. "Did you take her?" she begged, sobbing against his shirt. "Did you come today to tell me you meant to take Lizzy away?"

He did not answer. Darcy knew her reason would arrive when her emotions had been spent. Instead, he wrapped his arms about her and held her against him. "I would never punish you. If I had known we shared a child, I would have come, but it would have been for both the child and her mother." She fought to be free of him; yet, he held her in place. "You know my heart, Elizabeth," he bent his head to whisper into her ear. "If anyone knows me, it is you. I have shared more of myself with you than with any other person of my acquaintance. Even more than with my sister. I know others, those who have never exchanged even the slightest form of interaction with me, speak of me as an arrogant, uncaring person. I know how I appear to the world. You, too, once held such thoughts," he ventured, "however, I pray I have proved otherwise."

She sagged against him. "You must have her," she pleaded. "You would keep her safe when others would not."

"We will find her. I promise." He spoke with more calmness than he felt. Darcy knew in his heart he would destroy whoever had separated the child from her mother. Even if Elizabeth never was his, his vengeance would be forthcoming. "Let us see to Mrs. Harris. Perhaps the lady can tell us what has occurred."

She nodded her agreement and released her hold on his coat.

He turned her to where the woman remained unconscious upon the floor. Elizabeth broke away from him to examine Mrs. Harris's wound. "Fetch me the water bowl and a clean cloth," she ordered.

Darcy did as she instructed and then knelt beside her. Elizabeth dabbed the cloth in the water to wash the lady's face. "Mrs. Harris," she said in calmer tones than previously. "It is Elizabeth. Can you hear me?"

The woman's eyes fluttered open and closed several times before they focused on Elizabeth. "Mrs. ... Dartmore," she whispered in recognition before panic crossed her features. The woman pushed herself to a seated position. "Is Lizzy well?"

Elizabeth's features crumbled. "Do you know what

became of my daughter?" she asked through trembling lips.

The woman held her head in obvious pain. "I told her to run. Mr. Townsend came for her, but you'd never said you trusted the man. He pushed his way into the house. I kept telling him 'no,' but he would not listen. When I struggled with him, I told Lizzy to run home."

Elizabeth's hand shook, and he thought she, too, might faint. Therefore, he gave her a task to keep her focused. "I will remain with the lady. You return to the shop and search out Lizzy there. Send Jasper to fetch a doctor and instruct him to join me here. If you have Townsend's directions send them along with my man." He squeezed the back of her hand to make certain she was understanding him.

"I told him where Lizzy was," she admitted, tears returning to her eyes. "When I rejected his overtures, I told him I had to leave the shop to come fetch Lizzy."

"We will find her, love," he promised. "For now, you must assist me by doing what I asked. Do you understand." He spoke to her in clear, concise tones, although his heart was aching to take her again into his embrace. Darcy knew he must be strong for both of them. "I will remain with Mrs. Harris until the doctor appears, and then I will call personally on Mr. Townsend."

"Do not kill him, William," she pleaded. "I want my daughter back."

"Trust me, Mr. Townsend will see reason," he said. "Now hurry. Lizzy is probably waiting for you at the bookstore and is frightened her mother is not there to provide her comfort."

She nodded her agreement. "If Lizzy is there, I shall have Jasper bring you word." Then she was gone, running across the yard to the streets beyond.

Darcy watched her go — his emotions still reeling. He wished to follow to make certain no one brought harm to her ever again. Yet, there were more pressing matters hanging over his head. "Might I assist you to a chair, ma'am?"

"Who are you?" Mrs. Harris asked while struggling to her feet.

"I am Lizzy Anne's father," he said with a genuine smile, the idea of having a child had found purchase in his heart.

"Lieutenant Dartmore?" the woman asked.

He did not enjoy the pretense of using another's name, real or not; yet, if he did not comply, his daughter would be named a "bastard" by Society. "One and the same." He pulled a nearby chair closer to the lady.

"Everyone thought you dead," Mrs. Harris said as she hobbled the few steps to be seated.

"At times, I thought such was to be my fate." He knelt before her. "Might I fetch you something, ma'am?"

She shook off the idea, but winced from the movement. "I can certainly see your daughter in your features, lieutenant. You shall never be able to deny the child."

Darcy wished to ask more of his child, but he would learn it all soon enough on his own. The idea of his blood flowing through another was satisfying in so many ways, but it was also frightening in a manner he had never considered. The only other time he had known such fury as was coursing through him now was when Wickham had attempted to seduce Georgiana. Although he knew better than to allow his mind to think on the possibilities, he realized if someone, likely Lady Catherine or Matlock, had been bold enough to have him kidnapped to prevent his marriage to Elizabeth, the person would not hesitate to force Darcy's hand by taking his child. Making himself concentrate on the task at hand, he asked, "Might you tell me what occurred with Mr. Townsend?"

The woman appeared weak; yet, she related the tale. "Mrs. Dartmore was to retrieve Miss Lizzy after the bookstore closed for the day. Mr. Sheffield has been ill, and neither of us thought it was appropriate to expect the gentleman to tend the child while in his condition. In truth, although he says otherwise, Mr. Sheffield is too kind to his niece."

Darcy swallowed the words rushing to his lip. He wished to defend his former valet, but he set his instant anger aside for the time being. "What of Mr. Townsend, ma'am?"

"Right," she said. "We, meaning Lizzy and I, heard a knock at the backdoor and thought it was Mrs. Dartmore, but it proved to be Mr. Townsend. The gentleman said Mrs. Dartmore had sent him to bring Lizzy to the bookstore. He said Mr. Sheffield had taken a turn for the worse, and Mrs. Dartmore could not come herself. I told him I would come with them, for I wished to tend Mr. Sheffield myself. It was then Mr. Townsend insisted he and Lizzy go ahead, and I could follow. He appeared most eager to be gone."

"You said something about telling Lizzy to run," Darcy prompted. "Did Townsend do something to frighten the child?"

Mrs. Harris looked at the still opened kitchen door. "I should have known something was amiss when Townsend did not call at the front door." She frowned deeply. "When I turned to retrieve my cloak and bonnet from the hook, Mr. Townsend must have made some sort of grab for Miss Lizzy, for the child screamed and ran behind me for protection." The woman pulled herself up straighter. "Naturally, I chastised Townsend for being so foolish. After all, he has two sons of his own. Unfortunately, he ignored my protest and again moved to catch your daughter. When I stepped before him to order him from my house and to say I would return Lizzy Anne to her mother and he should consider his duty to Mrs. Dartmore complete, he struck out against me."

Darcy felt his hand forming a fist. Mr. Townsend would know Darcy's wrath.

The woman continued, "It was then Mr. Townsend shoved me from his way, and I struck my head against the china chest. I recall warning Lizzy to run, but not much after that. I must have lost consciousness."

A light tap at the door announced the arrival of the physician and Jasper. "I will leave you, ma'am," he said as he stood. "Thank you for your attempts to protect Elizabeth Anne." He briefly explained what he and Elizabeth had discovered regarding Mrs. Harris to the doctor and slipped a few coins into the man's hand. "If there are additional expenses, send a note around to Mrs. Dartmore at the bookstore, and I will see to the costs."

Then he joined Jasper in the yard, "Did Miss Elizabeth provide you Mr. Townsend's directions?" he asked softly.

"She did, sir." He handed Darcy a slip of paper. "The lady says this is the one the man provided when he first ordered books from the shop." As Darcy studied the address, Jasper continued, "I assisted the lady in searching the shop and the area surrounding it before I fetched the physician. Miss Elizabeth planned to retrace her steps before joining you at Mr. Townsend's home. She will meet you at the man's residence."

Darcy had hoped Elizabeth would have discovered the child at home, although he realized the half mile or so between Mrs. Harris's cottage and the bookstore would be difficult for a child of three or less to cover alone. The idea he did not know exactly when Elizabeth Anne had been born made him sad. He had missed so much of her life while he was imprisoned on *The Lost Sparrow*. First smile. First tooth. First steps. So many firsts of which he had been robbed.

"You are certain Mr. Townsend left Brighton a fortnight prior?" Darcy asked the man who ran the boarding house where Townsend had stayed. "Mrs. Dartmore is certain she observed him on the streets less than a week removed."

"The rooms be let to another these last ten days," the man said. "I kin show yous the register if'n you like."

Darcy waved off the idea. "We are simply attempting to make sense of what Townsend has told us."

"What of his sons? Emerson and Tobias?" Elizabeth demanded. She was obviously again very agitated by this turn of events.

The man looked upon her in sympathy. "Ma'am, to the best of me knowledge, Mr. Townsend had no children, at least, none that be residing with him under me roof. I don't let to families. Too noisy."

"William," she pleaded as she sagged against him. "Make this stop."

"I will," he said softly as he caressed her cheek. To the man, he said, "Is there anything else you can tell us of Mr. Townsend? Did he receive letters? Did he have visitors?"

"No letters, I knows of," the man shared, "and his only visitor was a man called 'Hardy.'"

"First or last name?" Darcy asked.

"Not certain, sir, but you might ask of the man at *The Dingy Rose*. Mr. Townsend favored the place."

Darcy handed the man several coins and walked Elizabeth outside into the encroaching night. He pulled her pelisse tighter about her. "I want you to return to the store."

"I would prefer to go with you," she protested.

"I doubt a place called *The Dingy Rose* is a place for a lady," he countered. "Moreover, you must be at the store in case someone sends a note requiring a ransom."

"A ransom?" she gasped. "But—"

His thumb made small circles upon her wrist. "I have thought upon the possibilities of why someone would steal away our daughter. Either someone thinks Mr. Sheffield would pay for the return of his grand-niece or someone has determined Elizabeth Anne is my daughter," he explained in calmer tones than he felt. He blamed himself for not arriving in Brighton earlier.

"But how?" she questioned. "No one knows of my being with Sheffield other than my father, and even he was not made privy to where we would settle."

Darcy attempted to keep his expression natural so as not to frighten her further. "When I called upon your father to beg for information of your whereabouts, Miss Bennet stopped me as I exited Longbourn's main gate. During our conversation, I asked if she knew the identity of the 'stranger' who reportedly called upon Mr. Bennet shortly before you departed Longbourn. Your sister told me she had recognized a man she identified as Sheffield, obviously from our time at Netherfield, when he arrived at Longbourn."

"So more than Mr. Bennet knew of Mr. Sheffield's offer?"

she reasoned.

"I do not think the others knew what Sheffield had done for you; Miss Bennet assumed he had delivered a message or some sort of settlement from my family," he explained, "but your sister had seen Sheffield from her rooms facing the main drive. Likely, others also had seen him. Most assuredly, one of the house servants let him into the house or a groom assisted in attending Sheffield's coach, which would have drawn attention."

"If Jane was at Longbourn, that means Mr. Bingley never returned to Netherfield," she said sadly. "I left my home and family so my sisters would have a future. It was all for nothing."

"I asked to see Bingley when I first arrived in London, and I was quite shocked he had not shown more fortitude than he did. I have essentially cut ties with him."

"I am sorry for it. Sorry for your loss of a friend, and sorry Jane has suffered so. My sister deserved a better life than to be a spinster. All that beauty and goodness wasted because she placed her trust in a man too weak to make his own decisions." Tears formed in her eyes. "Perhaps it was best to learn her lesson now than after she agreed to marry him." She shook her head in obvious remorse. "But as to my traveling with Mr. Sheffield, even Mr. Bennet did not know of my final destination, and we did not come to Brighton until after Elizabeth Anne was born. How could anyone learn of our whereabouts? As far as I know, other than the occasional letter from one of his brothers, no one is aware Sheffield is in Brighton, and, according to your former valet, even his brothers do not know we have traveled here together."

"Sheffield receives a pension from me," he told her. "Such is how I located him. Please know that before my return to England, Lord Matlock made himself the 'master' of my business affairs. He is likely to be aware of where Sheffield can be found. And then there is the matter of what those in your family told Lady Catherine."

"Lady Catherine? Why has Lady Catherine called upon my family?" Anger again returned to Elizabeth's tone.

He disclosed, "Both Lady Catherine and Lord Matlock

have called upon Mr. Bennet over the last month, each offering several thousand pounds to be used for your remaining sisters' dowries in exchange for information on your whereabouts."

"Because of my connection to you," she reasoned aloud.

"Yes," he said simply, despising the idea of his late mother's family harming those he affected.

"But surely Jane would not tell Lady Catherine of her suspicions of my being with Mr. Sheffield."

"No, but I fear your mother is not so circumspect. Mrs. Bennet told Lady Catherine that Mr. Sheffield had been more well-mannered than her ladyship when he called upon the household." He fastened the top two buttons on the pelisse. "I do not like to think either you or our daughter will suffer because of your connection to me, but, know, someone paid for me to disappear—my abduction was not simply a matter of opportunity—and I fear they are now attempting to cover their manipulations. I had hoped to reach you before anyone else did."

"Will they harm Lizzy?" she pleaded.

"I do not think it will come to that. Whoever staged our daughter's disappearance will use her to force our compliance." He snagged her chin to lift it so he might watch the dawn of realization arrive upon her features.

"Someone means to keep us apart?"

"I believe our relationship has caused others to react without caution," he confessed.

"I want our daughter safe," she ordered. "You will keep her safe, William. You will allow no harm to mark her."

"I will do everything within my power to secure Elizabeth Anne's return to your waiting arms." He kissed her forehead. "Permit Jasper to escort you to Mr. Sheffield. I will come to you as quickly as I learn anything."

"I believe I will call upon some of the other shopkeepers to see if they have seen anything of Lizzy. Perhaps one of them took her in."

"An excellent plan," he said, although Darcy doubted someone would not have returned the child if they had found her wandering the streets alone.

She started away but paused. "If you discover her, William, she will likely refuse to come to you on her own."

Even though the world was crashing in around him, he could not resist offering her a small smile. "Why is that, love?"

"I taught our daughter never to go any place with a stranger unless he knew our 'secret' words."

"Would you care to share the words with me?" He looked upon her lovingly. If it were not for the dire circumstances in which they found themselves, this would be a wonderful memory to cherish. "I would despise frightening my own child."

She half-smiled also. "Originally I thought to use the word 'Pemberley,' but I feared it might draw unwanted attention to how much our daughter resembles the Master of Pemberley."

"Also, a difficult word to pronounce for such a small child," he conceded. "What did you choose in its place?"

Theirs was an intimate conversation held upon a busy street. "Do you recall what you told Miss Bingley that you found pleasurable about my appearance when we were all together at Lucas Lodge?"

"It was the night I realized my complete obsession with you," he confessed.

"Those two words are the 'secret' words to your daughter's compliance. Elizabeth Anne liked the tale of how her papa defended her mama from the 'wicked witch' known as Caroline," she said with a pert lift of her chin, before walking away with Jasper at her side.

CHAPTER EIGHT

FRUSTRATED, DARCY RETURNED TO the bookstore. He did not expect to find Townsend enjoying a drink at *The Dingy Rose*, but he had hoped someone would know more of the man than they did.

"Did you learn anything?" Elizabeth asked when she opened the door to him.

He shook his head in the negative as he shrugged out of his coat. "People were purposely not speaking of the man, which likely means someone has paid for their silence. As many men are without work, they are willing to keep silent when the world erupts around them just for the pleasure of supporting their families."

She said testily, "If they really wished to support their families, they would not waste their few funds on drink and on the women who frequent such places."

Despite himself, he smiled. "Ladies are not supposed to know what men do in such places."

"Perhaps other women prefer to bury their heads in fluffy pillows," she replied with a snit of disapproval, "but I am not one of them. I would not tolerate a man who turned to strong drink when other solutions are required."

Darcy did not tell her men saw things differently from women, but he refrained from remarking on her observation. "I let it be known I would pay for information on Townsend's whereabouts or those with whom the man did business."

Tears filled her eyes. "What must Lizzy be thinking? It is dark. She must be so frightened, William."

He gathered her to him. "I know, love. We will find her. It is just going to take longer than either of us likes. You have my word I will bring our daughter home to you."

She rested her head against his chest. "I cannot live without her, William. The surgeon who was brought in by the midwife said there was a strong possibility I might never have another child." Darcy attempted not to react to her confession, fearing she would think he would reject her if she could not bear him an heir, but he knew he stiffened.

He stroked her back. "I promise I will use everything within my power to return Elizabeth Anne to her mother's arms."

As was typical of a man of his consequence, Fitzwilliam Darcy had taken charge of locating their daughter. In some ways, she was most appreciative of his influence; in other ways, she despised how he did it all without consulting her. Elizabeth knew it was his way of protecting her; yet, some of his exacting ways still grated against her nerves. Perhaps it was his training as the master of a large estate, or her lack, thereof, of knowing more of the world than how to run a manor house, that kept him a few steps ahead of her. Before she could think on the need for an evening meal, he had instructed Mr. Farrin to fetch meals from the nearby inn for all of them, even sending Jasper to carry one of the meals to Mrs. Harris and to assure all of the lady's recovery. He had also contacted the local magistrate to inform the man of Lizzy's abduction.

As the night wore on, he sent his men to an inn for rooms for the evening. Mr. Sheffield had returned below, leaving only the two of them. "I plan to remain," he announced as he sat in one of the armchairs across from her. His countenance held that same stubbornness she had observed when she had attempted to express her gratefulness for what he had done to save Lydia's reputation, and, by connection, her and all her sisters.

"It is late. If I am to continue to search for Lizzy tomorrow, I should attempt to rest," she said.

"Rest is advisable," he said. "You have had a trying day."

Although she knew him to be sitting across from her, her mind kept telling her none of what had occurred that day could be real. It was a nightmare she was reliving over and over again.

"Should you not join Mr. Farrin and Jasper at the inn?" she suggested. Elizabeth was not prepared to spend a night with him. Despite being grateful for his survival, she was not ready to fall into Mr. Darcy's arms again and never come out, especially, if his presence in her life had placed Lizzy in danger.

"I will sleep on the floor or in a chair," he said in customary calmness which occasionally drove her crazy, while, in reality, providing her confidence. "I will not leave until we know Elizabeth Anne is safe."

"Why do you insist on calling our child 'Elizabeth Anne' when the world calls her 'Lizzy'?" she charged.

His steady gaze held her in place. "For the same reason I have only called you 'Lizzy' upon one occasion—the evening I gave myself to you and you gave yourself to me—when I held you in my arms, and I knew we would end our days together. When I do the same with our daughter—hold her safely to me—when she becomes ingrained in my soul—becomes a living, breathing part of me, she will become 'Lizzy Anne,' and as I became 'William' to you rather than 'Fitzwilliam,' to our daughter, I will become 'Papa.'"

She understood: He required distance to keep himself calm enough to handle the chaos. At that moment, she both admired how he could control his emotions so completely and despised him for his coldness. "You cannot sleep on the floor."

"Elizabeth, for nearly four years, I often slept chained to the floor of a ship, a floor in a room with a fire will be a luxury."

"Chained?" She knew instant regret for never having asked what had occurred to keep him from their wedding. She supposed she really did not want to know, for fear knowing would make her forgive him, and, without her anger, she had no defenses against completely trusting him again.

"I was wondering when you would become curious as to what prevented me from pronouncing our vows."

Her brow knitted in shame. "It was wrong of me not to inquire. You deserved better of me," she admitted. "Would you speak to what occurred? That is, if you are comfortable in sharing it with me."

He paused as if considering how to answer. This was a different Fitzwilliam Darcy from the one she had come to love. There was a bitterness and a sadness about his countenance, and, despite her earlier observations regarding his "masterly" ways, he had lost some of his confidence. At length, he said, "As it is late, I will provide you the briefest of explanations." She understood: He did not want to dwell on the past, a past that had reshaped their relationship. Neither did she, but, until they could come again to some easiness between them, their future would be doomed before it began.

He tapped his finger against the table as if doing so would drive away the obvious pain he was experiencing behind his eyes, where, she knew, he saw everything from the last four years flash through his memory. "As you are aware, I returned to London to retrieve the ring I had designed for you at Rundell and Bridge's shop. What you do not know, or I am assuming you were not told, I received a message from Lord Matlock regarding problems with a shipment of silk and other items from the Far East in which we had both invested. We had already heard that the countess was ill and would not be attending the wedding and the new message said his lordship had been called home for some business that could not be neglected at the family estate. Therefore, I set out to visit both the jeweler and the docks with full intentions to return to Hertfordshire the following morning."

"The colonel received a message saying you had been delayed and would arrive late Saturday evening," she explained. "When you did not make an appearance for services on the Sunday before our wedding, I assumed your duties had delayed you. Although I had hoped you would arrive during the day on Sunday, I know you avoid traveling on the Sabbath unless your business is an emergency. Although I was disappointed not to have seen you before our nuptials, Mrs. Bennet had me running every which way to finish the details for the wedding breakfast. I thought you would leave at the crack of dawn and be in Hertfordshire well before our scheduled hour of half past eleven at the church."

"I sent no message to Fitzwilliam," he said.

"But it was on Darcy letterhead," she argued.

"Nevertheless, whatever my cousin received did not come from me. Unbeknownst to me, when I left Rundell's establishment, I was followed by two men to the docks."

"Robbery?" she asked softly.

He shook off the idea. "Your ring and my broken cane were found on the docks near the ship Matlock and I commissioned, but I was taken to the docks further down the Thames toward where the river flows into the ocean."

"Pressed?" Elizabeth sat heavily. She had never considered the idea of him being snatched away. She had played a thousand different scenes of his walking away from her in her head, but never once had she thought him kidnapped.

"Pressed into service upon *The Lost Sparrow*, a ship full of men with dark histories and questionable motives. I offered them a small fortune to release me, but they continually refused. I was kept aboard *The Lost Sparrow* for three years, eight months and two and twenty days — my feet never touching land until I made my escape and swam to safety when a British naval ship was in the same waters as us. *The Resolution* brought the *Sparrow* and its crew into custody in London on 3 August."

"Lizzy's birthday," she whispered in remembrance. "I wish I had known—"

He questioned, "Then our daughter arrived early."

She shook her head in the affirmative while attempting to keep the darkness of those days from showing on her face. He and she were very much alike in that manner. Elizabeth was certain he had only shared a fraction of what he had suffered during his confinement.

"In the beginning," she chose her words carefully, "Mr. Sheffield and I stayed in Cumbria while he searched for an appropriate location to purchase. He had wanted a shop in London, but when he took on my care, his plans changed. We could not be seen in London, for too many people we knew were there. I always despised the idea Mr. Sheffield abandoned part of his dream to save me, but both Lizzy and I would likely have died if he had not. Our daughter was born there."

"On his brother's estate?" William had asked.

"No. In a cottage we let. We were in Cumbria some eight months, throughout the remainder of my confinement and a bit longer until I was well again, and we could depart for Brighton."

"You were unwell after delivering Elizabeth Anne?"

Elizabeth did not dare to look upon him when she explained, "Lizzy had not completely turned when my pains started, and the midwife did not seem to know what to do other than to allow either me or the child to die. Mr. Sheffield would have none of her foolishness, so he dragged a surgeon in and stayed with me until the two managed to deliver our daughter safely. Unfortunately, what they first thought was childbed fever set in, but, later, my infection proved to be a different contagion. It was a terrible time for all concerned. While I recovered, Mr. Sheffield hired a wet nurse for Lizzy and tended me himself for more than a week."

"He has earned my undying loyalty," Darcy said simply.

In spite of the chaos around them, she could not resist teasing him. "Sheffield has seen more of me than have you. He bathed me and changed my gowns regularly when the fever laid me low."

He offered her a small grin. "I will have his tongue removed and him blinded before offering my former valet my loyalty."

There was still much to be said about their missing years, but she was not yet prepared to speak the words. "Why do you not use Lizzy's bed? It is small, but much better than sleeping on the floor."

"I would enjoy that. It would make me feel closer to our daughter."

She stood then. "I shall see you in the morning." Feeling conspicuous, she darted around him to enter her own quarters, preparing to close the door behind her before he thought to follow, but she foolishly looked back at him. He stood in apparent exhaustion. He rubbed his face with dry hands, and Elizabeth wondered again upon all he had suffered during their separation. She had thought him dead and no longer in pain, where each day she prayed no one would recognize her and name her daughter as illegitimate. Yet, he, too, had known the loss of his hopes for a bright future between them.

As he turned dejectedly toward Lizzy's small room, she realized how alone he was. Painful stoicism. She knew him, perhaps, as he had said earlier, better than anyone else. She recognized how having no control of this situation laid him low. Quietly, she entered the room and eased the door closed. "What am I to believe? How can I ignore the fact William's appearance stood as prelude to Lizzy's abduction?"

Darcy entered his child's room and stood quietly absorbing the essence of his daughter. He smiled when he noted the precise manner in which the room was organized. Certainly, Elizabeth would have assisted Elizabeth Anne in keeping order in the room, but he found himself drawn to the bookshelf where the books were lined up exactly as he would have done as a child. "My darling girl," he said reverently as he ran his fingers across the spines of a dozen books upon the shelf, "your father will not rest until he is able to hold you in his arms for the first time."

He glanced to the small bed and smiled. "Perhaps your father should sleep on the floor, after all." He tugged the mattress from the bed frame, which would not suit him, at all. "Will you be petite, as is your mother? Or will you be tall like your father? This mattress will not answer that question for a father who wishes to know you, at last." He laid the mattress out on the floor and began to undress, removing his boots, stockings, coat, waistcoat and shirt.

At length, Darcy sat upon the floor and inhaled deeply. "I promise you, little one, I will never give up. Your mother has done all she could to protect you. Now it is up to me to keep you safe."

Although he knew he would not sleep, he blew out the candle and curled his large frame into a tight ball and attempted to imagine the look of his child. Someone, and he held his suspicions as to who that someone was, had stolen away precious moments with his child — memories he would never be able to recover.

He did not know how long he had remained as such, but when the door opened to permit Elizabeth in, Darcy was not surprised.

"Are you asleep?" she asked softly.

Despite his misery, Darcy smiled. "No. I was just considering what all I had missed with my child. I wonder upon her countenance. Her features. Her mannerisms. I wish there was a portrait of her."

She took a step closer. "I have wanted to have her sit for one for some time, but Lizzy is always on the move. She is not an easy child to rein in."

Darcy rolled to his back, his legs hanging over the edge of the mattress. "There is not much room, but I would gladly share our daughter's bed with her mother."

"I would like to be closer to Lizzy on this evening when I do not know her fate," she admitted. "My room felt too empty, as does my heart."

"Then come," he said, lifting his arm to welcome her to snuggle in beside him.

Once she was settled on the small patch of mattress remaining, he turned on his side so they could speak honestly. "Tell me about Elizabeth Anne," he encouraged.

She sighed deeply. "I am excessively prejudiced," she began with what sounded of a smile in her tone, "but she is the brightest child I have ever encountered." Her hand came to rest upon his chest, and Darcy closed his eyes for a brief moment to savor the feel of her near him again. They had many bridges yet to cross, but that moment was the first time he had felt whole for longer than he could recall. "Usually Mr. Sheffield reads to her each evening — often the same story multiple times. He is so patient with her, and Lizzy is so attentive. She loves stories of castles and knights and dragons and just about anything under the sun. Inevitably, within a week of hearing the story, Lizzy is able to 'read' the book back to us." Elizabeth lightly stroked his arm as she spoke, and Darcy knew great contentment in the moment. "Naturally, she really is not reading the story, but she has memorized it, even knowing when to turn the page."

With pleasure, Darcy visualized his daughter's performance. "Go on."

"She has the wildest imagination, always coming up with stories to entertain herself when we visit the park — a tree becomes a giant and a stick is sometimes her sword and other times her scepter, a queen presenting orders to the giant to assist her in defending her kingdom." She laughed softly. "She has your mannerisms, William. You should see how she pulls herself up regally and eyes those who displease her. When she does so, Mr. Sheffield and I always provide each other a nod of approval when she looks down her petite nose at some injustice." She paused before adding, "I often tell her stories of her father — simple ones so Lizzy will know she is loved."

In spite of knowing a bit of disdain that she had essentially termed him "too proud," Darcy found himself smiling at the idea his child had inherited more than some of his facial features.

"Thank you, Elizabeth," he said in true gratitude, "for allowing bits of me to be displayed in our daughter, when I know you must have felt I had abandoned you and her. You allowed me into her life, even at the risk of damage to your own heart."

Although there was still much to be said between them, he nestled her closer to him. "We both require at least a few hours of rest if we are to find our daughter."

She nodded her agreement and aligned her body with

his upon the mattress, her head resting beneath his chin. With her beside him, Darcy allowed himself a few minutes of peace. So often he had dreamed of moments like this, minus the chaos awaiting them at dawn—moments of he and she lying in each other's embrace. Allowing his eyes to drift closed, he had nearly reached sleep when he felt her stiffen and realized her hand was draped across his waist and stroking his back.

"William?" she asked in distress.

He, too, grew rigid in remorse. "It is nothing," he said in stern tones.

She bolted upright. "It is something!" she insisted. "My God what did you endure?"

He attempted to make light of his condition so as not to tell her of the times he thought he would die. "Sometimes, as you well know, I lack forbearance and am too unmoving in my opinions."

"Your captors whipped you!" she said on a hiccupped gasp. "You could have died!"

"As could have you in delivering our child," he countered in even tones. He had always known he would have to share this part of his tale with her, but the idea of doing so in the mix of what had happened to their child had paled. If he had thought better of what he was doing when she entered Elizabeth Anne's room, he would have put on his shirt before he had asked her to join him on the small mattress.

"Dear Lord," she said as tears filled her eyes. "What sin did we two exact that brought us such punishments?"

Darcy knew, other than the anticipation of their vows, the sin was not on their part. Even that, awful as the realization must have been for Elizabeth when she came to know of her condition, he could not think upon their actions as a sin. They had conceived the child in love, and he would not think otherwise. *God is all about love and family.* He reached for her and edged her down beside him once more. "We cannot change our past," he said as he soothed the hair from about her face. "All we can do is bring Elizabeth Anne home and consider a future together."

CHAPTER NINE

A FIRM KNOCKING BELOW woke Darcy, but by the time he eased Elizabeth from his embrace so she might continue to rest upon their daughter's mattress and pulled a shirt on to descend the steps into the shop below, the messenger had departed, leaving Mr. Sheffield holding a sealed, folded-over piece of paper.

"A message for you, sir." He extended the note in Darcy's direction with a grin. "I paid the fellow the shilling you offered."

Darcy smiled upon his former servant. "I will see you reimbursed fully."

"I had no doubt, sir. Is Elizabeth well this morning?"

Irrational as the feeling was, Darcy knew a bit of jealousy, for Sheffield had been granted a familiarity with Elizabeth that Darcy had been denied. "She was still asleep when I came below, but I am certain she will rise soon, despite being awake half the night." Not wishing to answer questions on where he and she had slept, he asked, "How is your health?"

"Still a bit weak, but the fever has been gone for more than a day. I am prepared to assist you as required, sir."

Darcy accepted the man's continued loyalty with a gracious nod of his head. "You have proven yourself time and time again in a manner even those with titles felt below them. You protected my family when I could not. I am forever in your debt."

Sheffield bowed stiffly. "It was what you would have

expected of me, and Elizabeth and the child have provided me a family, something an upper servant in a fine house does not consider possible."

"What of Mrs. Harris?" Darcy asked. "I understand you two are courting. You could still claim a wife and familial connections, if that is your wish."

Sheffield shrugged. "I would not call our sharing the occasional meal courting, although I am certain others would." His former valet paused in that manner that always told Darcy a decision had been made by the gentleman. "Two things are apparent: Mrs. Harris is not much of a reader, and I wish to continue owning a bookstore and enjoying a variety of books. Secondly, I would never have placed Lizzy Anne with the lady. She never had children of her own and has often expressed the opinion that children should never be heard, nor rarely seen."

Although he did not comment on Mr. Sheffield's admission, Darcy easily recognized Mr. Sheffield's objections. Darcy had fallen in love with Elizabeth because she was well read and could converse on a variety of subjects. As to his former valet, Darcy suspected Mr. Sheffield had read half, if not more, of Pemberley's extensive library. "A woman with a mind for more than tea service and house calls is difficult to discover."

"But worth the search," Sheffield said. "Such is something I learned from serving you, sir. Thank you for demonstrating what was important in these trying times and for bringing Miss Elizabeth Bennet into my life at a time when I most required such an enchanting creature to make sense of my world."

Darcy was uncertain how to respond to Sheffield's declaration. He cleared his throat to say, "I should see to this message." He was certain of one thing: If he could convince Elizabeth to marry him, it would be essential to keep Albert Sheffield in Elizabeth's and Elizabeth Anne's lives. It would be a crime to separate the trio completely, and, moreover, Darcy would admit he, too, had missed Sheffield's ready advice. "By the way, I asked Mr. Farrin to bring breakfast to us from the inn. I did not want Elizabeth thinking she should tend to our needs.

Come join us when you are dressed."

When Darcy returned to the rooms above, Elizabeth was just coming out of their daughter's room. God help him! Despite the dark circles marking the area under her eyes, she was absolutely stunning. "Was there news?" she asked in hopeful tones.

"Yes, a message." He sat in a nearby chair and broke the crude dab of wax and unfolded the single page.

"What does it say?" Elizabeth demanded.

Darcy was not certain he could resist slamming his fist into the nearest wall. "Read it for yourself."

Elizabeth snatched the paper from his fingers. She read aloud, *"Don't knows if it heps, but Townsend speak of'en of returnin' soon to Kent. Say his benefactor live there."* She turned to him. "Kent, as in where Lady Catherine resides."

Elizabeth swayed in place, and Darcy scrambled to assist her to a seat. Shakily, she said, "Her ladyship warned me against pursuing a relationship with you when she called on me at Longbourn. She said I should never expect her to recede, going so far as to say she would not make herself scarce—would never go away—until I gave her the assurances she required." Her lips trembled and tears filled her eyes. "Lady Catherine declared my ambitions would never be gratified. She said I would depend upon her carrying her point. Oh, William, could it be so?"

Darcy would not tell her of his suspicions that his aunt had been involved in his abduction. "We must figure this out together. We already know Lady Catherine has again called upon Longbourn." He suggested, "We should dress before Mr. Farrin brings us breakfast." He placed a finger against her lips when she thought to object to eating in such a time. "Then *we* can decide how to proceed."

She nodded crisply, rose, and started around him, but he caught her arm to pull her into his body. Lifting her chin with two fingers where he might look down into the eyes that had enchanted him long before he knew up from down, he said, "I made you a promise last evening, and my resolve has not altered.

Elizabeth Anne will soon be in your arms again."

Tears spilled out of her eyes. "I pray so."

He released her then but did not move until she closed the door behind her. "If my aunt is at fault in this matter, there is nowhere she can flee where I will not hunt her down and have my justice."

Elizabeth stood looking about her room, feeling more vulnerable than she could remember since discovering she was carrying William's child. The room, which had been her private haven for the last three years, now felt as if she stood upon foreign soil.

Tucked away in William's arms last night, she had purchased the idea that at dawn Lizzy would be returned to her, but her worst fears had again reared its head. It had been so easy to believe all would be well, for she had hungered for someone to step in and right her world. Although she wished him well, the knowledge Mr. Sheffield would likely marry Mrs. Harris had had her, of late, wondering what the future held for her and Lizzy.

There was always something about Fitzwilliam Darcy that had spoken of his surety. Even when she did not approve of him, Elizabeth would have named him the most capable—most confident—man of her acquaintance. Naturally, he had filled her with a certainty that he would bring about her dearest prayer.

Heaving a deep sigh of regret, she dashed away her tears with the heels of her hands. "Whatever it takes, Elizabeth Anne, your mother is coming after you. I shall not rest until you are safe."

Darcy dressed quickly, not wanting Elizabeth to be alone with her fears. Although she might think otherwise, he knew her strengths and her weaknesses. She had withstood Lady Catherine's attack, and now Elizabeth was second-guessing how her temper had caused their child pain. Even after they recovered their daughter, and he held no doubt they would know success, just not as quickly as either of them would like—Elizabeth would never forgive herself for bringing on Lady Catherine's ire.

When he returned to the family area below, Mr. Sheffield was setting out the items Mr. Farrin had brought over from the inn. "I took the liberty of brewing tea. The tea pot is on the platter."

"You are quite handy," Darcy remarked as he poured himself a cup of tea.

"I always was," Sheffield responded with a smile.

"I know, and I was constantly appreciative of your care," Darcy said in all honesty, "but never so much as when I was forced to go weeks without a bath or a change of clothes."

"For what it is worth, sir, despite the so-called truth Lord Matlock shared with those at Darcy House, I never lost hope for your return."

The mention of his uncle had Darcy asking, "Could you explain what occurred at Darcy House when you arrived after the overturned wedding?"

Sheffield shot a quick glance up the stairs toward Elizabeth's quarters, before lowering his voice. "We did not arrive until very late in the day of what would have been your wedding. The house was at sixes and sevens, especially as Mr. Thacker had been dismissed by then. Lord Matlock had taken up residence in your study. He kept insisting you had been killed upon the docks, but I was suspicious because you had written to me from London and explained you might be an extra day or two in the City, for you had been charged with checking on a shipment in which both you and his lordship had invested.

"According to the information you shared in your instructions to me as to what you wished to wear for the ceremony and when you were expected to return, Lord Matlock could not attend the shipment because the earl was in Derbyshire at the time. Supposedly, there had been a fire at the stables. His note to you said he would not be able to attend your wedding because of his duty to his estate. However, his lordship was in London when the colonel, Miss Darcy, and I arrived.

"Certainly, a man could travel from Derbyshire to London

in two days, if he pressed his horses and the weather held, but it appeared odd to me as how Lord Matlock knew of your attack so swiftly. Would not it have taken an express from London to Derbyshire a full day, more likely two, to reach him with the news? And then there was a brief comment by Lady Matlock to the colonel, upon our arrival, of how her husband had overseen the search for and possible recovery of your body. A man cannot be in two places at once. I was asked for my resignation when your uncle discovered via the new butler that I had begun to express such opinions below stairs."

"It is as I suspected. I, too, have wondered about the tale that was repeated to me by Colonel Fitzwilliam and Lady Matlock." His ears noted Elizabeth's soft tread on the stairs. With a slight shake of his head he warned Sheffield not to speak his suspicions before Elizabeth. "Mr. Farrin and Jasper will return in a few minutes," he told her when she joined them in the kitchen. "We will set a course for Kent once we have eaten our breakfast. I assume you wish to accompany me."

"Most assuredly."

"Kent?" Sheffield asked with a lift of his brow.

Elizabeth explained, "The note from earlier said Townsend might be in Kent."

"Did it say where? Kent is not a small shire," Sheffield cautioned.

"We will stop at all the coaching inns until we discover someone who has seen Townsend and our child."

"Do we have a choice?" she remarked as she collapsed into a nearby chair and buried her face in her hands. Yet, before he could comfort her, a loud knocking came at the main door to the shop.

"I will see to it, sir," Sheffield said with a nod to where Elizabeth had succumbed to tears again. "Likely Mr. Farrin returning."

With Sheffield's exit, Darcy knelt before her and awkwardly wrapped his arms about Elizabeth. "I know, darling. This is too daunting after all you have endured."

"I have not seen my father — my sisters — or mama in nearly four years," she sobbed. "They do not even know of Lizzy's birth, and my parents could lose their grandchild before they even meet her."

He tightened his grip about her to tug her deeper into his embrace. "None of us will lose Elizabeth Anne. I know, at this moment, this feels impossible, but neither of us will rest — no matter how long it takes to bring our child home to you."

"You will not leave me until this is done well?"

"Not even then," he promised.

He rose when he heard Sheffield closing and locking the main door. Sheffield entered carrying a second message. "Another possible lead, I hope."

Darcy reached for it, but Sheffield shook off Darcy's hand. "This one is addressed to 'Mrs. Dartmore.'"

Elizabeth looked up expectantly. "For me?" She struggled to her feet to take the note from Sheffield. She reached for a knife on the table to break the seal.

Darcy waited in uneasy anticipation as she read the page and blanched white. "What does it say, Elizabeth?" Her hands began to shake, and he again brought her into his embrace. Removing the note from her fingers, he handed it off to Sheffield. Over her shoulder he watched as his former valet read the note, Sheffield's features taking on a thunderous expression. As Elizabeth sobbed into Darcy's shoulder, Sheffield held the note aloft where Darcy could read it.

Mrs. Dartmore, although we both know such is not your real name. Should I not say, Miss Elizabeth Bennet? If you wish the return of the child who bears your name and that of a fictitious father, you will send Mr. Darcy on his way. Turn him aside, not just for this day, but for all the days to come. Otherwise, this child will be placed with a family far away, and you will never see her again. If Mr. Darcy again seeks your company after your child is returned, everyone will shun the lot of you. You will be exposed as a fraud and the child as a bastard. I will be watching for Mr. Darcy's departure.

Darcy attempted not to stiffen in anger, but the emotion coursed through his veins, nevertheless. "Let us gather where we might discuss this turn of events."

"What is there to discuss?" she hiccupped between gulps of air.

He turned her toward the table. "We will sit. You will eat before you become ill, and you, Mr. Sheffield, and I will decide how best to proceed."

"How may I think of food when Lizzy Anne is in danger? I am not—"

"Hungry," he finished her protest. "However, you require your strength. You will be of no use to Elizabeth Anne, to yourself, or to me, if you collapse. Eat for your daughter," he instructed as he shoved her into a chair and placed a slice of toast before her on the plate. Taking up the knife he added butter and conserves. Meanwhile, Mr. Sheffield placed a cup of tea before her. "Just a few bites, love," Darcy coaxed.

"Drink your tea, Elizabeth," Sheffield instructed. "You require your wits about you."

"I have my wits about me!" she huffed.

CHAPTER TEN

"I HAVE MY WITS about me!" she declared, fisting her hands in her lap, and it was all Darcy could do not to laugh aloud. If he was not mistaken, his dearest Elizabeth's stubbornness had arrived. "How dare someone threaten Lizzy's future!"

He handed the earlier message to Mr. Sheffield to read, while he cautioned, "Although I assume you believe, as I do, that my Aunt Catherine, is behind this threat, I must state unequivocally her ladyship is not the author of this note."

"No," Elizabeth hissed, "Lady Catherine is not the author." She reached across the table to snatch the paper from where Darcy had left it on the table. "Your aunt has employed my cousin as her agent."

"Mr. Collins?" he asked. "How can you be so certain?"

She held up the paper where he might view it again. "Mr. Collins often wrote to my father—times when he announced his visits to Longbourn—his crowing about winning Charlotte's hand after my refusal—his warning me not to look above my station—and many more times than my father would have liked." She frowned deeply. "You know enough of Mr. Bennet's joy at the absurd to realize my father shared each of Mr. Collins's letters with me. Sometimes, except for that last one, with the whole family. Look at each of Mr. Collins's 's's.' Mr. Bennet called them 'a hanging s' because of how each nearly lies on its side and falls into the line of script below. And each of his 'l's' appear to

105

be crossed as if it were a 't.' Papa always said he did not know whether to think Mr. Collins too pretentious or not intelligent enough to include the correct letter formation."

Darcy took the note from her fingers to study it more carefully. "If I recall correctly, Collins is left-handed. See the smears on the paper, as if someone would not allow him time for the ink to dry before demanding him to continue?" He refolded the note and placed it on the table. "It is your decision, Elizabeth." He knew he risked his future—their future, for she had sent him away at Rosings Park, but, like then, he would protect her, no matter what it cost him. "Do you wish me to leave? I will understand, and, somehow, please know, I will discover a means, without anyone knowing, to send you the necessary funds to provide for you and Elizabeth Anne. I will never abandon my child."

She turned to meet his steady gaze with one of her own. "If such was my choice, would you marry?"

"I will not," he said with assurance. "Although we did not exchange vows, I pledged myself to you." He prayed she felt the same.

Mr. Sheffield cleared his voice as if to say something, but Elizabeth shook him off. "What of an heir for Pemberley? Even if we were together, I may not be able to provide you an heir."

"I should have been here days earlier, but when I arrived back in London after calling upon your father, I was delayed because Georgiana presented my cousin Fitzwilliam with a son. The line of succession can pass to Georgiana's children."

"Miss Darcy has married the colonel?" Elizabeth asked.

Darcy knew he frowned, and he explained. "Their joining would not have been my choice for my sister, but they appear satisfied. It is difficult for me to consider Miss Darcy is married. In my mind, she remains the girl who always followed me about." He sucked in a quick breath to steady his composure. "Fitzwilliam interfered with Lord Matlock's plans to marry Georgiana off to his oldest son, Roland, Lord Lindale."

"As I thought," Sheffield said softly. "I overheard two

conversations that had me wondering what his lordship had planned for Miss Darcy."

Darcy explained, "From what Fitzwilliam said, my uncle thought to align our families, matching Georgiana with Lindale and Fitzwilliam with my Cousin Anne. Initially, the colonel was able to forestall those plans as the search for what was my fate remained unclear, and then invoking his authority as one of Georgiana's guardians. When he feared my sister would be forced into an unwanted marriage while he was serving our King, the colonel resigned his commission and married his ward before Lord Matlock realized what Fitzwilliam had executed."

He sighed heavily, "As Lindale has refused to marry Anne, I suspect my return to the 'living' has again brought my aunt hope I will make my Cousin Anne my wife."

"I see," she said in tones that had him desiring the same type of assurances from her: a statement she would never marry another, but she made no such promise. Instead, she said, "It is obvious you must leave Brighton."

Darcy's heart dropped. "If it is your wish."

Puzzlement marked her features before a flush of color stained her cheeks. "I mean we must allow whoever is watching us to think I have sent you away, just as the person who ordered your removal has instructed. You will continue to search for Mr. Townsend, who I believe is more likely to have Lizzy than would Lady Catherine."

He reminded her, "All I know from the earlier message is Townsend was supposedly from Kent. I have no idea where to begin my search."

Sheffield cleared his throat to draw their attention. "Earlier, since saying Kent is a large shire, I have been thinking upon something Townsend said recently. Once, several weeks back, he was in the store, and we struck up a conversation about how it would be nice to have a day where one might go fishing. The weather of late has not been fit for much of any outside entertainments. I told him about fishing with my brothers in Cumbria when we were children and he mentioned something to the effect of how he enjoyed fishing along the islands off the Kentish shoreline. Said the fishing was better toward the Isle of Sheppey than it was near his home. I think he mentioned Tunbridge, or perhaps it was Tunbridge Wells. Then he quickly changed the subject, not talking about a favorite place or with whom he fished, as I had done. I thought it odd at the time, but, in retrospect, he likely realized what he had disclosed."

"It is a place to start," Darcy declared. "Thank you, Sheffield." He glanced to his lady. "And what role will you play, Elizabeth? I doubt you plan to remain at home when our daughter is missing?"

She finally lifted the bread with the conserves from her plate to take a bite. "If Mr. Sheffield is well enough to accompany me, I mean to make a call upon Rosings Park." She looked affectionately upon Darcy's former valet, and Darcy knew a bit of jealousy again. She had shared more of herself with Sheffield than she had with him. Learning more of each other was another thing he had lost when he lost his freedom. "If you are not yet well enough, please do not think you must attend me. The confrontation I anticipate will be far from pleasant. I have enough funds set aside to hire a coach and driver, if necessary."

Sheffield said adamantly, "We began this journey together, and I do not intend to desert you now. Lizzy Anne means too much to me not to continue. We will take my carriage."

Darcy said, "Then we should do some planning on how we mean to communicate with each other and how to deal with each of those involved when we catch up to them."

Darcy fought to keep the smile from his lips: His Elizabeth could have had a career on the stage. She dabbed her eyes with a handkerchief and gestured toward his waiting carriage. Over her shoulder, his eyes scanned the street, the other shops, and the narrow alleyways, searching for someone who could be watching them. Finally, his eyes fell upon a familiar figure in the window of the mercantile across the street: John Harwood, Lady Catherine's long-time man-of-all-work.

Elizabeth asked softly, "Did you see someone familiar?"

"My aunt's man-of-all-work," he said in equal caution.

"Mr. Harwood?" she asked.

"You know him?"

"Only by sight from when I tarried with Mr. Collins."

"Likely the man named 'Hardy' the boardinghouse owner had mentioned," he explained.

She nodded her head in understanding.

"When I depart," he warned, "watch whether he follows. I do not want him to trail you to Rosings Park."

She did not wish to look toward the man. "How may I be certain?" she asked with a frown.

He caught her to him as if he meant to exercise his will over her. For a few exquisite seconds, her body aligned with his before Elizabeth remembered she must resist him. It did Darcy's heart well to know she still could not resist the pull between them. She shoved against his chest, and Darcy reluctantly released her. With a crisp bow, he turned on his heels and strode away toward his carriage. However, he paused before reaching it to stand very still and stare in the direction where Harwood watched for Darcy's departure. He held his distance, but he made certain Harwood realized Darcy knew of the man's presence in Brighton. With a nod of his head, he turned and stepped into his coach.

As he looked out the coach's window, Elizabeth made to retreat inside the bookstore, but she turned at the door to watch his carriage depart. If he were not mistaken, there were *real* tears in her eyes this time.

She stepped inside to watch Mr. Harwood exit the mercantile. The man tugged his hat down lower on his forehead in an attempt to conceal his appearance, but he made the mistake of shooting a glance toward the bookstore's window, and she had seen him clearly. "Run home to Kent," she whispered as she watched Harwood mount to follow Mr. Darcy's coach. "Warn your mistress I shall not be dictated to by anyone."

With the "closed" sign upon the door, she returned to the

kitchen area in the back of the store. "Lady Catherine's man, Mr. Harwood, followed Mr. Darcy's coach," she told Sheffield.

"Harwood?" he questioned. "I know the man. Not the nice sort." Sheffield put away the cleaned dishes they had used for their breakfast.

"Do you think Mr. Darcy is in danger?" she asked in concern.

"Was the master aware of Mr. Harwood's presence in town?"

Elizabeth smiled easily. "Mr. Darcy is no longer your master, Albert."

"I served Mr. Darcy since he was twelve. He will always be the young master to me, just as he said Miss Darcy will always be the young girl who followed him about the halls of Pemberley," Sheffield argued. "You will understand when Lizzy Anne is in her twenties, but you still see her as the young girl wishing to crawl upon your lap for a hug."

"I suppose," she said with a grin. "To answer your question, Mr. Darcy was the first to spot Mr. Harwood in the mercantile."

"Good," Sheffield announced. "Mr. Darcy will know how best to mitigate Mr. Harwood's mission."

Elizabeth frowned. "Do you think Mr. Darcy is in danger?"

"If the master could survive what he shared of his ordeal, Mr. Darcy will experience no problems with Harwood. Moreover, Jasper and Mr. Farrin will protect him."

"I know you are correct, but I cannot keep from worrying," she admitted. "Do you think Lady Catherine will employ others to prevent Mr. Darcy from discovering Lizzy? I do not want either of them in danger."

"The more people Lady Catherine involves, the more she must open herself up to those who can incriminate her. In my years of observing her ladyship and hearing those below stairs speak of her while I was in service to Mr. Darcy, Lady Catherine trusts few, even those who have served her for years," he reasoned. "She prefers to intimidate. I imagine your defying her was a shock to her consequence."

Elizabeth did not want to dwell on her interactions with Lady Catherine. Instead, she asked, "How long will it take William to reach Tunbridge Wells?"

"Four to five hours," Sheffield shared.

"Then there is a possibility he may discover Mr. Townsend today," she reasoned.

"I pray such proves true," Sheffield cautioned, "but, if Lady Catherine is behind this madness, her ladyship will not relent willingly."

Although she would have preferred another answer, Elizabeth grudgingly agreed with Mr. Sheffield's estimation. "When do we depart?"

"We will leave the shop closed, which would make sense under the circumstances. I expect several of the gossipy sort will attempt to call upon us today. We will allow them to know we are at home, but we insist upon our privacy. I plan to call upon Mrs. Harris this morning to display my concern and to provide the lady our version of how Lizzy Anne's father made an unexpected appearance and why you have chosen to send him away."

"And what am I to do while you are out?"

"Pack a small trunk for yourself and a few toys and books for Lizzy. Our darling girl will require a bit of *home* once we find her."

"Naturally, you are correct," she conceded. "I simply want Lizzy's return." She sat heavily. "When will we depart?"

"We should be seen out and about for a few hours," he insisted. "I know you do not wish to go out, but perhaps you could rearrange the shelves in the shop. As long as a few view you through the window, they will not think it odd when you are not seen upon the street for several days. We will wait until everyone breaks for their midday meal. In that manner, fewer will take note of our leave-taking. The carriage will be waiting for us at the opening in the common alley at that hour."

"How long will it take us to reach Rosings Park," she inquired.

"It is more than seventy miles to Rochester and Higham. You must postpone your altercation with Lady Catherine until some time tomorrow."

"Would it be too obvious to seek out Mr. Darcy in Tunbridge Wells?" she asked in what she knew were hopeful tones, but Elizabeth could not resist praying for an early end to this madness.

"Mr. Darcy provided me a place to call upon where he will leave word if he has found any information of Townsend and Lizzy. Otherwise, we should continue on with our role in confronting Lady Catherine."

They had departed Brighton later than either she or Mr. Sheffield had liked. After his call on Mrs. Harris, Sheffield had seen their trunks were stored away safely; however, as he had predicted, there had been a steady stream of fellow shopkeepers, and even a few customers, calling at the back entrance. As they did not want others to know of their plans and being concerned more than one person had been hired to spy on them, 'they' had, more truthfully, Mr. Sheffield had, accepted the callers' well wishes and prayers, while all she could do was to pace the floors, silently wishing them all away, despite their best intentions. As she, literally, traced her steps over and over again, Elizabeth attempted to recall what exactly she and Lady Catherine had said to each other on that fateful day.

"You can be at no loss, Miss Bennet, to understand the reason for my journey hither. Your own heart, your own conscience, must tell you why I come."

"Indeed, you are mistaken, madam. I have not been at all able to account for the honor of seeing you here."

"Miss Bennet," her ladyship had cried angrily, *"you ought to know I am not to be trifled with. But however insincere 'you' may choose to be, you shall not find 'me' so. My character has ever been celebrated for its sincerity and frankness, and in a cause of such moment as this, I shall certainly not depart from it. A report of a most alarming nature reached me two days ago. I was told not only your sister was*

on the point of being most advantageously married, but you, Miss Elizabeth Bennet, would, in all likelihood, be soon afterwards united to my nephew, my own nephew, Mr. Darcy. Though I 'know' it must be a scandalous falsehood, though I would not injure him so much as to suppose the truth of it possible, I instantly resolved on setting off for this place, that I might make my sentiments known to you."

Elizabeth recalled coloring with astonishment and disdain before answering. *"If you believed it impossible to be true, I wonder you took the trouble of coming so far. What could your ladyship propose by it?"*

"At once to insist upon having such a report universally contradicted."

Coolly, Elizabeth answered, *"Your coming to Longbourn, to see me and my family, will be rather a confirmation of it; if, indeed, such a report is in existence."*

"If! Do you then pretend to be ignorant of it? Has it not been industriously circulated by yourselves? Do you not know that such a report is spread about?"

Elizabeth managed to keep the smile from her lips. *"I never heard that it was."*

"And can you likewise declare there is no 'foundation' for it?"

"I do not pretend to possess equal frankness with your ladyship. 'You' may ask questions which 'I' shall not choose to answer."

"This is not to be borne, Miss Bennet. I insist on being satisfied. Has he, has my nephew, made you an offer of marriage?"

Elizabeth had wanted to laugh. If Lady Catherine had known what had occurred at Hunsford Cottage, she would not be asking such an inane question. *"Your ladyship has declared it impossible,"* she responded in order to needle Mr. Darcy's aunt.

"It ought to be so; it must be so," the grand lady had declared. *"While he retains the use of his reason. But 'your' arts and allurements may, in a moment of infatuation, have made him forget what he owes to himself and to all his family. You may have drawn him in."*

Elizabeth wished to tell her ladyship she had managed to earn Mr. Darcy's affections by despising him. Arts and allurements were far from her repertoire. Rather, she said, *"If I* have, I shall be the last person to confess it."

"Miss Bennet, do you know who I am? I have not been accustomed to such language as this. I am almost the nearest relation he has in the world and am entitled to know all his dearest concerns."

Elizabeth was beginning to lose patience with this conversation, and she had no intention to bend to Lady Catherine's will. *"But you are not entitled to know 'mine'; nor will such behavior as this, ever induce me to be explicit."*

"Let me be rightly understood. This match, to which you have the presumption to aspire, can never take place. No, never. Mr. Darcy is engaged to 'my daughter.' Now what have you to say?"

"Only this; that if he is so, you can have no reason to suppose he will make an offer to me."

Lady Catherine hesitated then. *"The engagement between them is of a peculiar kind. From their infancy, they have been intended for each other. It was the favorite wish of 'his' mother, as well as hers. While in their cradles, we planned the union: and now, at the moment when the wishes of both sisters would be accomplished in their marriage, to be prevented by a young woman of inferior birth, of no importance in the world, and wholly unallied to the family! Do you pay no regard to the wishes of his friends? To his tacit engagement to Miss de Bourgh? Are you lost to every feeling of propriety and delicacy? Have you not heard me say that from his earliest hours he was destined for his cousin?"*

Elizabeth wondered for a few brief seconds what Mr. Darcy would have said to this madness, but she was alone in defending herself. *"Yes, and I had heard it before. But what is that to me? If there is no other objection to my marrying your nephew, I shall certainly not be kept from it by knowing his mother and aunt wished him to marry Miss de Bourgh. You both did as much as you could in planning the marriage. Its completion depended on others. If Mr. Darcy is neither by honor nor inclination confined to his cousin, why is not he to make another choice? And if I am that choice, why may not I accept him?"*

*"Because honor, decorum, prudence, nay, interest, forbid it. Yes, Miss Bennet, interest; for do not expect to be noticed by his family or friends, if you willfully act against the inclinations of all. You will be

censured, slighted, and despised, by every one connected with him. Your alliance will be a disgrace; your name will never even be mentioned by any of us."

Irritated beyond reason, Elizabeth had said curtly, "These are heavy misfortunes. But the wife of Mr. Darcy must have such extraordinary sources of happiness necessarily attached to her situation, that she could, upon the whole, have no cause to repine."

"Obstinate, headstrong girl!" her ladyship had wailed. "I am ashamed of you! Is this your gratitude for my attentions to you last spring? Is nothing due to me on that score?" Her ladyship had sat on the bench, and Elizabeth had had no choice but to follow suit. "You are to understand, Miss Bennet, that I came here with the determined resolution of carrying my purpose, nor will I be dissuaded from it. I have not been used to submit to any person's whims. I have not been in the habit of brooking disappointment."

By this point, Elizabeth's patience had worn thin. "'That' will make your ladyship's situation at present more pitiable; but it will have no effect on 'me.'"

Lady Catherine barked, "I will not be interrupted. Hear me in silence. My daughter and my nephew are formed for each other. They are descended, on the maternal side, from the same noble line; and, on the father's from respectable, honorable, and ancient — though untitled — families. Their fortune on both sides is splendid. They are destined for each other by the voice of every member of their respective houses; and what is to divide them? The upstart pretensions of a woman without family, connections, or future! Is this to be endured! But it must not, shall not be. If you were sensible of your own good, you would not wish to quit the sphere in which you have been brought up."

Fury had rushed through Elizabeth's veins, but she made herself not physically lash out against Lady Catherine. "In marrying your nephew, I should not consider myself as quitting that sphere. He is a gentleman; I am a gentleman's daughter; so far we are equal."

"True. You 'are' a gentleman's daughter. But who was your mother? Who are your uncles and aunts? Do not imagine me ignorant of their condition."

Elizabeth had so wished to strike the woman. To demand an apology. Yet, she knew in many ways Lady Catherine de Bourgh had the right of it. Through tight lips, she said, *"Whatever my connections may be, if your nephew does not object to them, they can be nothing to 'you.'"*

"Tell me, once and for all, are you engaged to him?"

Though Elizabeth would not, for the mere purpose of obliging Lady Catherine, have answered this question, she could not but say, after a moment's deliberation, *"I am not."*

Lady Catherine seemed pleased. *"And will you promise me never to enter into such an engagement?"*

"I make no promise of the kind." It had felt good to say the words aloud, for another offer of Mr. Darcy's hand had been her most cherished wish.

"Miss Bennet, I am shocked and astonished. I expected to find a more reasonable young woman. But do not deceive yourself into a belief that I will ever recede. I shall not go away till you have given me the assurance I require."

She had stood her ground. *"And I certainly never shall give it. I am not to be intimidated into anything so wholly unreasonable. Your ladyship wants Mr. Darcy to marry your daughter, but would my giving you the wished-for promise make their marriage at all more probable? Supposing him to be attached to me, would my refusing to accept his hand make him wish to bestow it on his cousin?"* Elizabeth knew such was not true, for she had already refused his hand—months earlier, and Mr. Darcy had made no attempt to join with his cousin in that time. *"Allow me to say, Lady Catherine, the arguments with which you have supported this extraordinary application have been as frivolous as the application was ill-judged. You have widely mistaken my character if you think I can be worked on by such persuasions as these. How far your nephew might approve of your interference in 'his' affairs, I cannot tell, but you have certainly no right to concern yourself with mine. I must beg, therefore, to be importuned no farther on the subject."*

"Not so hasty, if you please," Lady Catherine had insisted when Elizabeth made to return to the house. *"I have by no means*

done. To all the objections I have already urged, I have still another to add. I am no stranger to the particulars of your youngest sister's infamous elopement. I know it all: that the young man's marrying her was a patched-up business, at the expense of your father and uncles. And is 'such' a girl to be my nephew's sister? Is 'her' husband, the son of his late father's steward, to be his brother? Heaven and earth! Of what are you thinking? Are the shades of Pemberley to be thus polluted?"

Elizabeth resentfully stated. "You can 'now' have nothing further to say. You have insulted me in every possible method. I must beg to return to the house."

Elizabeth had risen, but Lady Catherine had followed her to her feet. Her ladyship was still highly incensed and would not concede her efforts to be futile. "You have no regard, then, for the honor and credit of my nephew! Unfeeling, selfish girl! Do you not consider that a connection with you must disgrace him in the eyes of everybody?"

In truth, Elizabeth had considered that reality, but she would never permit Lady Catherine to know her ladyship's words had found their target. "Lady Catherine, I have nothing further to say," she repeated. "You know my sentiments."

"You are then resolved to have him?"

Elizabeth had turned on her then. She had hissed, "I have said no such thing. I am only resolved to act in that manner, which will, in my own opinion, constitute my happiness, without reference to you, or to any person so wholly unconnected with me."

"It is well. You refuse, then, to oblige me. You refuse to obey the claims of duty, honor, and gratitude. You are determined to ruin him in the opinion of all his friends and make him the contempt of the world."

She had replied, "Neither duty, nor honor, nor gratitude have any possible claim on me, in the present instance. No principle of either would be violated by my marriage with Mr. Darcy. And with regard to the resentment of his family, or the indignation of the world, if the former were excited by his marrying me, it would not give me one moment's concern, and the world in general would have too much sense to join in the scorn."

In reflection, Elizabeth wished she could take all those

words back. Wished she had never confronted Lady Catherine de Bourgh. For her ladyship had finished the conversation with a threat to which Elizabeth had not paid close attention. Such was now her nightmare. *"And this is your opinion! This is your final resolve! Very well. I shall now know how to act. Do not imagine, Miss Bennet, that your ambition will ever be gratified. I came to try you. I hoped to find you reasonable, but, depend upon it: I will carry my point."*

"I am grieved we could not reach Tunbridge Wells this evening," Mr. Sheffield said as he squeezed the back of her hand. They had taken refuge at an inn still in Sussex, unable to reach Kent before an evening storm had driven them from the road.

She nodded sadly. "At least, we have reason to believe Mr. Darcy arrived in Tunbridge Wells and has continued the search for Lizzy." Tears pooled in her eyes. "Even so, I cannot bear to consider how frightened Elizabeth Anne must be without her mother and her Uncle Albert to tuck her into her bed with a kiss."

"Just be comforted by the idea Mr. Darcy will never rest until he finds his daughter. The master is singular when it comes to family," Sheffield declared with a hitch of emotion in his voice.

Elizabeth belatedly realized if she and Lizzy became part of Mr. Darcy's household, Mr. Sheffield would be alone in the world. He had done so much for her, the idea made her sadder. She smiled weakly. "I have no doubt. If I require any evidence to the gentleman's tenacity, I have only to look to our unconventional courtship." They sat in silence for several minutes before she asked, "Should I have told Mr. Darcy what measures we executed to protect Elizabeth Anne?"

CHAPTER ELEVEN

Darcy knew exhaustion when he laid out upon the thin mattress in the room he had claimed in the inn on the outskirts of Tunbridge Wells. It had been both a frustrating, as well as a fulfilling day. As he had expected, Mr. Harwood had followed Darcy's carriage at a respectable distance until Darcy led the man to the local blacksmith shop. When he entered the establishment, he introduced himself and explained to the proprietor, "A man has followed me from Brighton, and I think it best if the local constable speaks to him to learn his intent."

"Are you certain he means mischief?" the blacksmith asked in obvious concern.

Darcy kept his countenance sincere. "I noted him when I entered my coach in Brighton, and he has been behind me ever since. The man is on horse and has had multiple opportunities to overtake me and proceed forward to his business in the area, if that was his purpose. Instead, he sits upon his horse, at this very moment, overlooking your front door. Why do you not step outside and pretend to examine my team and have a look for yourself?"

The man appeared suspicious, but he did as Darcy suggested, returning a few minutes later. "Roan-colored horse in the tree line off to the left."

"That is the one," Darcy confirmed. "The thing is if I attempt to capture him, he will simply ride away; however, as he has proven to be so determined, I suspect he will return. I certainly would not want to lead him to my family's door. I do not wish to place you and yours in danger, but do you have a means to summon the local sheriff or magistrate to arrest the man without setting up an alarm?"

The blacksmith sent his son with a note and instructions to the local sheriff to come around the back road on Mr. Cooper's land, which backed up to the blacksmith's place, so he would come up behind the fellow.

It had cost Darcy several hours and ten pounds between rewarding the sheriff and the blacksmith for their service, but he had convinced the sheriff to detain Mr. Harwood for three days to permit Darcy time to depart the area. After all, until Harwood committed an actual crime, he had as much right to be on the road as did Darcy, or so Darcy was told by the sheriff. Obviously, when Harwood was brought before the magistrate, he invoked Lady Catherine's name; yet, Darcy swore he had never encountered Harwood in the last four years upon his aunt's estate. "Not a lie," he told himself as he turned upon his side, searching for a more comfortable position upon the bed. He already missed holding Elizabeth in his arms. "One night was not enough."

Unfortunately, his search for Townsend had been equally twofold as his dealings with Harwood. Even so, he finally had learned Townsend had returned to his mother's home near Pantiles. "I will call upon the house early tomorrow morning and pray Townsend and Elizabeth Anne are there or someone within knows where to find the man."

<hr>

They had departed Sussex early, pausing briefly at an inn on the far side of Tunbridge Wells for a late meal, a change of horses, and, more importantly, a message, left especially for them by Mr. Darcy. They had waited until they returned to the coach before reading the note.

My dearest Elizabeth,

I pray your journey to Tunbridge Wells was a safe one. Please know you are constantly in my thoughts and prayers.

She felt a bit awkward reading Mr. Darcy's more intimate words to Mr. Sheffield, but her friend simply nodded his head to encourage her to continue.

I made progress with Harwood in that the local sheriff has agreed to detain the man for three days to permit me time to leave the area. Most assuredly, Harwood protested against my complaints, but was placed in the local gaol, nevertheless. Lady Catherine should have no warning of your intended call upon Rosings Park.

"Such should prove to our benefit," Sheffield observed.

Elizabeth admitted, "I have worried over Lady Catherine expecting our call. I do not want her to take over the encounter before I have a chance to speak my disdain."

I have located and called upon Townsend's mother this morning. The woman, initially, was not cooperative, but I proved most persuasive. Although she could not say for certain whether her son had a child with him, neither could she deny it. When he returns to Kent, Townsend essentially stays in what would be a worker's hut on his mother's small property. The woman provided me permission to view the hut, and there was a small clue left behind: the tip of a green ribbon, as if the ribbon had begun to unravel. You said Elizabeth Anne had green ribbons tying back her braids. This provides me hope, and I pray it will you, as well. Our daughter may be frightened, but it appears Townsend is tending to her needs for there were dirty plates on the table with relatively fresh remnants of food on them.

"I wonder what Mr. Darcy offered Mrs. Townsend to secure her cooperation," Elizabeth mused.

"The master's late father taught his son well," Sheffield assured. "Mr. Darcy knows when to use a heavy hand, as with Mr. Harwood, or when to extend his promise of assistance, and when his warning of dire circumstance for an opponent's refusal is appropriate. He is not a hard man, but I pity those who cross him."

Elizabeth sighed heavily. "Whatever it takes to bring Lizzy home is fine. Just as long as my child is safe."

As Mrs. Townsend was not certain of her son's destination, I plan to travel eastward, parallel to the coast and then turn northward to meet with you in Higham. Be cautious around my aunt, as we are both aware, her ladyship will not be an easy foe to fell. If I learn anything, I will send word by express to inform you of any changes to my plans.

She stopped there as Mr. Darcy added a private message that brought a flush of color to her cheeks and tears to her eyes.

Although she was certain Mr. Sheffield took notice of her reaction to Mr. Darcy's message, he said, "Then we continue on to Rosings Park as we planned."

Darcy attempted to trace Mr. Townsend across Kent, but there had been no sightings of a man or Darcy's daughter. "It seems to me a man traveling with a small child would be required to stop periodically," he grumbled as he again stepped down before an inn.

"Should we change out the horses, Mr. Darcy?" Mr. Farrin asked.

"I am beginning to think we chase a ghost," he admitted reluctantly. "Change out the horses. We should set a course for Rosings Park. I do not want Elizabeth to encounter Lady Catherine alone."

"Certainly, sir." Mr. Farrin climbed down from the seat to see to the team.

"I will ask of Townsend inside." Darcy's steps had become heavier with each denial of Townsend's presence.

"May I be of assistance, sir?" The innkeeper rushed forward to greet him.

"Do you have horses to let?" he asked.

The innkeeper frowned. "I fear not, sir."

It was Darcy's turn to scowl. Another disappointment. "Very well," he said with a calmness he did not feel. "Might you answer a question then?"

"Yes, sir."

"I am seeking a man of about my age traveling with a small female child of three years. Have you seen him?"

The innkeeper opened his mouth to respond, but Jasper appeared at Darcy's side. He said softly, "You should come, sir. Mr. Farrin says he requires your attendance immediately."

Darcy eyed his long-time servant and asked the question resting upon his lips without saying a word.

"Yes, sir." Jasper responded.

Leaving the innkeeper to his duties, Darcy followed Jasper out into the inn yard where Mr. Farrin conversed with a groom. Farrin made the introductions. "Mr. Darcy, this is Mr. French. He believes he has seen Mr. Townsend and the child."

"Aye, sir." The groom cleared his throat in importance. "Perhaps two hours past, a man rides in on a horse, with a child up before him on his lap. The wee lass be cryin' and sayin' she wanted her mama and her Uncle Elbert."

"Albert," Darcy corrected, his heart racing in anticipation. "Did Mr. Townsend say where he meant to take the child?"

Darcy expected to hear the words "Rochester" or "Higham" or something indicating Lady Catherine's estate; however, Mr. French uttered, "Queenborough. Said he was to show the child the well. I's didn't think of what he say until later, after he rode away once he watered his horse."

"Queenborough?" Darcy questioned. "The town or the former castle?"

"Could be the town, for there be lots of wells there, but I be thinkin' of the collapsed well the Royal Navy deepened back in the late 1700s. Likely not, but that be me first thoughts."

"Dear God!" Darcy felt as if someone had struck him hard, knocking the breath from his chest. "Jasper. Farrin," he called as he raced toward the carriage. "The Isles of Sheppey! I should have started there!"

It was late morning when Mr. Sheffield's coach had entered the gates of Rosings Park. Sheffield had napped on and off all afternoon; however, Elizabeth had not complained, for she knew him not fully recovered from the ague, which had brought him low for nearly a sennight. She was blessed: The dear man had shored up his energies for this journey, for he, like Mr. Darcy, had promised to protect her. Moreover, conversation was not required between them. Although she was more social than he, her mind was so full of what was happening with Mr. Darcy and Lizzy, she had had no reason to give voice to her fears again. Albert Sheffield not only understood her angst; he shared it.

They made good speed along the lane, and she turned her head to glance out the carriage window just as Charlotte Collins stepped from Hunsford Cottage. Her long-time friend raised her hand to shade her eyes to study their coach.

Elizabeth pulled herself up straight. "Might as well begin here," she growled. "Good a place as any." She pounded on the roof of the coach to signal for the driver to halt.

She was already unlatching the door before Sheffield could drag himself from his sleep. "What is amiss?" he mumbled.

Elizabeth ignored him and jumped down awkwardly without the steps being set to storm across the lane toward where recognition brought a smile to Charlotte's countenance. Her friend was striding toward Elizabeth with her arms open. "It is you! I thought never to see you again." Charlotte caught Elizabeth in a natural embrace, before Elizabeth could stop her. Her friend hummed with pleasure, and so would have Elizabeth if it had been any other day and any other circumstance. She had truly missed Charlotte as much as she had missed her family in Hertfordshire. However, when her friend pulled back to look upon Elizabeth's features, Charlotte's expression changed. "Not that I regret seeing you; yet, why are you in Kent?"

Elizabeth ignored both Charlotte's question and her welcome; instead, she broke away to continue her charge upon the cottage. "Where is he?" she demanded. "Where is my cousin?"

Charlotte appeared puzzled, but she gestured toward the neatly-tended cottage. "I believe my husband is in his garden."

Elizabeth did not wait for her friend. She hiked her skirts and scrambled through the gate and around the house. As Charlotte had predicted, Mr. Collins was bent over his vegetables. So angry she could barely see, Elizabeth rushed at the man—shoving him to the ground, then kicking him. "You contemptible creature! I should order you whipped!" She kicked him again. "Better yet, I should take up the whip myself!"

It was then Mr. Sheffield caught her up in his embrace, locking her arms at her side, although she continued to fight him. She was so full of anguish that Elizabeth simply wanted someone to be punished for her trials.

"Elizabeth!" Charlotte demanded. "What mean you by this madness?" Her friend knelt beside Mr. Collins. "What offense has my husband executed against you?"

"You do not know, do you?" Elizabeth accused while she squirmed to be free of Sheffield's hold. "You do not know what crimes your husband has committed?"

"Know? Know what?" Charlotte stood to look between Mr. Collins and Elizabeth.

Mr. Collins struggled to his feet. "I have done nothing to deserve such treatment, but what must one expect from the Bennets. Two daughters who have known such shame no decent man will approach the other three!"

Elizabeth growled again. "You proudful toad! You think I do not know how your father all but disowned you because you were such a disappointment to him. It was my father, you twit, who stood against yours. Mr. Bennet knew the value of having a son, where yours was willing to send you away to live with others. Such was the source of their falling out." She turned to Sheffield and indicated she would be calmer, and he released her, before she turned back to Collins. "Somehow you learned what my father did for you. Do not deny it. Such is why you extended the proverbial olive branch to my family. You knew your father had erred, and, in your totally incompetent manner of approaching the world, you meant to offer your gratitude." She stiffened as she looked upon the man. "Then you betrayed all things holy. You should not wear the robes of a cleric. You do not deserve the honor of serving your parish."

Charlotte stepped before her husband to block Elizabeth's view. "I think you have gone too far, Elizabeth. I must ask you to leave this property."

Elizabeth reached into the pocket sewn in the side seam of her dress to remove the note she knew written by Collins. "Not until you read this message delivered to my home yesterday morning. You should be made aware of the kind of man you married."

"I already know enough of Mr. Collins's nature," Charlotte declared stubbornly.

Sheffield said softly, "It would be easier if you would agree, ma'am. Surely you are aware of Elizabeth's obstinate nature."

"And who are you, sir?" Mr. Collins demanded. However, he remained partially concealed behind his wife, using her as his shield. "I view no ring on either of your fingers. Is the gentleman your protector, Cousin Elizabeth? Have you become a kept woman?" he said in accusation.

Sheffield's hand caught Elizabeth's elbow to hold her in place. "I am Mr. Darcy's valet and do upon occasion, when the gentleman himself is not available, serve as the lady's protector, but not in the sense of degradation that you infer. Yet, we are both aware I have been made known to you. You, obviously, can name my identity; otherwise you would not have known the directions displayed upon the outside of the note in your wife's hands." Sheffield tucked Elizabeth into his side. "Please read the message, Mrs. Collins. We await your opinion."

Elizabeth held her breath as her long-time friend and confidante unfolded the note to read its contents. "You have a daughter, Elizabeth?" Charlotte smiled sadly. "We lost ours."

"I am grieved for your loss, Charlotte. You, as a mother,

will certainly understand how I feel. I have a daughter," Elizabeth said simply, "but someone has stolen her away. I must find her, Charlotte, before it is too late."

"And Mr. Darcy?" Charlotte asked, a frown forming on her features as her eyes returned to the paper.

"Very much alive and searching Kent, brick-by-brick, to locate his child," Elizabeth explained. "Mr. Collins knows something of where my daughter has been taken."

Elizabeth heard the click of a gun. She turned to discover Mr. Sheffield's driver holding a pistol on Mr. Collins, who had, obviously, thought to make his exit or, more likely, report Elizabeth's accusations to Lady Catherine at the great house, while she attempted to convince Charlotte of the urgency of their mission.

"I would suggest ye rejoin yer wife, sir," Mr. Jacobsen said.

"Mr. Collins," Charlotte accused in sharp tones. "You wrote this note."

"I did not," he said with a sickening smile on his lips, evidently meant to convince his wife of his innocence.

"Mine was not a question, sir," Charlotte corrected. "You have executed Lady Catherine's dirty work again. It is bad enough you harangue her tenants when she instructs you to do so, but to commit such a crime! I recognize your handwriting. Do not deny you are, if not the author, the transcriber, of this note. I have corrected enough of your sermons to be well aware of your script. It is one thing to feed her ladyship's vanity in order to maintain your position, but it is quite another to send threatening notes to those who have treated you fairly. And how could you be involved in stealing away a child from her family? Can you not imagine the terror that little girl experiences? What if she were your child? Our child?"

He said in excuse, "I had no choice. Such was Lady Catherine's wish."

Charlotte charged at her husband then, much as Elizabeth had done earlier. "You placed Lady Catherine's Bedlam-like demands before the welfare of our family? Before the welfare of your relations? You conspired to separate your cousin from her child!"

"The child was born without the benefit of wedding vows," he protested.

"Are you certain?" Mr. Sheffield said quietly.

"Lady Catherine says it is so," Mr. Collins insisted.

Charlotte snapped. "Then it must be written as surely as if it was the finger of God damning the child. Heaven forbid Lady Catherine de Bourgh would approve of an opinion not of her own making! And even if it were true that Elizabeth's child was Mr. Darcy's by-blow, your duty as a cleric is to pray for her and the child's eternal souls, not set as judge! When did our God set you in judgement of others? Jesus did not judge Mary Magdalene. Instead, he welcomed her among those who followed him."

"Be reasonable, Charlotte," he entreated. "Lady Catherine will turn us out without a reference if I do not do what she asks. I had no choice."

"You always have a choice, Mr. Collins," Charlotte said in steely tones. "The difference is whether you are man enough to stand against those who defame others. You will make this right, or I will take your child and return to my father's house in Hertfordshire." It was only then that Elizabeth realized Charlotte was again with child. Lying with a man such as Mr. Collins would never appeal to Elizabeth, but Charlotte was different. All her friend had ever wanted was children and a house of her own.

Mr. Collins attempted to stand his ground. "You are my wife, Mrs. Collins. You may not leave without my permission, and I will never tolerate your removing my child from this house."

"And I will not tolerate a man who practices such evil against his relations. I would not want our child to know such a man as his or her father. I want my children to be raised with honor. Moreover, I doubt my father or my brothers will care for your posturing, Husband," she declared. "Sir William Lucas raised his children with values."

Mr. Sheffield added, "Do not forget Mr. Darcy, sir. Once he has located his daughter, Mr. Darcy will move heaven and earth to destroy all those who stood against him. You would do well to tell Elizabeth what you know. It may be the only thing to save you."

"Lady Catherine will not allow anything to occur to me or the others who serve her. She is my patron," Collins asserted. "She is the daughter of an earl and the widow of a baronet, permitting her precedence over her nephew. Her word is her bond."

"Since when?" Charlotte said sarcastically.

"You cannot think to compare her ladyship with her nephew," Sheffield argued. "Mr. Darcy is one of the wealthiest men in England. Even his uncle, Lady Catherine's brother, fears Mr. Darcy. You should also," Sheffield warned in ominous tones. "A wealthy gentleman always trumps the widow of a commoner."

Elizabeth enjoyed the manner in which Sheffield played with Mr. Collins. The gentleman was a powerful ally.

Collins pronounced another cut to Elizabeth's reputation. "Do you mean to continue to be Mr. Darcy's mistress?"

She did not permit Collins to know his words had found a target. Instead, Elizabeth laughed confidently. "If you wish to meet Mr. Darcy on a field of honor, say those words to the gentleman. Have you not realized by now, Cousin, I am to be the Mistress of Pemberley?"

"Mr. Darcy cannot marry someone who has born a child on the wrong side of the blanket," Collins said with a smirk.

"You say another disparaging word about my child, and I will borrow Mr. Jacobsen's pistol and make Charlotte a widow," Elizabeth threatened while taking a menacing step forward. "In addition to curbing your nasty disposition, it would be worth the penalty to view you six feet under in order to save Longbourn from your rule. Mr. Bennet's tenants certainly do not deserve a master who thinks only of himself. If you were dead, Mr. Bennet can live out his years without the specter of you and your incompetence hanging over his head. Then, if she is so blessed, either Charlotte's son will inherit or Longbourn will pass to a different line of cousins — men of integrity — men who understand the meaning of 'honor.'"

Charlotte frowned again. "You will apologize to your cousin for your unforgivable remark, Mr. Collins."

"I will—" he began, but swallowed his denial when Charlotte pointed her finger at him.

"I said," Charlotte enunciated each syllable distinctly, "you will apologize to Elizabeth, and you will tell her what you know of her child's whereabouts."

"But, Mrs. Collins—" he thought to protest.

"Now," Charlotte growled, and Elizabeth wished to smile, for she had heard her friend use that same tone and same stance more than one time with Charlotte's younger brothers and sisters. No one, not even Sir William, spoke back to Charlotte when Elizabeth's friend used that particular tone. Like Charlotte's brothers and sisters, Mr. Collins had crossed his wife's reasonable nature one too many times. "I shall not ask it of you again."

Mr. Collins's color paled more than usual. Evidently, the man had foolishly brought out this side of Charlotte's temper previously. With his head down, he did as his wife asked. "Lady Catherine's new groom, Mr. Townsend, is to abandon the child on one of the islands in the Medway Estuary. Near Queenborough."

"Abandon!" Charlotte and Elizabeth shrieked together.

Elizabeth reached for Mr. Sheffield's waiting hand. "We must go. Now." He was already waving Mr. Jacobsen toward the coach. Holding her hand, Sheffield tugged her along behind him, lifting her into the waiting carriage before shouting orders to Jacobsen and following her inside.

In less than a minute, Jacobsen had turned the coach around and was headed back the way they had come — toward the entrance gate of Rosings Park. Belatedly, Elizabeth realized she had not said her farewells nor expressed her gratitude to Charlotte.

As if reading her mind, Mr. Sheffield said, "Mrs. Collins will understand. She possesses a mother's instinct. The lady will likely be satisfied to have been of use to you."

Elizabeth nodded her acceptance, although she knew, somehow, she must say the words to Charlotte. She owed her friend that much. "How long to Queenborough?" she asked as she turned her attention once again to the passing tree line.

"Three hours, give or take, with tolls and all," Mr. Sheffield responded. "Hopefully, the ground stays dry, even if there is a chill in the air and a dampness not customarily found in England this time of year, we should make decent time if we miss the rain."

"Yet, there is only a few hours before nightfall." She sighed heavily in despair. "Will this madness ever end?"

"It will. A few more hours. Continue to stay strong for Lizzy."

"But my sweetest girl is so young," she protested. "Will she ever recover from this upheaval?"

"Children are generally more resilient than we give them credit for being," he said.

"But, as you said moments ago, it is so cold. I did not even think to consider whether Townsend took her coat." She broke into tears. "What kind of mother am I?"

He reached across the coach to pat the back of her hand. "You are the very best of mothers. I am so proud to be a part of your life."

Elizabeth smiled weakly. "Why did you never consider marrying me?"

"The years between us," he said simply.

"Not so far," she said, allowing the madness of the last few days to settle again. "There is only eighteen years, and we rub along together well."

He smiled upon her, but it was the brotherly smile he had always presented her. "When you were twenty, the differences felt broader than they do today," he said with a shrug of his shoulders. "Moreover," he continued, "I am vain enough to wish my wife to prefer me to all others, especially to a man to whom I have presented my respect."

"I am hopeless, am I not?" Her bottom lip trembled with emotions. "I have only truly loved Fitzwilliam Darcy."

"The master is a fortunate man—more fortunate than many, for he will spend the remainder of his days with you and Lizzy."

"Ahoy in the coach!" a voice called out. A single rider approached, pressing his horse to overtake them.

Looking out the small window in the rear of the coach, she asked in anxiousness, "A highwayman?"

Sheffield had released the latch for the side window. With his head out the opening, he said in a loud voice, "I do not think so. The rider has a red scarf about his neck, the agreed upon signal from Mr. Darcy."

"Then stop the coach!" Elizabeth ordered. "Mayhap William has found our Lizzy."

CHAPTER TWELVE

"Mr. Darcy," his coachman pleaded. "This is a dangerous endeavor. I must advise you against entering the well."

Darcy continued to release the buttons on his waistcoat. His greatcoat, dress coat, and hat rested upon the ground near where his carriage sat ready. "I did not realize the well had collapsed further," he admitted. "I know my efforts are likely futile, but I cannot walk away until I attempt to discover for certain whether my daughter is lying at the bottom. Even if she has not survived this abuse exacted against her, Elizabeth Anne should look down from heaven and know her father loved her enough to enact the impossible in her name."

Both his coachman and footman nodded sharply, tears evident in their eyes. "We will support you, sir." Jasper said. "Do what you must. We will not abandon you."

Mr. Farrin backed the coach close to where the Queenborough Castle well once stood. Traces of the bricks and the hole were all any of them could see: A gaping hole—one reportedly more than a hundred feet deep.

Darcy tied the rope about his waist as Jasper placed a three-inch wide tree limb through the back wheels of the carriage to keep it from rolling. They had tied the other end of the rope to the carriage's chassis. Mr. Farrin stood at the head, holding the horses in place, prepared to pull Darcy out if he encountered difficulties.

"We only have fifty feet of rope, sir. Not enough to reach the bottom," Jasper cautioned.

"I understand." If Elizabeth Anne was alive at the bottom of the well, Darcy would purchase every length of rope in Kent in order to reach her, and if she died at the hands of Townsend, he would pay to have an expert climber retrieve his child's body, see her buried properly, and, then, personally hunt down Townsend and exact his own revenge. Upon *The Lost Sparrow*, Darcy had learned several unique methods of torture, and he would see each performed on Townsend before the man died. "Perhaps there is enough to learn the truth. That is all I ask."

He tied a lantern to the rope about his waist before moving to the edge of the opening to kneel down and yell into the black opening. "Elizabeth Anne, if you hear me, darling, please answer me. I know you are frightened, but I am here to see you returned to your mother's arms. Please answer me."

He listened with his whole self, but there was not even a whimper. Disheartened, Darcy swallowed his sorrow and turned where he could drop himself into the abyss. Inching downward, the rope sliding through his hand burned, but the pain was familiar, one he had experienced often in his years aboard *The Lost Sparrow*. Odd how those years of drudgery and bottomless hopes allowed him the confidence to search for his daughter.

"A little more," he called as he permitted himself to slide into the darkness, the air in the well colder than he had expected. He shivered, but rather his reaction came from the cold or from the dread of the unknown, he could not say.

"Only ten more feet of rope, sir," Jasper called from above, and Darcy slowed his descent. Releasing the lantern, with trembling fingers he finally managed to light the candle within and then close the latch. The lantern offered only a weak flicker of light, barely cutting through the thick blackness of the expanse below him. "Elizabeth Anne," he called his voice bouncing off what remained of the walls. "Fine eyes!" Yet, there was no response.

He lifted the light away from his body, calling out. "Look up, sweetheart. Do you see the light? Call out if you do!" He listened with all his heart, but there was nothing. "Fine eyes!" he called once again on a watery plea. The silence that followed nearly had him releasing the knot in the rope about his waist and permitting his earthly body to join what he imagined to be the broken body of his child at the bottom of the pit. "I wish I knew for certain," he whispered. "I wish I knew if you are below, my child. Dear God, am I to know more hardship? How might I support Elizabeth when I feel as if all I wish to do is to abandon this world?"

He bowed his head then and wept. His heart breaking. At length, he murmured a passage he recalled from the book of *Revelation*, "He will wipe away every tear from their eyes, and death shall be no more, neither shall there be mourning, nor crying, nor pain anymore, for the former things have passed away." He sighed heavily and waited for God's answer.

※

"There!" Elizabeth pointed as Mr. Sheffield's carriage bounced through yet another rut in the road. Mr. Jacobsen had permitted the horses their heads.

Mr. Sheffield held onto the strap to keep himself upright, pounding on the roof to signal for Jacobsen to stop.

The messenger had indeed been sent from Mr. Darcy, stating the gentleman had learned that Townsend meant to take Lizzy to the Queenborough Castle's abandoned well. *"What Townsend plans to do at that point, I cannot say,"* read his message.

It was then that they—she and Sheffield—had set off on a mad dash across Kent. "Fitzwilliam will go to great lengths to learn if Lizzy has been placed in the well when Mr. Collins says otherwise. I cannot lose him, Albert," she had said, at least, a dozen times over their thirty miles' journey.

At length, the carriage slowed and the spectacle before them had unfolded. Albert beat her to the door this time, crawling down awkwardly, before turning to lift her from the opening. As quickly as her feet hit the ground, she was calling his name.

"Fitzwilliam! Dear God, Fitzwilliam! She is not in the well! Do you hear me, William? Lizzy is not in the well!"

Darcy's tears flowed easily, and his body shook from the despair filling every part of him. Reluctantly, he blew out the candle and resigned himself to the barren existence awaiting him. He reattached the lantern to his person and prepared himself to be pulled to the surface when he heard what he thought was Elizabeth calling his name. Had she found their child at Rosings? He lifted himself up to climb up the rope if necessary.

She was nearer now. "She is not in the well. Do you hear me, William? Lizzy is not in the well!"

Hope bloomed in his heart again. "Thank you, God," he whispered before he called to those at the surface. "Pull me up!" He could feel the slight tug on the rope as Jasper steadied the rope attached to the brace under his carriage.

"Pull him out!" Elizabeth's frantic pleas filled the air above his head. "Mr. Sheffield," she ordered, "assist me with the rope while Jasper removes the limb blocking the wheels!"

Although Darcy doubted her and Sheffield's combined strength was strong enough to pull him out without the assistance of his coach and his servants, the fact Elizabeth Bennet would risk her life to save him healed another fissure of his bruised existence.

"William?" she called in a strained voice.

"I am here," he answered, as the rope began to move upward. He leaned back so he might "walk" up the remaining wall of the well rather than to be slammed into the bricks.

"William?" Her worry-filled face showed over the edge of the open well. "Please practice care."

Each of her gestures of affection provided him the strength to carry on, which had been foolishly lacking but a few moments earlier. Finally, Jasper reached into the well and, quite literally, jerked Darcy to the surface.

"Thank you, Jasper," he grunted as he elbowed his way up and over the well's roughly defined opening. With what felt like a lifetime, and perhaps it was, he was flat on the ground upon his stomach, and Elizabeth was draped over him, whispering his name, her tears sliding down his neck.

As quickly as he could free himself from the rope about his waist, he rolled over to capture her to him. Lying on his back in the grass upon a cold damp ground with the woman he dearly loved draped across him was a moment he had dreamed of many times — naturally, without the audience and the cold, but a dream fulfilled, nevertheless. However, this idyllic memory would only be complete if their child was near. "Did you recover Elizabeth Anne at Rosings?"

His words must have reminded her of their dilemma, for she stiffened and sat up. "We did not reach Rosings."

He sat also. "Did my message turn you around before you confronted Lady Catherine? When I heard your call, I thought you had news of Elizabeth Anne. In fact, I had hoped she was with you."

Sheffield reached a hand down to Elizabeth and then one to him as the man explained, "Elizabeth encountered her cousin before we made it to the great house." Sheffield smiled easily. "Knocked Mr. Collins to the ground and kicked him a few times before I could reach her." He winked at Darcy. "You must remember, sir, never to rile the lady."

"So noted," Darcy said with a caress of her cheek. "Now, tell me, love, what did you learn from the estimable Mr. Collins?"

She glanced to the sky and frowned. "It is a long story, and we do not have much time. It will be dark soon. In short, Collins says Townsend, who is supposedly employed by your aunt, was instructed to capture Lizzy and to leave her unattended upon one of the islands at the mouth of the Medway Estuary."

"My dearest Lord," he groaned. "Will this never end?" He turned to his servants. "We must be to Queenborough Harbor immediately." To Sheffield, he said, "Once your horses have cooled, please follow. For now, Elizabeth is coming with me. I want to know what happened at Hunsford Cottage before we reach the coast. We are headed into a smuggler's den on Burntwick

Island, and I require information before I must negotiate with men who have defied more than one government excise man. The smugglers are said to have no regard for the law and my presence on the island will not be welcomed."

"You understand, sir," the man said for the third time since he had agreed to let Darcy the small dinghy, "the men on Burntwick will not take well to a stranger among their mix." The boat was likely one left behind or stolen from a larger vessel, but it was the only one available.

"I understand," Darcy assured, handing the man the coins upon which they had agreed. If your dinghy is lost in the approaching storm or destroyed in retaliation by those on Burntwick, Mr. Sheffield, here, will see you have a replacement." He reached for Elizabeth's hand. Although, Darcy remained hesitant about taking Elizabeth with him, he did not press the issue. He knew it would be fruitless to attempt to convince her not to travel with him to the island. Whether bonds of marriage had been pronounced or not, they were committed to each other: They had been a couple even long before she had finally accepted his proposal. In fact, he suspected some day, in the future, mayhap even long after they were gone, their love story would be the one by which all others would be judged. "Are you prepared, my dear?"

"I am prepared to know the return of my daughter," she announced as she stepped carefully into the dinghy. If the high tide had not already arrived, their journey would have been easier. Burntwick was a flat, raised marshland barely a mile long and less than a mile wide that at one time was part of the parish of Upchurch and attached to Kent's mainland. There was a narrow channel, called Stangate Creek, that separated the island from the Chetney Marshes. One of their fears for the child was if Lizzy was alone on the island, she might wander into an area that would become cut off by the high water and would not know what to do. Unfortunately for them, at high tide the island was separated into several smaller islands by the water.

Over the last twenty years, at various times, the island had been used by the government for a quarantine base for ships sporting some sort of onboard infection before the ship was permitted to enter the Thames, preventing the infection to reach London. The Capital had seen enough of plagues and contagions over the centuries. More importantly, of late, the North Kent Gang, a notorious group of smugglers, would not be happy for outsiders to appear suddenly upon 'their' island.

Darcy shoved off and deftly stepped into the boat, quickly settling himself on the seat and taking up the oars.

"Do you think Mr. Townsend is one of the smugglers?" she asked.

"My encounter with Townsend was brief, but from what all I have learned of the man, I doubt it. Those on the island are smugglers, but most who form such a gang are men just eking out a living. The custom duties on tea and spirits and a variety of other goods affects all Englishmen, but not equally. From what I observed of the home Townsend's mother resides in, he does not share what money my aunt provided him with the lady. She lives in impoverishment. I am assuming he has been in Brighton for some time?"

"A few months," she confided.

"Even staying at the boarding house, food, drink, and his passing his time at *The Dingy Rose* must have cost Lady Catherine a fair sum," he observed.

After that, they remained silent for the remainder of their short journey, each lost in his or her own thoughts. "Allow me to go first," he said as he directed the dingy onto the marshy beach. "My boots are more appropriate for the damp ground." He nimbly stepped out of the boat and tugged it up onto the beach. When she stood, he lifted her into his arms and carried her to the drier area.

"The blanket," she said looking back to the boat.

"I will fetch it," he assured as he set her on her feet. Despite the trials remaining before them, he smiled upon her. "I find I am quite satisfied to follow your orders."

She glanced upward, "We must hurry. We are racing against both dusk and what appears to be another storm rolling in."

However, before he had the opportunity to respond, the sound of two clicks of guns coming close together said they had company upon their right and their left. "This be not the place for a lovers' tryst," a voice announced.

Darcy slowly raised his hands. "We have no tryst planned. We have been told a man who has stolen our three-year-old daughter away has abandoned her on this island. All we wish is an opportunity to search for her."

"There be no child on the island." The man gestured toward the dinghy. "I suggest you return to the mainland while you may."

Uncharacteristically, Elizabeth buried her face in her hands, rather than to argue with the man. "Please, sir," she wailed with a well-placed sniffle, and Darcy realized the sham she practiced. He worked hard to hide the surprise at her display of emotions. "We have trailed the man from Brighton, across Sussex—" Another sniffle followed by a hiccup. "From Tunbridge Wells to Rochester and now here. We cannot simply leave without knowing for certain!" She turned and buried her face in his shirt. Darcy held her close—close enough to know there were no damp tears upon his shirt, even though her shoulders heaved and shuddered in apparent distress.

"Why would someone steal away your child? You be someone important?"

Darcy shook his head in the negative. "I am no titled gentleman, but I am willing to pay for your assistance in the search for my child or for any information you may have on a man called 'Sidney Townsend.'"

"Townsend? He involved?" The man frowned in obvious disapproval.

Darcy nodded, as he gently stroked Elizabeth's back, keeping her close in case the situation turned sour.

"Yes, Townsend from near Tunbridge Wells. Supposedly

a groom at Rosings Park near Rochester." He would not mention that Rosings Park was owned by his aunt.

The man's eyebrow shot upward. "Townsend, a groom? That scoundrel can barely sit a horse. If'n the owner of Rosings Park be such a fool as to hire a man with no skills, mayhap I shud seek employment there."

Darcy asked, "May I employ you long enough to search the island? The cloud bank indicates a storm approaches, and it is becoming dark. Once we lose the light, our hopes of finding the child fade."

The man motioned to his partner. "We each search this island every evening." He likely meant they made certain others did not come for the stash of goods they had hidden somewhere upon the strip of land. "No one has sent up an alarm of discovering an excise man or a child." The fellow's eyebrow rose in challenge, meaning he would not permit Darcy to wander about the place.

It was Darcy's turn to frown. "We were specifically told by someone involved in this caper that Townsend had been ordered to abandon our child upon an uninhabited island in the Medway Estuary."

The man looked off to the east. "If I didn't want someone found 'till it be too late to change the outcome, I'd choose Deadman's Island, not Burntwick. No one alive goes there unless he be burying the remains of someone who died upon a diseased ship."

Darcy's heart plummeted. "For that very reason, I never considered Deadman's Island." His voice broke when he belatedly realized his aunt would be cruel enough to order his child placed in such an environment. If Lady Catherine paid to have him pressed upon a pirate ship, she would not consider his illegitimate child worthy of being spared.

He felt Elizabeth clutch his lapels in distress. "Fitzwilliam," she pleaded.

He looked to the man, a total stranger, but one he had the uncanny suspicion was more than a smuggler—he was an honest man. "May I trust you to see my wife returned to the mainland where her uncle awaits us. I cannot chance having her infected on that island." He knew the likelihood of any disease remaining from the bodies was next to nil, but Darcy did not want her on such a place. It was bad enough his daughter could be hiding somewhere on an island named "Deadman's."

She pounded his chest in a fit of rage. "You cannot think to leave me behind," Elizabeth protested. "You cannot ... I cannot ... please."

He knew she would not change her mind easily, but he had made his decision, nonetheless. "Listen to me, Elizabeth." He gave her shoulders a solid shake to force her to respond. "It is nearly two miles to Deadman's Island, and a storm approaches. It will be upon me before I can reach the island. I require you to return to Sheffield's side. If I do not reach Elizabeth Anne, then you and Sheffield must take up the task. Our daughter should not lose both her parents in an act of madness. Through no fault of her own, our child lost her father once already. She does not really know me, and my loss would be sad, yet, not memorable. However, she would be broken to lose her mother. Elizabeth Anne requires you to be strong, and so do I. Tell me you understand."

Tears filled her eyes. "I understand," she said through trembling lips. "But how will I know if you have her?"

He was desperate to be gone and said the first thing to come to his mind, no matter how preposterous it was. "After the storm passes, I will light the lantern and place it on the highest point on the island as a signal we are together. If she is there, I will carry her to your waiting arms in the morning."

"Where should I go to watch for the light?" She followed him toward the dinghy.

He doubted anyone would see a candle burning from so far, but he said, "Queenborough is less than a mile removed. Choose somewhere along Shepherd's Creek. Just know if I am not successful, you and Sheffield must seek out our daughter with the dawn."

"You will be successful," she declared as she rose up on her tiptoes to kiss him briefly.

When she wrapped her arms about his waist for a final embrace, he spoke to the men who trailed behind them. "I ask again. Do you give me your word to see my wife safely returned to her uncle?"

"Aye, sir," the man declared firmly. "We'll see it done properly. Before the storm."

Darcy set Elizabeth to the side to reach for one of his cards. "If you discover Townsend, deliver him to this address in the Capital. Either my cousin, who is in residence there, or I will see you paid handsomely. Just be forewarned my cousin is a retired colonel of the army."

The man pocketed the card and presented Darcy a toothy grin. "If'n we discover Townsend, we'll wait fer yer return befoe we deliver the ne'er-do-well." He motioned to Elizabeth. "We should be gone before the storm, ma'am. Follow me."

Darcy watched her leave with the man, belatedly realizing he did not ask either man for his name. He risked much by not taking her with him. He risked more, however, if he were to be so foolish. Dragging the dinghy back toward the water, he, again, climbed in and took up the oars. He had never visited Deadman's Island. Few had. Like Burntwick, he knew Deadman's Island was crisscrossed by narrow tidal channels, which meant it was currently separated into several smaller islands because of the high tide. Some channels could be crossed by simply trudging through the standing water. Others were swiftly running streams. The island, itself, was marshy and covered by mudbanks. At one time, prison hulks moored there. Those who died were left upon the island to decompose in shallow graves.

"Please, God," he prayed as he turned the rowboat toward where he hoped to know an end to this nightmare. "I keep turning to you, God, and, in your infinite wisdom, you keep sending me messages. This time I ask that you extend your hand over my child. Protect her until her earthly father can do his duty to her and her mother."

As quickly as he left the shallow creek for the open water, the wind whipped up, and within minutes the first bands of rain arrived. "Under these conditions, this could take me more than an hour," he groaned as he fought to keep the dinghy upright. "Yet, I shall not stop until I am either at the bottom of the sea or I find Elizabeth Anne. Neither her mother nor I can live without the child."

CHAPTER THIRTEEN

WITH EACH STROKE OF the oars, Darcy repeated his prayer, the one protecting his daughter from harm. When the rain started, he had shoved the blanket, the lantern, Elizabeth Anne's doll, and the food Elizabeth had packed for them beneath the seat upon which he sat, hoping to keep it all relatively dry. Thankfully, the rain had not been as heavy so he had expected, but the winds had him fighting not to be driven into the Kentish coastline. He was soaked, not from the rain, but from his efforts to reach his child.

After what felt forever, Deadman's Island came into view. Under the dark skies, it appeared more daunting than he had expected. The thought of a three-year-old left alone on such a place had him uttering a mix of prayers for the child's safety, along with a string of curses, wishing Townsend and the man's employer to the fires of Hell for the atrocities practiced against his family.

With a final burst of effort, he rammed the dinghy upon the so-called beach, actually a strip of marshland, just as it had been on Burntwick Island. Jumping out, he dragged the small boat onto the dry land so it would not float away. He paused only long enough to catch his breath and to shake out his arms to be rid of the cramps tightening his muscles in painful spasms.

Glancing up to the sky, he realized the rainstorm had moved inland, and the sky was brighter than when he had set off from Burntwick; however, the wind had not abated. In fact, it was, from his experience on the sea, what his fellow sailors would have called a "gale."

Pulling his coat tighter about him, Darcy began to search the area closest to where the boat rested, carefully sweeping back and forth across the island, constantly calling his child's name, although he was uncertain whether his words were being snatched away before anyone could hear them. Often, he paused to listen for a return cry, but, other than the occasional whistling sound of the wind as it shoved its way between openings created by cracks in the rocks or between remnants of abandoned structures—likely left over from the prison hulks, there was nothing moving except him, swirls of dead vegetation, and a myriad of insects that buzzed about his head.

Starting out again, he beseeched, "Elizabeth Anne!" What he hoped was dust, but was likely rotting bones and debris from prison hulks slapped him in the face, and he paused to wipe it from his mouth and eyes. "Please answer me!" he continued. "I know you are frightened, but your mother and I are here for you." Naturally, he realized the child would not understand the hidden desperation in his words, but he worked hard to keep his tone the type that would induce his daughter to show herself, for if she was not near, he had no idea where next to search for her. He absolutely could not tell Elizabeth he had failed her again. She would never forgive him. Hell, he would never forgive himself!

He kicked up bones from a shallow grave, one where someone had died from some sort of agonizing disease. He had witnessed more than one crew mate suffer from scurvy and malaria. "Elizabeth Anne! Please, darling!" He turned in a slow circle, his eyes searching each rock and piece of lumber—each plant and scraggy tree—until, at length, they landed on a bit of yellow sticking out from a drab background. She was hidden behind two uprooted trees, whose branches were laced together, as if they chose to fall down in each other's arms.

His first instinct was to rush over and grab her up into his embrace, but Darcy set his anticipation aside to approach slowly. She had experienced enough tragedy for any one lifetime. "Elizabeth Anne," he said steadily, "I know you are behind the tree. Will you not come out, darling?"

At once, she began to whimper, and so he dropped down to his knees on the other side of the fallen trees in an attempt to coax her out without scaring her more. He wanted her to accept his protection—as her father. "I know you are frightened. I realize you do not know me, and I must imagine how dearly you want your mother."

The word "mother set off her tears, and it was all Darcy could do not to reach over the limbs and snatch her into his arms to comfort her, but it was too soon. "Where's mama?" she hiccupped. "Mr. Towsand say Mama was here, waitin' for me, then he left. Mama not here."

Darcy swallowed the curses rushing to his lips. Telling her he would take her to her mother had been his first choice to convince his daughter out of hiding. He must find a safe place for her from whatever animals roamed this island and from the storm. The wind had not slowed. "Your mama is on the shore watching for your return. With the wind and the rain, I did not want to risk her life. You require your mama, do you not?"

"And Uncle Allbirk."

Darcy smiled with her pronunciation of Sheffield's name. "Your Uncle Albert is protecting your mama right now from the storm."

Her little lip trembled. From the cold or fear, he did not know. He could tell she had on a cape, but, with the dark, he could not tell whether it was heavy enough to protect her or not. "Who 'tect me?" she asked sadly.

"Your mama thought I could do the job if you would permit it."

"Who you?" she asked, her sweet face crunching up in an obvious new round of fear. Dirt and dried tears showed upon her cheeks.

"If I tell you who I am, I do not want you to be afraid. Can you be a brave girl, like your mama?"

"Mama brave?" she asked.

"Oh, my darling child, your mama is one of the bravest people I know. She brought a beautiful little girl into the world. That takes someone special, do you not think?"

She stood for a brief second, and he could view more of her, but she nearly lost her balance when a gust of wind barreled down upon them. He was prepared to grab her, if necessary, but catching her to him would also bring about more fears, and Darcy would not have her unwilling to go with him. She squatted low again.

"Mama loves me," she reasoned.

"Very much," he assured. "And although you and I have just met, just like your mama, I love you."

The wind sent a shiver of cold down his spine. He was certain his daughter must be equally as uncomfortable.

"Who you?" she repeated.

"I am your father," he said softly.

She bolted upright and prepared to dart away. Her eyes were as round as saucers. "Mr. Towsand said there be dead people here. My papa is dead."

Darcy moved slowly to keep her calm. "I am your father, Elizabeth Anne." He spoke in quiet tones. "I will prove it to you. Your mama told me you would not trust me unless I knew the secret words. Is that not correct?"

"You know words?" she asked. Her eyes darted left and right, likely seeking another place to hide.

He held himself perfectly still. He could easily catch her, but he wanted her to trust him. However, the wind had again grown stronger, and dusk was upon them. He knew he should speed things along, while practicing care. "Years ago," he began as he edged forward, "when your mama and I first met, there was a lady who thought I did not like your mama."

"The witch Caroline?" she asked.

He was thankful to have cut ties with the Bingleys, but, God help him, it might be worth one social call just to hear his daughter call Caroline Bingley a "witch."

"Yes, the witch Caroline," he said with a smile. "Anyway, I told the witch Caroline—." The name was growing on him. "I had been mediating on the very great pleasure which a pair of fine eyes in the face of a pretty woman can bring a man. The pretty woman was your mother, and the secret words are 'fine eyes.'"

She bolted then, but not away from him. Rather, right at him. Darcy caught her and scooped her into his arms. He kissed the side of her head and unbuttoned his coat. "Let us warm you properly." He tucked her inside and wrapped the coat about her.

"You really my papa?"

"Most assuredly."

"We find Mama?" she asked as she snuggled deeper into his warmth.

"We must wait until the wind passes," he said as he turned his steps toward where he had left the dinghy. "But we have a blanket and some bread and cheese and what your mama says is your favorite doll to keep us company until we may leave this place."

"I love Mama," she said against the lawn of his shirt.

"I love your mama, also," he said kissing her dark curls. He had not had a good look at all of her features, but, from what he could tell, she was formed in the image of his grandmother, Emilia Darcy. There was a portrait of Emilia in the Pemberley gallery, and he anticipated the pleasure of having a picnic lunch with his daughter before the portrait and telling Elizabeth Anne of the remarkable woman who was his daughter's great-grandmother.

"I love Uncle Allbirk, too," she said through a muffled sigh.

"He is one of my favorites, as well," he shared. If Albert Sheffield asked for the moon, Darcy would attempt to package it up for him.

When they reached where he had left the boat, he retrieved the blanket and the doll and food. Wrapping his child in the blanket to keep her warmer, he set her out of the way of the wind.

Then, he tore off some of the bread. "You hold your doll and eat, while your papa builds up some place to hide from the storm."

"Yes, Papa." Those two words reached into his chest and took root, bringing love back into his life. She was too young to understand how a man thought to be dead could finally be so full of life. All Elizabeth Anne knew was her mama had given him the secret words, which meant he could be her "papa." It was an idea that made his chest swell with pride.

While his daughter watched, he tugged the boat closer to a rock formation and tilted it upward to lean against the rocks, but be out of the way of the wind. The inside faced the rocks. "Are you prepared to crawl into your papa's special hiding place?"

She eyed the structure skeptically, but she followed him inside. He crossed his legs and set the blanket on his lap. Placing her in the middle of it, he draped the ends around her and leaned against the rocks to support himself and her. "Is that not better?" he asked, breaking off some of the cheese and handing it to her.

"You make a 'pecial hidin' place before?" She took a big bite of the cheese.

He caressed her head and rested it against his chest. "When your papa was a little older than you, my mama and papa would use blankets to make special hiding places in my nursery. We would sit together, just like you and I are right this minute, and we would have cakes and play games. Those were some of my best memories." Memories he would enjoy replicating with his child.

"Mama say you like tapple tarts, like me," she said around a mouthful of bread.

It should not surprise Darcy that Elizabeth had taken note of his food preferences, but it did. Moreover, it pleased him she had shared bits of him with their daughter. "Apple tarts are my favorite."

"Uncle Allbirk likes berry bread best."

"Yes, he does. Thank you for reminding me of that fact." He kissed the top of her head.

"This is Miss Jane." She handed him her doll.

Darcy said, "Miss Jane is the name of your mama's sister." He wondered if Elizabeth had suggested the name to their child.

"Mama have sister?"

"Yes, your mama has four sisters," he explained.

"I want sister."

Darcy would enjoy more children, but Elizabeth thought there would be no others. He reminded himself to be satisfied with what God had provided him. "Your papa's sister, your Aunt Georgiana, had a baby this week. You have a new cousin. Would that be a good gift for now?"

"Another girl?" Her voice sounded sleepy.

"No, a boy."

"You 'ave house, Papa?"

He stroked her hair and bent to whisper in her ear. "I own the most magnificent house you will ever see. Think of a castle. And horses. And sheep. And lovely things to eat."

"And more dolls?" she murmured.

"As many as you want. And pretty dresses." He continued to whisper his dreams for her into her ear as she fell asleep cuddled into the curve of his body.

Elizabeth watched the island for the signal Mr. Darcy promised, but, so far, there was no notice. She and Jasper sat in Mr. Darcy's coach, both wearing coats, hats, gloves, and covering themselves with blankets. Mr. Farrin and Mr. Jacobsen tended the teams of both coaches, and she had demanded that Mr. Sheffield seek comfort at the nearby inn. Although her friend protested, she had insisted. The gentleman had yet to recover fully from his recent contagion.

"How long do you think it will be before Mr. Darcy sends the signal?" she asked aloud.

Mr. Farrin had maneuvered Mr. Darcy's coach as close to Shepherd's Creek as was possible in the marshlands, without it becoming stuck in the watery soil. As she had refused to be far from the coast, the coachman had insisted the carriage would provide her some protection from the wind and storm.

"The rain has stopped," Jasper reminded her, "but the wind has increased. Mr. Darcy may not be able to keep the lantern lit until this weather passes over us. Even if he does set the light, we might not be able to see it. A single light so far away is questionable, ma'am," he cautioned.

"I know you speak the truth, and you wish to decrease my worry; yet, I shall not rest until I know they are both safe."

"Mr. Darcy will not fail you, ma'am. Those of us at Darcy House and at Pemberley know him a man of his word."

Darcy woke from one of the most contented dreams he had experienced in many years. A warm bundle along his front filled his lungs with the sweet scent of cheese and a little girl. Unfortunately, his legs were numb from being twisted beneath him. He thought to straighten them, but realized he was still hidden behind the dinghy, and there was no extra room to purchase. He opened his eyes and looked around. He was sitting on damp ground and holding his precious daughter. "Life is perfect, little one. You make it that way." He nuzzled her head.

Fully awake now, he listened for the wind, but it had finally calmed. "We should return you to your mother, my darling girl." He shifted Lizzy away from his chest and placed her down on the ground, carefully working a part of the blanket loose to protect her head.

Free to move more fully, he slowly unfolded his large frame, turning upon his knees to crawl through the narrow opening he had created, to stand once more upon Deadman's Island. Gingerly, he stretched his arms over his head. and felt the tenderness in his back and arms from his rowing efforts a few hours prior; however, he remained pleased. The pain was well worth it. Elizabeth would be thrilled.

"Elizabeth!" he chastised himself. So consumed with holding his child, he had forgotten to set the lantern. She would be frantic. "It would be foolish to light it now," he instructed himself. "Just deliver your child, and all will be well." He prayed she would not be too angry with him.

Therefore, he caught the side of the dingy and turned it to half walk and half tug it toward the water. During the joy of having Elizabeth Anne safe, he had not considered the edge of the water would be farther removed than when he arrived on the island last evening, as the tide had gone out. However, at length, the boat was in place. He returned then for the food and the lantern, which he lit and placed in the bow to light their way and to signal those on shore of their arrival, specifically, to signal Elizabeth. Finally, he carried the sleepy child to a special place in the bottom of the dinghy.

"You leave, Papa?" she murmured.

"Not without you, my girl," he said as he placed her down. "We are going to find your mother," he assured softly, removing the curls from her face. "Rest now."

Within minutes, he shoved off, using the oars to turn the small boat toward the mainland, allowing the lantern to light his way back to Elizabeth and what he hoped would be a new life.

Darcy could not refrain from smiling as he watched Elizabeth cutting up Lizzy's food into bite-sized pieces. Last evening, he had not even thought of breaking the cheese and bread into smaller pieces so his child would not choke on them. He had a great deal to learn about being a parent and was prepared to be a ready student.

Elizabeth had been pacing the beach when he carried their daughter to her. She had frozen in place when she noted his approach. "Lizzy Anne is home," he said softly, jarring her into action.

"Oh, William, you found her." She rolled back the blanket to look upon their child. He knew it was killing her not to grab her daughter from his grasp and kiss the child all over. "Was she frightened? Was it terrible on the island?"

"I would not wish to spend the night there if I had not been holding this special gift from God. Nor the day."

She had traced a line along their child's cheek. "I pray this incident will not cause her to have nightmares."

"I attempted to add memories. I propped the dinghy against a rock formation to make us a special hiding place. Then I told her of my mother and father making a similar place with blankets for me as a child. Told her Pemberley was like a castle. I promised her all the dolls she wanted and pretty dresses for her to wear."

She raised her eyebrow then. "What if I choose not to marry you?" she challenged. "Will you take Lizzy from me?"

"I would never torment you in that manner," he said in all honesty. "However, I cannot promise I shan't make a nuisance of myself and offer you my hand in marriage, at least, once per day. Likely more often. Nor can I promise not to employ our daughter to wear down your resolve."

She rose up onto her toes to kiss Elizabeth Anne's head. "You would use my child against me?"

He leaned to the side to brush a kiss across her forehead. "No, but I would use our child to win your heart."

"You already own my heart, Fitzwilliam Darcy," she said softly. Her eyes locking with his. "However, I fear Lady Catherine will not cease her manipulations until she has her way. I refuse to place Elizabeth Anne in danger again. If that means we live apart, then so be it."

"All I ask is you do not provide me your answer until you view for yourself what I have planned for her ladyship."

They had traveled to Rosings Park at a less frantic pace than the ones they had both employed the day before to reach Queenborough. Unsurprisingly, Mr. Liles and Mr. Ruffe, the two smugglers he had trusted with Elizabeth's life, had made an early appearance at the inn with Sidney Townsend in tow.

"That was quick, gentlemen." Darcy had asked the men to wait until Elizabeth escorted their daughter on a walk into Queenborough before he met with the men. He would not have Lizzy Anne encounter the scoundrel again.

"We seen no reason not to enjoy a hunt," Liles said with a grin. "With the storm, there be no other employment to kept us busy."

Darcy glanced to Townsend, who sported more than one bruise and laceration upon his person. "It appears your prey put up a fight."

Mr. Ruffe shrugged his shoulders in an act of dismissal. "Not much of one. None of us believe a man should take a child from its mother. You possess a fine lady, sir, if'n you don't mind me sayin' so. She be very kind to us, last eve. Made certain we had a meal at the inn and all."

Darcy smiled easily. *His* Elizabeth had enchanted two of the North Kent gang. "I am blessed as a man may be." He looked to Townsend. "I fear I do not have enough coins with me to pay for your services, gentlemen, and I assume you would not wish a bank note."

Mr. Liles presented Darcy a toothy smile. "Ruffe and me thought we might carry an express to that colonel you mentioned. Been awhile since either of us be in London. You said he could see us properly paid."

"Excellent plan. Allow me to send my servant to fetch the local magistrate while I write instructions to my cousin and my housekeeper to see you also are fed a proper meal." He paused to calculate in his head. "I, too, hope to be in London later today or tomorrow, at the latest. It may not be necessary for you to speak to the colonel, if you wish to delay just a bit. After all, it is Saturday, and the banks are closed."

"We cud wait to travel," Liles reasoned, "if'n it mean we continue to deal with you."

"If I were at my home, you would be easily presented admittance, and I have access to funds my cousin does not," he explained.

"Then we travel later today, not wishin' to travel on the Sabbath."

"Neither do I," Darcy explained. "Such is the reason I mean to reach Rochester soon and be done with the madness that has plagued my family for four years. You may call on me after services tomorrow. For now, allow me to offer you these coins in good faith."

Darcy gestured Jasper forward. He instructed, "Please ask the magistrate to join me here."

"Yes, sir." Jasper rushed away to do Darcy's biding.

"If'n you not mind, we best leave before the magistrate arrives. Wouldn't want to permit him to know we had anything to do with this."

Darcy understood. The men before him likely had had more than one run-in with the law. "We will meet again tomorrow." Liles and Ruffe nodded and then disappeared into the busy town.

"Don't I possess any rights?" Townsend protested.

"Not of which I am aware," Darcy said casually. "In case my aunt did not tell you, I am a rich man, and money can purchase anything—even the gallows upon which you will swing for your crime of kidnapping my child."

"Her ladyship is rich also," Townsend protested. "She will see to my release."

"Although I believe it a poor system, in England, a *man's* wealth always outweighs a *woman's*," Darcy declared. "And if you think Lady Catherine holds honor and will not place this caper upon yours and Harwood's shoulders, you are a fool. Moreover, I possess plans for her ladyship. Her reign of power is coming quickly to an end."

"She is your family," Townsend argued. "You would not wish your family's name brought into account."

Darcy leaned forward to press his point. "My family has grown smaller in the last month. I have even cut an *earl* from those I call 'family.' If I can banish an earl, I will have no qualms in bringing down my wrath upon the widow of a common baronet."

Townsend's brows burrowed. "You would not," he protested.

"I would," Darcy declared. "My allegiance is to the woman you know as 'Mrs. Dartmore' and my child."

"Your bast—" Townsend began.

But Darcy's fist arrived before the loggerhead could finish the word. He yanked Townsend's head upward by the hair of the man's head. "Listen to me," he hissed. "Do not even think that word in relation to my child. It would suit me just as well to place a bullet between your eyes, and, if you think I am too deep into Society's pockets to make good on my threat, you should know I survived four years upon *The Lost Sparrow*, one of the most dangerous and ruthless pirate ships on the sea." He noted how Townsend's pupils dilated in surprise. "Now, here is how we are going to finish this. You will be presented the choice of hanging for your crimes or knowing transportation. While you are contemplating your decision, you should consider the fact that three members of *The Lost Sparrow*, which is now in dock and under the authority of the British Royal Navy, have already provided the government signed statements implicating Lady Catherine de Bourgh in my kidnapping. My aunt has no hope of escaping my vengeance and neither do you."

CHAPTER FOURTEEN

IT HAD TAKEN LONGER for them to depart Queenborough than Elizabeth would have liked—not that she was anticipating their upcoming confrontation with Lady Catherine de Bourgh, but because of the total devastation marking Fitzwilliam Darcy's countenance. The time he had spent with the magistrate laying out the charges against Townsend had taken an obvious toll upon him. Mr. Darcy had set himself the task of discovering who had betrayed him and who had stolen away his child. Now, it would be necessary for him to divorce himself from all those he had once trusted. His world had gotten smaller, and she knew he had executed all this for her.

As they looked on while the gentleman bid his farewells to the magistrate and his men, Sheffield whispered, "The master's whole life has been turned upon its head. Only you can restore his strength—his will to continue on."

"Yet, will he not view what we did as another betrayal?" she pleaded.

Sheffield shrugged his response. "I am certain Mr. Darcy will be surprised at the depth of details we performed, but, beyond his shock, I believe he will know relief. We always knew some day we would be asked to explain ourselves." He kissed her forehead in affection. "I will take Lizzy Anne with me. I have a small bag of lemon sugars in my pocket. She and I will read a book and enjoy our ride. Please let me know if you wish me to make an explanation to Mr. Darcy. After all, our escapades were my ideas."

Therefore, Elizabeth had asked Jasper to retrieve the small leather satchel from her trunk before they set off for Higham. "How long before we reach Rosings Park?" she asked Mr. Farrin as he handed her into Mr. Darcy's carriage. The gentleman himself had personally carried their daughter to Sheffield's carriage, making certain both their child and Sheffield had enough blankets and warm bricks to make their journey comfortable.

"About three hours, ma'am. A bit over twenty miles, but the roads are generally good in that part of Kent so perhaps sooner."

She nodded her gratitude, but she wondered if she would survive three hours in the same carriage as Mr. Darcy. She had yet to permit him a kiss or anything more than the comfort of his embrace during all this madness. There was still so much to say to him. So much to explain. For just a moment, she panicked and slid across the seat to disembark, choosing to ride with Sheffield, but. before she could reach for the door latch, Mr. Darcy crawled into the coach and tapped on the roof to signal for Mr. Farrin to begin their journey. Jasper closed the door and climbed up on the box, and they were rolling out of the inn yard.

"Elizabeth Anne presented me three kisses before she settled in beside Mr. Sheffield," he said proudly. "She called me 'Papa' again."

Elizabeth smiled knowingly. "What did you promise her?"

He grinned largely. "It is our secret. She made me swear not to tell her mama."

"You plan to spoil our child," she accused.

"Please do not make me promise not to shower her with a few pleasures she might have done without because I was not there. I missed too much of her life, Elizabeth. I can never have those moments."

She reached across the coach to squeeze his knee. "No reason exists for you to purchase her love, William. Lizzy shall simply be happy to have you in her life."

He turned his head to look out the window. "Will she?" he asked, and she noted the tears that had formed in his eyes. "Before I came to Brighton, Elizabeth Anne remained safe."

She said softly. "I imagine Lizzy will be a bit more frightened of strangers than usual, but she is young and quite intelligent. I am certain she will outgrow this mishap. We must simply be vigilant and assist in her healing."

"I am not speaking only of what Townsend executed against her. We can show her how the law has sent Townsend away, and he will never harm her again. Of what I speak is how my presence in her life changes her from the beloved child of a lieutenant in the British Royal Navy to the by-blow of a wealthy man. In many ways, I have ruined her chances for a future that will not bring her shame. Perhaps I should go away again. I cannot bear to think I have brought harm to her."

The tears escaped his eyes then, and he buried his face in his hands. "Why did we not wait for our vows?"

"Because we were in love, and we were both too certain of how our consequence would prevail."

He did not look up when he said, "I still love you, but perhaps I should leave you with Sheffield. Disappear from your life."

"Mr. Darcy," she said in sharp tones. "If you were foolish enough to make good on your threat, then Lady Catherine will have won. Her scheme would know success. She will have separated us, which always has been her purpose. Even if you would finally agree to marry your cousin, my lie will have been exposed. It is not as if Lizzy and I can return to Brighton and continue to be 'Dartmores.' Moreover, my doing so would not be fair to Mr. Sheffield. He is a man built for a family, one of his own, not one borrowed from another. Is that what you wish for a man who served you for nearly twenty years? Is that what you want for me and your daughter?"

"You know it is not," he argued, wiping away his tears. "If I had my wish, I would make you my wife as quickly as the law would allow our joining, but doing so would not protect Elizabeth Anne. She was born out of wedlock. My wealth will protect her to some extent, but not completely. I struck Townsend today because he called our Lizzy a 'bastard.' I fear I cannot strike every man who does so, for there will be many."

His words had touched her heart almost as deeply as had his promises of affection. What she was about to tell him would either make or break their relationship. "What if we possessed a means to legitimatize Lizzy's birth?" she asked, fully demanding his attention.

"Tell me. Anything. I will do anything. No matter the cost," he assured. He sat forward in interest.

"There will be no financial cost, per se; yet, there will be a cost to you and me," she stated. "We will spend our lives, theoretically, living in sin, and we will require the assistance of your sister and my father, as well as my Aunt and Uncle Gardiner."

His features changed from confusion to true interest. "Perhaps you should tell me what you have in mind."

She dug in the satchel resting on the seat beside her and withdrew two rolled documents. "Let us begin with these." She handed them over and waited until he had read each of them. Elizabeth had never been so nervous in her life. Would he agree to what she offered?

"Are these forgeries?" he asked.

"Not exactly," she responded.

He kept both papers upon his lap and leaned back into his seat as if seeing her for the first time. "Then you must explain further."

Elizabeth swallowed her concerns, meeting his steady gaze with one of her own. "It all started when my father thought to press Mr. Sheffield into marrying me. It was then that I told your former servant I suspected I was with child. By that time, I had missed my monthlies twice, and my Scottish relatives had refused to take me in in my condition, but they had suggested in their letter to Mr. Bennet that if we could bring the father of the child up to snuff, they would be glad to stand as witnesses to our joining in Scotland."

"I am listening," he said, again looking closer at the pages resting upon his knees. "If I am not mistaken, this is Sheffield's script, is it not? He taught me to mimic his style of writing. When I was young, I could use both hands equally for throwing a ball or eating or writing, although, like Mr. Collins, I showed a slight preference for my left. Father and Sheffield decided it would be best if I developed my right hand for writing letters of importance so as not to leave ink smears on legal papers. Smears that later could be misconstrued as changes in the document. How many times I traced my name on the paper where Sheffield had written it out for me, I do not care to fathom. Traced whole phrases and sentences also. Soon his penmanship and mine were very much the same, except I never quite manage the swirl on the 'F' in 'Fitzwilliam.'"

She confirmed his suspicions with a nod of her head. "In the beginning, we, meaning my father and Mr. Sheffield and I, considered some sort of marriage by proxy; Mr. Sheffield and I even thought to travel to the Continent for such a marriage, but, even if we could have found a means to prove you alive and in agreement to our joining, England does not recognize a marriage by proxy as valid under the church law. Both parties must be able to say whether he or she agrees to the marriage. In a proxy marriage, that cannot happen."

"No one marries by proxy except our kings and queens," he grumbled.

"Yes. As neither of us can claim such aspirations, another means was required." She presented him a smile. "Mr. Sheffield has learned both about investments and manipulation at your hands. He meant to protect our child, especially if I had carried the heir to Pemberley. He said you would want your son to have Pemberley and without proof of marriage before his birth, our child could have no claim on his proper inheritance. Moreover, if our child had been a boy, then I could remain with him in your home, as his guardian, and no one could displace either him or me. Mr. Sheffield and I agreed we would only place a claim on Pemberley if the child was a boy. What we executed in your name, Fitzwilliam, was to protect your son, if we had been so blessed. Instead, we—you and I—can use it to protect our daughter."

When they stepped down before Rosings Park, he was still a bit dumbfounded by what Elizabeth had shared, but as Elizabeth had essentially agreed to spend her life with him when she chose to share the documents with him, his heart had been properly fortified by the idea. He was quite proud of how she had gone to great lengths to protect the child they had created.

"I am certain Miss Lizzy would enjoy a bit of exercise. If you would not mind, Sheffield, mayhap Elizabeth Anne would enjoy the garden," he suggested. "If it becomes too cold, you could probably beg a cup of tea from Lady Catherine's cook. She will recognize you as my valet."

"I believe I would also enjoy a stretch of the leg. Come along, Lizzy Anne."

Darcy watched them walk away. "Into the lion's den," he said as he offered Elizabeth his arm.

"As long as we are not to be the sacrifice," Elizabeth said with a weak smile, but he could tell by the tightness of her features, she was not so brave as she would like.

Darcy released the knocker and waited for Lady Catherine's butler to respond.

"Mr. Darcy. Miss Bennet," the man said. "I was unaware of your expected arrival, sir." He glanced to the two carriages. "Should I send someone to unload your trunks and prepare rooms?"

"That will not be necessary," Darcy said, as he stepped past the man. "We shan't be staying. I simply require a few moments with my aunt."

"Her ladyship is in her favorite drawing room. Should I announce you?"

Darcy smiled. He knew Lady Catherine's butler would likely lose his position if he did not provide her ladyship with some form of warning, but Darcy wished the element of surprise. "The most I can offer you, Mr. Charles, is to follow a few steps behind you down the hall. If she asks, which I doubt she will after our business is done, tell her ladyship I refused to wait."

Mr. Charles swallowed hard. "As you wish, sir."

Darcy kept Elizabeth close as they followed the butler up the stairs and down the hall. "Breathe," he whispered in her ear. "Within the hour all will be well."

"An hour?" she questioned nervously just as Mr. Charles opened the door to the drawing room and announced them.

Darcy tugged her through the door so Mr. Charles could close it behind them and make his quick exit. Anne and Mrs. Jenkinson rose to their feet, but Lady Catherine simply glared at him where she sat in her favorite chair, lording her will over the room.

"How dare you bring that woman into my house!" her ladyship accused. "And after what you still owe your cousin!"

Darcy's eyes settled on Anne. "I apologize, Cousin," he said blandly. "I did not realize you still held hopes of an offer of my hand. After all, I have been from England for nearly four years."

Anne shot a quick glance to her mother before responding, "I am simply happy for your return, Darcy." His cousin seemed to sense something had changed, for she presented a look filled with unspoken questions. If he had his way, she would be free of Lady Catherine's autocratic rule soon. "We all thought you dead, especially after your footman was found in the Thames. It is most joyous to discover otherwise. We were pleased to hear the news from Uncle Matlock."

"I am glad you welcome my return, but your mother could have told you years ago that I remained alive. After all, she paid my captors to keep me from England," he accused.

Anne gasped, "Mother, tell me this is not true!"

"Naturally, it is not true," Lady Catherine declared with her customary authority. "Just a twitch of Darcy's mind, likely an assumption learned from Miss Elizabeth Bennet."

Darcy tightened his hand resting upon Elizabeth's, warning her not to respond. "Odd that," he said with more calm than he felt. Before this time, he had never considered striking a woman, but, if his aunt were a man, he would gladly challenge her ladyship to a duel, or, at least, a round of bare-knuckle sport, just for the pleasure of seeing her suffer. Or, better yet, permit the same degradation as he had suffered on the pirate ship. "Moreover, I have forwarded the confessions of both Mr. Harwood and Mr. Townsend to my agent in London. Both men are likely secured and imprisoned in the Capital by now. Each man has implicated you in the abduction of my daughter." He had sent word to Tunbridge Wells to inform the magistrate there of Harwood's part in Elizabeth Anne's kidnapping and had asked that Harwood be transported to London for necessary confinement. Although he had not personally spoken his threats to Harwood, he was certain the man, like Townsend, would see the benefit of transportation as punishment over hanging for his crimes.

"You have a daughter, Darcy?" Anne asked in continued bewilderment.

He brought Elizabeth's gloved hand to his lips for a brief show of affection. "Elizabeth has presented me a replica of my paternal grandmother, Emilia Darcy. My daughter's ancestry cannot be denied." It was very important to him to claim Elizabeth Anne publicly before family.

"Your bastard!" Lady Catherine hissed.

He leveled a deathly glare on his aunt. "Beware, your ladyship. The last person who used that term in reference to my child is missing several teeth."

"You would not strike a woman!" Lady Catherine declared in confidence.

"Would I not?" he asked with a tilt of his head as if considering doing just that. "Amusing, only a moment ago I was wondering how well you would do with a cat-o'-nine-tails. Would you care to view how the scars appear when they are healed?"

"Do not be vacuous, Darcy," she warned.

"No. I think you should view what your schemes exacted upon your sister's son." He began removing his coat, cravat, and waistcoat, handing them to Elizabeth as the room looked on. He noted how Mrs. Jenkinson hid her eyes behind her hands, but he was surprised to note that Anne appeared braver than he had expected. More curious than he expected. He continued to speak as he undressed. "You paid men to press me into service upon a ship that sailed under a variety of flags, looting and stealing from others." At length, he tugged his shirt free from his breeches.

"That is enough, Darcy!" Lady Catherine ordered. "Whatever point you wish to make can be made with words, not physical displays of your person!"

"I have just begun, Aunt. Do you not wish to know how your money was put to good use? You wanted me humbled, and, believe me, the captain and the first mate attempted to do just that." He caught the ends of his shirt and raised it to his waist. "By the way, did I forget to mention that three of the men you paid to remove me from my duty to Elizabeth are currently in the custody of the British government? They have been most cooperative. Much more cooperative than I was when I was aboard *The Lost Sparrow*." He jerked his shirt over his head and turned to allow his aunt to view what he had suffered at her hands. He heard Anne squeal in distress and noted Mrs. Jenkinson attending to his cousin, but he did not move. His eyes were on Elizabeth. "My sin—the one I executed to merit this punishment, was to love a remarkable woman. A woman who has answered all my prayers. You see, Aunt, the men you hired could take chunks of the skin off my back, but they could not stop my heart from loving Elizabeth Bennet." He returned his shirt to its proper place and reached for his waistcoat. "You arranged for your own kin to suffer such punishments because you wish to control everything within your reach."

"I never meant—" she began, but there was no real regret upon her countenance, which only enflamed him further.

He turned to his cousin. "I love you, Anne, but I could never love you as a man should love his wife — not as my father loved my mother. Not as Sir Lewis loved Lady Catherine. The differences in the marriages of our parents were how the Fitzwilliam sisters reciprocated. Where Lady Anne Fitzwilliam was satisfied to be a simple 'Mrs. Darcy,' Lady Catherine Fitzwilliam was never giving enough to be a mere 'Lady de Bourgh.' She is too consumed with her own consequence."

"How dare you?" Lady Catherine growled. "What do you know of my marriage?"

"More than you care to learn. My father warned me against trusting you, but I foolishly did not take his advice. And while we are on the subject of marriage, I will ask the same of you: What do you know of my marriage?"

Lady Catherine snarled, "So you finally married Miss Elizabeth. Is that what you came to tell me? You married the trollop?"

Darcy charged at her, his hand ready strike. "That is twice in the last quarter hour that you have defamed my family."

"I shall have you arrested for threatening me," his aunt dared to say.

"Please summon the local sheriff. Even better, I will instruct Mr. Charles to do it for you." He was nose-to-nose with his aunt. "I believe the magistrate will be interested in my accusations against you. As you said earlier, I possess 'physical' proof of my afflictions. He will also wish to hear the confessions of those arrested previously. Personally, I doubt, even for you, that any local form of the law will go against the word of the British Royal Navy."

"What is it you want, Darcy?" she huffed.

"Two things," he pressed his hand against her shoulder, pining her to the chair and forcing her to listen to what he had to say. "First, ask me what you should know of my marriage."

He had to present his aunt credit: Her ladyship did not flinch. "You wish to tell me something you deem important, so be about it and then leave my house forever."

He did not release her. Instead, he loomed over her.

Losing Lizzy: A Pride and Prejudice Vagary

"Allow me to share a tale of two people who have suffered at your hands and only because you meant to inflict your will over them. My story begins the August before my supposed nuptials in November of 1812 when Miss Elizabeth Bennet and her relations visited Pemberley. Actually, my tale begins earlier when I was here for my annual visit to Rosings and learned that the most enchanting creature I had ever come to know was also in residence at Hunsford Cottage. You did not know then, but I will bring you up to snuff now, that I proposed to Elizabeth one evening at Hunsford." He smiled at Elizabeth. "The lady held some legitimate complaints regarding my actions, but I let her know I would do anything to win her regard." He was not speaking an untruth: He had confessed everything in his letter to her, and it did, eventually, change her truth of his character. "I will not bore you with all the details, but, let us say, I prevailed, and was accepted. I convinced my lady to agree to a mad dash to Scotland before she could change her mind." He turned back to his aunt. "We were already married when you began your campaign to separate us."

"I do not believe you." His aunt's confidence had slipped a notch, but he knew he would be required to be ruthless in order to know her confession.

"Would you hold the wedding certificate where her ladyship might view the date and our signatures, Mrs. Darcy?"

Elizabeth placed his coat and cravat over the back of a chair, removed one of the certificates from the satchel and unrolled it. She carried it to where his aunt sat. "Your ladyship," Elizabeth said sweetly. "Please note the date 1 August 1812 and your nephew's signature along with mine."

"This cannot be. Surely this is some sort of gambit you practice," she argued.

"There can be no dispute. The marriage is recorded in the church records of that year," he countered.

It was satisfying to watch his aunt's eyes widen in recognition. "Then why, if you were already married, did you agree to marry in Hertfordshire?" she demanded.

Darcy took up the response. "When we returned from Scotland, there was a message from Elizabeth's elder sister reporting Miss Lydia's elopement with Mr. Wickham. We made a quick decision. I would hunt the couple down, for I held knowledge of Wickham's haunts. It would be my employment to force my former school chum to marry Miss Lydia so as to save the remainder of Elizabeth's sisters. Two elopements would have spelled disaster for my new relations. Therefore, Elizabeth returned to Hertfordshire, and I went searching for the wayward couple. Naturally, we had to allow time for the Wickhams to make their appearance in Hertfordshire and depart for Northumberland before I made my return to Longbourn. Initially, we thought simply to make the announcement of our marriage, but so many things remained contingent upon a public acknowledgement of our joining, we agreed to a second marriage."

Elizabeth rolled the certificate and returned it to its leather case. "Do you not recall, your ladyship, my responses when we argued in the garden at Longbourn? I am certain both Miss de Bourgh and Mrs. Jenkinson recall the incident, for they awaited you in the carriage. You were set to have my agreement to deny Mr. Darcy. You asked if I was resolved to have him, and my response was, 'I am only resolved to act in that manner which will constitute my happiness, without reference to you or any other person so wholly unconnected with me.' I remain of that persuasion."

"Why would Mr. Bennet agree to such a farce?" Lady Catherine questioned.

"Because he loves all his daughters," Elizabeth continued, "and by that time I knew I was with child. What harm was there to permit others to think we married in November, rather than three months earlier. My mother would have two daughters married, and Mr. Darcy and I would have been in Derbyshire when our child was born. No one would have been the wiser."

Darcy took up the tale. "Unfortunately, you meant to have your way—to practice your will over my life and Elizabeth's life. You had me kidnapped off the streets of London, and, even when the captain of *The Lost Sparrow* wished to return me to England, you continued to pay him for his services — continued to have me detained."

His aunt growled, "Miss Elizabeth disappeared. I could not take the chance you would return to England and seek her out. Her father refused all offers of money to finance his other daughters' futures in order to protect the second. You say he loves 'all' his daughters, but he would see the three still at home living in penury rather than to tell me Miss Elizabeth's whereabouts."

Darcy's smile returned. "Like me, Mr. Bennet knows quality when he views it. Elizabeth has always been his favorite."

Elizabeth accused, "It was only when my mother mentioned Mr. Darcy's servant that you knew where to find me." It was Elizabeth's turn to be angry. "You knew I would not deny Darcy if he came for me; therefore, you paid kidnappers — Townsend and Harwood — to steal away my precious child and abandon her on Deadman's Island to die of starvation or worse. You cared not that she was but three years of age and posed no real threat to you."

"She did pose a threat," her ladyship countered. "Darcy would never desert his child — legitimate or otherwise. He would have expected Anne to tend another woman's child."

"Mother, how could you have done all this?" Anne pleaded. "Darcy, you must know none of this was my idea."

"You are as much a victim of your mother's acid-like whims as am I. As is Elizabeth," he assured. He straightened then, but remained close, where he could crowd his aunt's chair, preventing her from rising. "Now," he said, as if someone had prompted him to continue, "for the second thing I require of you, Aunt." She opened her mouth to object, but he ignored her, speaking over Lady Catherine's continued objections. "You must provide me your choice of whether you wish to retire to the Continent *never* — and I repeat, *never*, to return to England again. Naturally, you will be permitted your dowager's allowance, and, if you practice frugality, you may live out your days comfortably — "

"I shall not leave Rosings," she insisted.

Darcy continued his speech without acknowledging her protest. "*Or*," he emphasized, "you may take your chances with a very public trial."

"You would not act against your mother's only sister," her ladyship argued.

"Certainly, I would. You acted against my best interests. Fair exchange."

"Matlock will not tolerate your mistreatment of me and Anne."

Darcy corrected, "You will notice, Cousin," he said as he momentarily turned his attention to Anne, "as always, your mother places her interests before yours in her protest; yet, it is of no consequence, know that you will never receive mistreatment at my hands. Rather, I plan to free you from the ties that have held you in place for years. For all intents and purposes, I mean to see you to the inheritance that should have been yours by now. From no fault of your own, you are well past the five and twenty years required for you to inherit Rosings Park with Sir Lewis's will. Your father loved Lady Catherine, but he was wise enough to know her nature. You are able to inherit through the original establishment of the de Bourgh baronetcy, which can pass through the female line. Such is the reason your mother thought, first, to have us marry, so she could remain at Rosings, while you would be with me at Pemberley. In my absence, she meant to tie you to Lindale, who also did not have a need for the estate, for he is to inherit Matlock's earldom and all it entails. Most recently, she would have matched you with Fitzwilliam, until the colonel took matters into his own hands and chose to wed Georgiana instead."

"I would not know what to do if I were placed in charge of Rosings, Darcy. I do not have the head for such matters," Anne said softly.

"Do not worry. I propose that Fitzwilliam and my sister move in with you at Rosings. He can oversee the estate and assist you in meeting eligible men, but I insist our cousin remain in control of Rosings for a minimum of five years. Such will provide you time to discover a man who wants you for you and not for your inheritance—a man willing to wait five years to claim his control of your fortune and this estate is more likely to speak honestly of his affection for you. If you choose not to marry, Fitzwilliam will see to the estate or will employ a person to operate it for you. Such will provide the colonel time to sharpen his skills as an estate manager and place him in a better position to know success at Yadkin Hall when he assumes control of that estate, which is to be his inheritance. Naturally, I will lend a hand so all three of you will know success."

"Fitzwilliam knows nothing of estate management," Lady Catherine protested.

"Yet, you were willing to have him marry Anne," Darcy countered. "I suppose you reasoned if the colonel was presented as Anne's husband, then you could remain at Rosings Park's helm. You simply wished to exercise your preferences over a man of little experience beyond the battlefield. You never once considered, what would have become of the two of them if you up and died suddenly. You cared not for what chaos might have ensued. In order to keep Rosings Park under your control, you would have sacrificed the future of your daughter and your nephew. Yet, I assure you, Fitzwilliam learns quickly. More importantly, he is quite amiable. He has a way with people, which will prove a nice change for Rosings' tenants." He shook his head in disgust. "Your world is very small, Aunt. It consists of only yourself, and I feel very sad for you."

"Matlock," Elizabeth said softly from her place behind him.

"Your reminder is much appreciated, Mrs. Darcy." He enjoyed saying her name. He had waited for what felt an eternity to do so. "As to Matlock, I have not yet decided upon his 'punishment,' but as I have proof from a variety of bankers that his lordship has had his hand in my accounts on multiple occasions during the years of my absence, I doubt his influence will be of much use to you."

"Mr. Darcy," Elizabeth said, "as I assume you near the

conclusion of your dealings with her ladyship, I shall make certain Lizzy and Albert are well. It is a chilly day outside."

"I shan't be long," he said.

"If you hold no objections, I believe I would like to introduce my daughter to Mrs. Collins. This will likely be the only time when such an opportunity will show itself, and I would despise her not knowing our daughter. When we were younger, she and I often spoke of marriage and children. Would you mind retrieving us from Hunsford Cottage?"

"If such is your wish, I will be along shortly."

"Your ladyship. Miss de Bourgh. Mrs. Jenkinson." Elizabeth turned to leave after her curtsey, but Anne rushed forward to join her. "Might I walk with you, Mrs. Darcy? I would enjoy meeting your daughter, as well."

"Anne!" Lady Catherine called. "Come back this instant!"

"A walk will do me well, Mother," his cousin called. She did not turn around to look at any of the occupants in the room. He imagined it was Anne's first act of defiance. Instead, his cousin caught Elizabeth's elbow, and they exited the room arm-in-arm.

"Go with her!" Lady Catherine ordered Mrs. Jenkinson, before she turned her attention back to him. "Now, what is all this nonsense of turning Rosings Park over to Anne?"

"Not nonsense, my lady," he said as he retrieved his coat to slide his arms through the sleeves. He stepped behind the screen to return his shirt to his breeches. "You have yet to tell me which is your preferred choice: The Continent and a sensible allowance paid quarterly or the English legal system? I will expect your decision by the time I step from behind this screen." Between the slats of the panels, he watched his aunt stand and tiptoe toward the servants' door. "Return to your seat, my lady, or I will summon the magistrate and place the choice of a public trial in action."

"You have lost your reason, Darcy," she declared as she sat once again.

"I lost all rational thought when you set yourself against Mrs. Darcy and my child." He leveled his gaze upon her as he stepped from behind the screen to face her once again. "My shirt is returned to my breeches. What is your choice, Lady de Bourgh?" His choice of words was meant as a reminder that she was a commoner—whether she was a baronet's wife or the daughter of an earl. Only members of the peerage were considered anything beyond the gentry or the working class.

She lifted her chin regally. Even in defeat, she meant to prove him wrong. "I suppose I must choose Europe, despite the devastation left behind by the war."

"Remember, if you return to England by any means other than in a box bearing your body, I will see you arrested and prosecuted for your crimes." He crossed to ring the bell cord. "Also understand that your allowance must last through each quarter for which it is allotted. There will be no advances and no pleas for more." He turned to her. "This must seem a severe punishment, but keep the image of the scars on my back with you. There are worse punishments than going without a few luxuries." He said without emotion, "I have the agreement drawn up and the witnesses waiting below. Let us begin."

CHAPTER FIFTEEN

HE HAD ASSURED ANNE that he would send a carriage for her tomorrow to bring her to London, but his cousin had decided she and Mrs. Jenkinson would arrive at Darcy House some time this evening. "After her ladyship finishes wishing you upon a short ladder to purgatory," Anne giggled. It was the first time Darcy could recall hearing that particular sound escaping his cousin's lips.

"You are welcome at any time. Just know I have installed three men of business and a new land steward at Rosings until the Fitzwilliams can arrive. Nothing will happen to your inheritance."

She glanced back to where the upper storeys of Rosings Park could be viewed over the tree tops. "It shall all feel odd," she admitted. "All I have ever known—"

"Fitzwilliam and I will protect you."

"Do you think I might have an allowance also, Darcy? I would enjoy making a purchase that does not require my mother's prior permission."

He caught her to him for a quick embrace. "We will set up a proper allowance when we meet your new men of business, who will aid in your transition to heiress."

"As long as Georgiana permits me to hold her son, I shall be happy. Her ladyship always thought I was too frail to be around children."

Darcy swallowed his sigh of resignation: His cousin would have a long road ahead, one where she would finally experience a life of normalcy. "Until this evening then." He turned to assist Elizabeth into his coach, and Sheffield lifted Lizzy Anne inside.

"If you hold no objections, I believe I will return to Brighton, sir," his former servant said with customary decorum.

"Absolutely not," Elizabeth declared before Darcy could open his mouth to express the same sentiments. "We began this journey together. William has promised me that we would be to Hertfordshire tomorrow. I want my whole family to have your acquaintance. They owe you so much. Neither Lizzy nor I would have survived without you."

Sheffield shrugged in obvious defeat. "I have never had a female purposely make me feel guilty with as much skill and excellence as you, Elizabeth. You should beware of her arts, sir."

Elizabeth laughed. "Trust me, I learned from the best. You will understand when you take Mrs. Bennet's acquaintance."

"Very well," Sheffield said. "I suppose it would be pleasant to speak to Mrs. Guthrie and the others again."

"William," Elizabeth pointed her finger at first him and then at Sheffield, "do not permit Albert to sleep in the servants' quarters. Both of you hear what I say."

"Yes, Elizabeth," he and Sheffield said together.

"I am warning you, Albert Sheffield, I will drag you from the servants' quarters by the lobe of your ear and deposit you in a proper room if you do not follow my request. I will not relent on this matter."

Sheffield nodded his understanding and stepped back to permit Darcy to climb into his coach. When Jasper closed the door and climbed up on the box, Darcy said with a grin, "You were very forceful, Mrs. Darcy."

"Why you call Mama Bisses Barcy?" Lizzy Anne asked.

Darcy lifted the child to his lap. "Because our last name is *Darcy*. You are Elizabeth Anne Rachel Darcy." He had learned his child's full name when he had viewed her baptismal records.

His child looked to Elizabeth for confirmation. "Your papa

is correct. We are Darcys."

Lizzy frowned, but she did not dwell long on the idea. Instead she asked, "You have castle bigger than that one?" She pointed to Rosings Park, which grew smaller as they departed the main road of the estate. His daughter craned her neck for one last look at the manor house.

"Ask your mama," he suggested.

"Your papa has one of the largest and finest houses in all of England," Elizabeth said with a smile.

"Bigger than the King?" Lizzy asked in awe.

Darcy laughed, "Not quite that large, but large enough for you to have plenty of places to play." He adjusted his hold on her. "We are going to our house in London. The King also lives in London, but not in our house."

"We see baby?" she asked.

"Yes, you will see your new cousin," he responded with a grin.

Lizzy told Elizabeth. "Baby's a boy."

Elizabeth chuckled. "You have told her of the Fitzwilliams' son."

"The child is her cousin," he said with a smile. "Lizzy will have a family."

"I like famee," his daughter concurred. She yawned loudly.

"Papa will hold you," he said softly. "You nap, and soon we will be at Darcy House."

"The house has our name," she murmured as she snuggled into his body.

He allowed the natural sway of the coach to rock the child to sleep. Within minutes, Lizzy's eyes fell closed, and she hummed a soft snore. Darcy had not known such contentment since he had been a small child upon his mother's lap.

"It may take more than one day for me to make the necessary arrangements for my sister and Fitzwilliam and come to an 'understanding' with Lord Matlock," he cautioned. "You told Sheffield we would return to Hertfordshire tomorrow. I do not want to disappoint you."

"I did not think tomorrow was possible," she admitted. "After all, it will be the Sabbath. I simply wished to keep Sheffield with us for a few more days. I do not wish him cut from our lives."

"I agree," he said with a nod. "I am losing my aunt and uncle. Each has played a major role in my life since my father's passing." He sighed heavily. "I want those I can trust to play a role in Elizabeth Anne's future, no matter his or her station in life."

"Mr. Sheffield is a gentleman's son, as are you," she argued.

"Yes, he is. I did not mean to sound as if I disapproved of Sheffield's upbringing."

"I know," she said in honest tones. "It is just that I have something to confess."

Darcy eyed her suspiciously. "Please do not tell me you hold a *tendre* for my former valet."

She laughed softly. "I adore the man, and he holds my deepest gratitude, but not my heart, Fitzwilliam Darcy. Only you. Yet, that does not mean I do not worry for the gentleman's future."

He smiled easily at her. "And what future do you believe Mr. Sheffield deserves?"

"A wife. Children, naturally," she said with such ease, proving she had thought long and hard on her conclusion.

"Women always think every man requires a wife and children to know satisfaction," he countered. "If the practice of primogeniture did not rule the aristocracy and upper society, I suspect more than one man would have been happy to spend his days in bachelorhood."

"I do not think every man deserves a wife and children. Men, such as Mr. Townsend would be a poor candidate for any woman." She frowned deeply. "I still believe Charlotte Lucas's choice a poor one, and you cannot tell me Mr. Wickham is the type to want a wife or children if someone did not pay him to act honorably."

"All good points," he conceded.

"By the way, have you any knowledge of whether the Wickhams have presented my parents with a grandchild or not?"

"I do not. I did not think to ask of the pair when I spoke to Miss Bennet, and, she, thankfully, did not inquire of Mr. Bingley. I am not certain what I could have told her that she did not already know, and, as she did me a good turn, I would not have wanted to inflict more pain on her."

"Thank you for that," she said softly. "And as to the Wickhams, I suppose my mother will bring me up to snuff quickly enough." She shrugged, "I pray our maneuverings did not bring sorrow to Lydia's dreams." She visibly shook away her doldrums. "The point I wish to make is, Mr. Sheffield would make some woman a devoted husband and would provide love to his children."

"I assume you believe Sheffield should choose someone other than Mrs. Harris?" Darcy was enjoying this conversation because it provided him insights into Elizabeth's mind. It was as if they had taken a step back in time to the days when they were still learning something of each other's values. "I cannot say I was impressed with the lady," Darcy admitted. "For what it is worth, I believe Sheffield is also less than happy in thinking the lady is his only choice."

"Did he say something to you of the prospects of marrying Mrs. Harris?" she asked in interest.

"Just that the lady is not much of a reader," he shared.

"Is that all?" Disappointment marked her features. "I was hoping he had come to his senses."

"You do not understand the working of a man's mind nor how we communicate with each other. When men speak of marriage, Elizabeth, such complaints regarding a woman's lack of common interests is as good as a refusal for a man to propose."

She presented him a large grin. "It is difficult to learn such nuances in a household of women. Then it was certainly true that your comment about my 'fine eyes' was an overture of your affections?"

"It was. My affections have not waned, my love." Heat flashed between them before they both reined it in. They still had a long way to go before they could claim the remnants of what once rested easily between them.

"Then Mr. Sheffield," she said in quiet tones, "requires a woman who is a reader."

"I would think a man who owns a bookstore would wish to be able to discuss books with his wife," Darcy concluded. "What have you in mind, Elizabeth?"

"I was just considering how both Jane and Mary are avid readers."

He teased, "You will not enjoy my observation."

"And it is?" she challenged.

"Just that you may be Mr. Bennet's favorite daughter, but you possess some of your mother's tendencies to manipulate those within your care, as if you are a chess master."

She ignored his taunt but did display her concern. "Do you think either Jane or Mary a bad idea?"

"I do not," he admitted. "If Sheffield would develop an affection for either, I would be happy to welcome him into our family. Either way, Sheffield will always be Lizzy's 'Uncle Albert.'"

"I promise to allow nature to take its course," she said smartly, "except for one matter I deem of importance."

"That would be?" Darcy could not resist smiling. He would be the fortunate one: the man who woke up to such a woman every day.

She blushed but did not look away. "I wish you to discover a bookstore similar to the one known as Brooke's. Do you know it?"

"Yes, it is the one I frequented before my abduction."

She nodded her understanding. "Before he called upon my father, Mr. Sheffield had thought to purchase Brooke's with his savings. While still in your employment, he planned to hire someone to run the store for him, and when it was time to retire, he would assume those duties."

"Admirable," he said in honesty. "I had no idea Sheffield was wealthy enough to think of purchasing Brooke's." He grinned. "I must be overpaying my staff."

Another rush of color flooded her cheeks. "I should probably not disclose this, but many of Society do not realize their servants possess ears."

He stifled the laugh ready to escape his lips, for he did not wish to disturb his child. Yet, it was difficult not to wish to kiss Elizabeth's lips when she quirked them in amusement.

"But—" she began.

"So, what exactly did Sheffield overhear that made him rich enough to consider purchasing Brooke's when it became available?" he asked, thoroughly enjoying their conversation. This was to be his life, and Darcy could not wait to embrace it fully.

She smiled largely. "Sheffield invested in the same ventures as did his employer, and he sold when you did."

"How very astute of him," he said with a large smile. "Perhaps, I should ask for a fee as I am the one who did the research on the various proposals."

She gestured his tease away. "Permit me to finish my tale, sir."

He nodded his agreement.

"Sheffield had a small inheritance from his mother's dowry and had saved for the purchase, but when he agreed to assist me, his expenses increased dramatically. We let a cottage in Cumbria for nearly a year. Furniture. Travel to Scotland and the necessary payments for someone to antedate the marriage and other ways to assure you and I were in the area on the appropriate date. My medical care. A wet nurse. Even when he lost the opportunity to bid on Brooke's, he might still have chosen London, but we feared someone would recognize me. With my luck, I would have come across my Aunt and Uncle Gardiner or the Bingleys or someone from your family." She paused to gather her thoughts. "As the Meryton militia had departed Brighton shortly after Lydia's debacle, when the store there became available, Brighton proved a viable choice for both of us. Sheffield purchased the building and all its contents. As he would make the best with Mrs. Harris as his wife, Mr. Sheffield would be satisfied to return to Brighton, but, in my opinion, neither the lady nor the seaside town is the gentleman's dream."

Darcy's smile dimmed, and he turned serious. "Mr. Sheffield would never accept my financial gratitude. His pride is as big as his heartfelt care for you and Elizabeth Anne."

"I agree. Sheffield would refuse. Moreover, Brooke's is no longer available, but certainly there must be one just as perfect for the man. Might I add a search for another establishment where Sheffield can hang his sign of ownership to your list of changes in our lives to accomplish?"

"Permit me to consider how best to proceed without destroying the gentleman's sense of honor. I would have agreed to assist him even if he was still my valet, but your story compels me to know success in this matter," he assured.

They had spent the remainder of their journey deciding how they would proceed with their relationship. They had agreed they would carry forward the idea that they had eloped to Scotland, providing Elizabeth Anne her legitimacy while denying themselves vows of marriage. Because neither of them considered 'living in sin,' despite their continued commitment to each other, a viable option, at length, it was decided they would marry in a private ceremony as quickly as possible. Yet, as English law required residency in the parish of either the man or the woman for four weeks prior to the ceremony, they would spend the next month as a couple in the eyes of the world, but, in private, this time, they would postpone the duties enjoyed by a man and his wife.

Neither of them wished to wait to share himself with the other, but they both felt strongly that if they did not properly speak their vows, it would destroy their future happiness.

At length, the two carriages pulled up before Darcy

House, and Darcy assisted Elizabeth down before lifting Lizzy into his arms. He knew his neighbors likely watched his every move. Samuels hurried down the steps to assist Jasper with the trunks. He instructed, "Bring in those belonging to Mr. Sheffield also." Then, he escorted his family into Darcy House for the first time.

"Mrs. Guthrie," he said as he handed off his hat to the lady. "This is your mistress, Mrs. Darcy." To Elizabeth, he said, "Our housekeeper, Mrs. Guthrie."

His long-time servant curtseyed. "Welcome, Mistress. Your room is still in good order, but I will have a maid set the fire for this evening."

Darcy gave his daughter a little squeeze. "And this is Miss Elizabeth Anne Rachel Darcy, my daughter. We call her 'Miss Lizzy.'" He kissed his child's cheek. "Miss Lizzy will require a place in the nursery along with Mrs. Fitzwilliam's son. If the boy's nurse cannot also tend Lizzy, then assign one of the maids to her. We will only be in residence for a few days. My wife wishes to visit with her family in Hertfordshire before we retreat to Derbyshire."

"I shall see to the details, Mr. Darcy."

He glanced over his shoulder to where Sheffield waiting. "I am certain you recognize Mr. Sheffield."

"Yes, sir."

He grinned. "Although I could desperately use his services, Sheffield is to be treated as a guest during his stay with us."

Mrs. Guthrie's features displayed her surprise, but, as any good upper servant would, she nodded her understanding.

"One last thing," he ordered. "My cousin, Miss de Bourgh, and I assume her companion, Mrs. Jenkinson, will be joining us later for an extended stay. The ladies will require rooms, as will her footman and coachman. Please apologize to Cook for upsetting her plans for supper."

"Certainly, sir."

"Where is my sister?"

"I believe she and Mr. Fitzwilliam are in her sitting room."

He nodded his gratitude and started up the stairs with Elizabeth on his arm and Lizzy nestled against his shoulder.

"Sheffield," Elizabeth called without looking around. "You may visit below stairs, but—"

"I understand, Mrs. Darcy," Sheffield said with a laugh. "I would not dare go against your will."

CHAPTER SIXTEEN

THEY WERE ACTUALLY IN London for three full days before they departed for Hertfordshire. Before Anne arrived on that Saturday evening, Darcy had taken Fitzwilliam aside and explained the part Lady Catherine had played in Darcy's trials, as well as the restrictions he had placed upon her.

"And you are willing to permit others knowledge of all this if her ladyship does not comply?" Fitzwilliam asked.

"I would not wish to place either Elizabeth or my child in a position of public shame, but I cannot relent. Lady Catherine's spitefulness nearly cost me my life. It did cost me three years of memories with Elizabeth Anne and Elizabeth. What would you do if our aunt had robbed you of the memory of holding your son for the first time?"

Fitzwilliam casually sipped his brandy, but Darcy noted how his posture was no longer relaxed and there was a hardness in his tone when he spoke. "Likely more than you have executed against her ladyship."

"Trust me, I wished to tear her apart, limb-by-limb. Yet, there were others who did not deserve the public notice a trial would have brought to our doors. Many more than my family. You. My sister. Your son and future children. Sheffield. Anne. All her ladyship's servants. Your mother. And more than we care to consider."

Meanwhile, Elizabeth, bless her heart, convinced

Georgiana that the day he rode ahead to Pemberly and had left her with the Bingleys had been the day of their elopement—that they had been corresponding, and he knew of her traveling in the area with her aunt and uncle. Elizabeth had suggested that they had become reacquainted in Kent, and he had proposed, but she had asked for time to consider his offer.

"Did you not take notice of how distracted Mr. Darcy was after he returned from Rosings Park? My mind was certainly everywhere but on Mrs. Collins's kind efforts to entertain me."

"My brother did appear from sorts," Georgiana admitted. "I thought him still angry with me for my foolishness at Ramsgate."

"Nothing of the nature," Elizabeth assured. "Fitzwilliam and I should not have written to each other," Elizabeth said with a straight face, while not providing the details of how they had gone about the correspondence without anyone knowing of it, especially her father. "However, we had an 'understanding.' I promised him I would make my decision by the time I joined my relations in the Lake District. However, the Gardiners' plans changed, and your brother and I were so close—. The Gardiners and I traveled to Matlock and Dovedale. My relations knew of your brother because, as you recall, my aunt lived in Lambton when she was younger, and they were aware I had spent time with Fitzwilliam in both Hertfordshire and Kent. They did not question when he called upon me in Derbyshire, and they were more than happy to permit him to escort me on an outing about the shire. Little did they know, we planned a race to the border to marry. As the day progressed, he sent them word of our impetuousness and guaranteed we would return the following day. They were not best pleased, as I was not of age to marry in England without my father's permission, but they accepted our affection as genuine.

"Your brother wished us to meet in private, but the Bingleys had traveled with you. He and I planned to make our announcement after the day you and I shared tea. Unfortunately, on that day I received news of my sister's elopement with Mr.

Wickham. Do you not recall how nervous both Fitzwilliam and I were when we were all together with the Bingleys? It was foolish of us to postpone our announcement, but two elopements in the same family and so close together would have ruined my sisters. We knew our true wedding date, and we saw no harm in a public ceremony in order to save my family's reputation."

Georgiana teared up then, even more so when his sister realized how much he and Elizabeth had suffered. His sister had studied the marriage certificate they had shared with her. "Those days were so black for me. I realized William cared very much about you when he whisked me off to Lambton to take your acquaintance, but then the Bingley sisters spoke so critically of you and to you. I did not know what to think. Yet, you protected me when Miss Bingley mentioned Mr. Wickham, and I thought we could be friends. I was barely sixteen years and so ashamed of my foolishness in dealing with the man. I was thankful for your hand of friendship, but I did not think I deserved it." She looked down at the marriage license in her lap. "This is surely William's signature, so it must be as you say. I would know my brother's handwriting anywhere. I recall how contrite he was when he left me with the Bingleys. Apologetic, but eager to leave. Now, I understand why."

Obviously, Elizabeth offered no such fabrications to her relations when she called upon the Gardiners after church on Sunday. She simply pleaded for their cooperation to protect Elizabeth Anne and made them the necessary promises that she and he would marry within the next month.

Her part in setting their lives aright had been easier than his.

All he really accomplished on Sunday was to make an appearance at his club and let it be known he was interested in investing in a bookstore in London, no preferences, except he wanted it to be one where both those of the upper class and those of the working class might feel comfortable patronizing. That done, he had returned to Darcy House to learn Mr. Ruffe and Mr. Liles were waiting for him in the kitchen. Once Jasper had escorted the pair to Darcy's study, he dispensed with their payment quickly, when he landed on an idea that just might work. With a few questions and a willing response, he employed Mr. Ruffe for a much more important job.

"You wish me to sit in a room at an inn located in Dry Drayton for a bit over three weeks?" the man asked in dismay. "My meals and my drink furnished. I'm to be known to be there, but not draw too much attention, so others will not question when you replace me there? Nothin' personal, Mr. Darcy, but we don't much look alike."

Darcy assured, "Unless you do something uncalled for by becoming involved in a fight or losing your earnings in a game of cards, most people will not take note. Are you willing or not?"

Darcy made no further explanation of what he intended to do: He simply confirmed Ruffe's duties.

"No other jobs—no murders or thievery?" Ruffe asked suspiciously.

Darcy laughed easily. "Just sit and eat and drink. I will pay the bill. Rest for a few weeks. Your absence might draw the Queenborough magistrate off your mark." He had chosen Ruffe over Liles because Ruffe was not married and his absence from Kent would not prove a hardship for his family.

Ruffe questioned, "And you'll see me mam has money for me brothers and sisters while I'm gone."

Darcy assured, "Mr. Liles can deliver the money with a note from you when he returns to Kent, but I require you are in Dry Drayton today."

On Monday, along with a magistrate from the proper part of London involved, he had called upon three different men of business and demanded a return of the funds they had illegally transferred from his accounts. He assured each that an accounting of their transactions had been provided the magistrate himself and action would be taken immediately if they did not comply. He also demanded their removal from London, and all of England. All accounts were to be reimbursed within a fortnight, and the men were to disappear off the face of England by that time or they would be arrested and prosecuted. He repeated the procedure for an associate member of Darcy's bank. That particular gentleman was charged with bank fraud, and the bank managers were put on notice to install more stringent measures to protect their customers or face similar charges. The man was arrested on the spot before enough members of Society for the word to circulate that Darcy was back in London and exacting his revenge on those who had crossed him.

At length, he tracked his uncle down at his lordship's club. Matlock was not best pleased to view him sliding into the seat beside the earl. "Go away, Darcy," his lordship grumbled. "I do not wish to speak to you."

"Such suits my purpose perfectly well," Darcy countered. He glanced about the room and noticed a number of eyes upon them. Until now, Darcy had not ventured out much since his return to London. He had not wanted to be distracted by the questions visibly resting on the lips of many of their onlookers. "Perhaps we should take our conversation to the park across the street." He stood then. "Join me, my lord," he instructed. "I doubt you wish others to overhear what we must discuss."

"The countess has already warned me of your disdain," the earl said with a scowl.

"I am glad to hear it. Yet, her ladyship does not know my decision on how we will go forward," Darcy countered.

"Do you mean me to accompany my sister to the Continent?"

"Ah, it is as I expected: Lady Catherine still believes someone can force me to relent. Only one person has that power over me, and as she has also been wronged by the two of you, I doubt 'mercy' is yet in her vocabulary." Darcy leaned down and lowered his voice to say, "Although I cannot condone her measures, at least, I understand the bit of mania Lady Catherine practiced against me and mine. I have yet to comprehend how you became involved."

The earl dropped his voice. "I believe the park is an

excellent idea."

Darcy motioned the servant to fetch the earl's coat and hat. They made their way from the club to the nearby park in silence. It was only when they sat on either end of the bench located out of the way of the few pedestrians willing to encounter the frosty afternoon that the earl spoke. "Lindale has borrowed heavily from a money lender."

"And, as usual, you made to save him from my cousin's indolent tendencies?" Darcy was doubly thankful the colonel had rescued Georgiana from such an existence. "I suppose you initially borrowed money from Lady Catherine." The puzzle was coming together. "Was it her ladyship's idea for you to send me on a wild goose chase at the docks? Was that the price you paid for the loan?"

"He is my heir," Matlock offered in excuse, but made no effort to apologize for his part in Darcy's torment. Darcy shuttered his heart to deny his uncle mercy.

"And what type of earl will Roland be? You have failed to instill in Lindale even half the responsibility Fitzwilliam displays," Darcy chastised.

"I could not permit my eldest son to know street justice," the earl argued.

"I might feel some sympathy if your manipulations had assisted Lindale to a better place — had him regretting his actions, but, from what I have heard from others, he keeps two mistresses and spends the majority of his time in the gaming halls." He shook his head in sadness. "Have you considered insisting upon Lindale living within his means? Providing him no advances on his quarter allowance?" He sighed heavily when his uncle refused to respond. "You obviously have not. Instead, you chose to rob your nephew of nearly twenty thousand pounds — rob me of the funds I, initially, had set aside for my sister's dowry," Darcy hissed. "You took the funds meant for Georgiana's husband, your younger son, the one who has brought glory to the Fitzwilliam name, and presented it to Lindale, so your eldest son might continue his profligate ways and ruin everything your father and grandfather set about doing for the Fitzwilliam legacy. What have you executed to prevent the complete ruination of the earldom?"

Matlock shook his head in the negative. "My pleas are ignored."

Darcy sighed heavily. "Then I have no choice but to demand proper payment. Perhaps if Roland views his too proud father brought low, your elder son will learn a valuable lesson."

"I do not have twenty thousand pounds, Darcy," the earl admitted despondently.

"I did not expect you would," Darcy said in sadness. "Yet, such will not have me forgiving the debt. As with Lady Catherine, I am offering you but one real option: First, you sell off the unentailed properties, including your London home, and any of the smaller estates, with the exception of Yadkin Hall, which is Fitzwilliam's inheritance and is not to be touched. Perhaps, you will be required to sell off only a few to return my twenty thousand dollars or perhaps you will be called upon to strip the earldom of its glory."

"Where am I to live when Parliament is in session?" his uncle demanded.

"If you receive enough for your properties, perhaps you will be able to afford a fashionable home outside of Mayfair. Yet, in truth, personally, I do not care much about your consequence, my lord. Share the house Lindale employs when he is in London, that is, if the viscount can still afford it, or let rooms in your club. I doubt your countess will care much to be seen in London after word goes out through the usual circles of your being in debt to me and how I am calling in immediate payment. Many will likely begin to wonder what crime you have committed. Mayhap they will recall I went missing for nearly four years and wonder if somehow you were involved. I shan't say a word unless my funds are not restored. If not, many will learn the truth in the newsprint in a very public trial." Darcy fidgeted with his cane. "Just so you know, those you employed to do your dirty work have either been arrested or made to pay for their errors in judgment. That is, all except the real culprit where you are concerned: Lindale. If you are too weak to rein in your heir, you are likely to know more than the loss of your properties, your youngest son, your elder sister, and your late sister's children.

"However, I would think a reasonable man would be capable of reading the writing on the wall, but it has been many years since you displayed that type of reason. Go home to Derbyshire, my lord. Assist your tenants to a better life. Become the type of earl your father expected you to be. Insist your heir does the same. Use your power in the House of Lords for the good of England, not to line the pockets of a few corrupt peers. Just do not expect me and mine to be a part of your future."

Darcy stood then. "I will expect payment in full by the end of Twelfth Night, my lord. Three months. Not one day more."

"You are certainly George Darcy's son. I never met a harder man," the earl said softly. "You are very much cut in his image."

"I am also Lady Anne's son," Darcy said in regret. "When my father would have recognized the false face you offered me, my mother, your sister, would have pleaded with me to trust you—which I did. Yet, you forget how unforgiving Lady Anne Fitzwilliam Darcy was when people meant to harm her family. Even she would have presented you the direct cut and more for placing her family in danger. Likely, you would know a punishment worse than Lady Catherine's." Darcy started away but turned one last time. "Before you lose face in Society, please place your influence behind Fitzwilliam. I believe he would be an excellent member of the House of Commons and would bring back some of the glory of your family name, much more so than will Lindale. Such focus will provide the colonel the knowledge he did not lose a promising career when he married Georgiana. Fitzwilliam is built to serve and will be a credit to your family and England, where Lindale's future and that of the earldom is questionable."

On Wednesday morning, they departed London for

Hertfordshire. They would have left on Tuesday, but there were still details of the arrests to be decided. Moreover, he had a lead on a possible investment for Sheffield. He watched in amusement as Elizabeth fidgeted on the bench across from him. It had been heavenly to sleep beside her the last few nights. It would be perfection when they could share more than a few kisses and long conversations.

"Mama 't-witch," Elizabeth Anne said with a frown.

Darcy tugged the child closer to his side. "Your mother is excited. It has been a long time since your mama has seen her mama and papa."

The child looked up at him in concern. "Her mama and papa like me?"

"They will absolutely adore you," he assured.

Mr. Farrin maneuvered the carriage through the Longbourn gates, and Elizabeth slid to the coach's window, released the latch, and stuck her head out the window for a better view. She glanced back to him with a smile. "I wonder if Jane has noted our approach and set up an alarm."

"More than likely," he said. It had been so long since he had viewed such joy on Elizabeth's face, he was glad to have been the one that presented her this moment. "Fine eyes," he whispered to Lizzy Anne and pointed to Elizabeth.

Lizzy giggled. "Fine eyes, Mama."

"What a wonderful compliment," Elizabeth said with a caress of their daughter's cheek. Then, the carriage was slowing. He cautioned, "Permit Jasper to set down the steps. I do not want you breaking a leg to reach the ground. I will follow with our daughter."

From somewhere near the house, he heard Miss Bennet call, "It's Lizzy! I told you it was Lizzy! Elizabeth is home!"

His daughter tapped his arm as Jasper set the steps, and Elizabeth scrambled from the carriage. "How they know my name?" Lizzy Anne asked in disbelief. Darcy climbed down, taking in the image of Elizabeth in Jane's arms, with the other Bennets flowing through the door. He sighed heavily: He would never know the embrace of his mother or father again, and, likely, there would be few from his newly-married sister, who would reside several days' ride from Pemberley. "Come, little one." He caught Elizabeth Anne in his arms. When she was situated with an arm about his neck, he said, "Mama's sisters sometimes call her 'Lizzy.'"

Sheffield joined him to watch the reunion. "Mayhap soon I should travel to Cumbria. It has been more than four years since I have spent time with my brothers." Before either of them could say more, they looked up to view Miss Bennet striding toward them, and Darcy heard Sheffield's quick intake of air. "She still possesses the face of an angel," he said as if thinking aloud.

Darcy did not comment, but he thought: *Elizabeth had the right of it.*

Miss Bennet said with a smile upon her lips, "I knew you would bring her home. I told Mr. Bennet you would. Thank you for keeping her safe." She squeezed his arm and stroked it with affection as she spoke.

Darcy nodded to Sheffield. "If you wish to express your gratitude to anyone, it should be to Mr. Sheffield. It is he who provided Elizabeth a home since she departed Longbourn. I just convinced her to return."

Miss Bennet turned her smile on Sheffield, and his former valet blinked rapidly. Darcy knew that moment. Such had been his response to Elizabeth when he took her acquaintance at the Meryton assembly. In retrospect, he should have known then it was foolish to fight his attraction to her, for no other woman he had ever met had sent a zing of recognition through him as he had felt in that moment.

"Pardon," Miss Bennet said a second before she embraced Mr. Sheffield. "I know we have not been properly introduced," she said with a blush realizing she had reacted against propriety. "I am simply so full of joy, I cannot contain myself. Thank you, sir."

Sheffield cleared his throat. "Your actions are perfectly understandable, miss—perfectly acceptable."

Miss Bennet looked back to Darcy, and her eyes finally fell upon Elizabeth Anne. "Oh, my," she whispered as realization arrived. She glanced again to Sheffield, but with a shake of her head she knew Sheffield was not the child's father. Then she smiled upon him. "And—" She blushed again. She knew immediately when Elizabeth Anne had been conceived.

He smiled upon her and relieved her from asking the obvious. "Miss Bennet, may I introduce you to your niece, Elizabeth Anne Darcy." To his daughter, he said, "This is your mama's sister, Jane. Your Aunt Jane."

"Like my doll?" Lizzy Anne asked.

"Exactly."

"Come." Miss Bennet pulled his arm. "Everyone will want to know Elizabeth's child." As they started away, the lady reached a hand back to Sheffield, to include him in the gathering and the celebration, and he scrambled to come along beside her to catch Miss Bennet's hand and place it on his arm. Darcy noted the smile the lady presented his former servant and the look of astonishment mixed with pleasure on Sheffield's countenance. It was a beginning.

When they joined the chaos, Mrs. Bennet turned her attention to him. "Mr. Darcy, we thought you had forsaken our Lizzy."

"Never, ma'am," he said with a gentle smile. This woman was to be his new mother. She was nothing like the elegant Lady Anne, but God had provided him a family, at last. It was not the one he had thought to have, but it was the one he required to heal his soul. "I love your daughter to distraction," he assured. He turned where Lizzy Anne could look upon all those gathered outside of Longbourn. His daughter appeared a bit apprehensive, for, like him, she had been raised alone, until this day only claiming Sheffield and Elizabeth, but she also appeared excited by the possibility. "Would you care to take the acquaintance of your granddaughter, ma'am?" he said to Mrs. Bennet. Darcy kissed his daughter's cheek. "Sweetheart, this is your grandmother, your mama's mother."

Lizzy Anne's features screwed up in apparent skepticism. "A grandmama? I never had a grandmama." He noted how Mrs. Bennet's eyes filled with tears.

"Yes, darling," he said softly to encourage Lizzy Anne's cooperation. "Why do you not tell your grandmother your name?"

His daughter remained uncertain, but she said, "Lizbeth Anne Bachel Darcy."

"Rachel?" Mrs. Bennet clutched at her chest. "My mother's name." She turned to where Mr. Bennet still embraced his second daughter. "Mr. Bennet! Mr. Bennet, come now. You must meet your granddaughter!"

Everyone's head turned their way, and, quickly, he and Lizzy and Mrs. Bennet were surrounded by the Bennets. Lizzy Anne's grip tightened about his neck. Meanwhile, Elizabeth fought her way to his side. She reached for her father's hand, and all grew quiet. "Papa, this is your granddaughter. My and Mr. Darcy's daughter."

Tears formed in Mr. Bennet's eyes. He spoke to Elizabeth, but his eyes devoured the sight of his grandchild. "I was so worried when you left Longbourn."

"You knew Elizabeth was breeding when you permitted her to leave us?" Mrs. Bennet demanded.

Darcy had thought Mrs. Bennet would have been shocked and would demand their immediate removal from her home, but she acted as if she were appalled by the decision her husband had made: As if she were incensed by the idea of Elizabeth being forced to leave in her condition. Perhaps, Darcy had misjudged the woman as easily as she had misjudged him. She would never be what could be called a "sensible" woman, but she had one admirable quality: She was willing to fight for the welfare of her children. On that, they could agree.

Elizabeth said, "Papa saw to my safety," she said to the gathering. "Now, may we all go inside? You each require an explanation, Mr. Darcy, Mr. Sheffield, and I could use a cup of tea, and, I imagine, my child would enjoy a cake or two, would you not, Lizzy?"

"She is a 'Lizzy' also?" Miss Kitty asked.

Mrs. Bennet said proudly, "The child is Elizabeth Anne Rachel Darcy." She caught Elizabeth up in a quick embrace that appeared to embarrass both of them. "Thank you, Elizabeth, for presenting your daughter my mother's name."

"I wanted her to have a part of you, Mama," Elizabeth said softly. "And a part of Darcy's family. 'Anne' was the Christian name of Mr. Darcy's mother."

Darcy set Lizzy Anne upon her feet. She held back for a second when Mr. Bennet bent to offer the child his hand. "I am your grandpapa, and I have been waiting a lifetime to know you. Would you like to come with me and see the house where your mama grew up?"

Their child glanced up to him and Elizabeth. They both nodded their encouragement, and Lizzy Anne walked away with Mr. Bennet. All turned toward the house, and Elizabeth leaned against his side as he braced her steps to follow.

"Another Elizabeth has won your father's heart," Darcy said with a smile.

"We still must make our explanations as to how we married before Lizzy was conceived," she whispered. "We must pray Mr. Bennet will cooperate."

"As this scheme was half his idea, he has little choice."

"Yet, at the time of the arrangement, we all thought you dead," she reminded him. "The new reality for my father is that we will be living together under his roof, without the privilege of an actual marriage ceremony."

Darcy glanced to where the last of the Bennets and the servants entered the house. "We will allow our daughter to soften Mr. Bennet's heart. Now come along. They will be wondering why we tarry."

"There will be many questions," she reminded him. "Is this what you want?"

"I want you and my daughter. I do not believe I can be whole again until we are together as a family. As to the questions, we will answer them all," he assured her as he placed her hand on his arm to escort her inside. "However," he leaned closer to whisper, "there are two things you should know before we go inside."

"And those are?" She paused on the steps leading to the threshold.

"First, like Bingley before him, Mr. Sheffield believes Miss Bennet has the look of an angel. Moreover, he blinked in pleasant surprise when your elder sister presented him with an impromptu embrace out of gratitude for tending to you."

"Blinking is good, correct?" she asked.

"I blinked that way when my eyes fell upon you at the Meryton assembly," he confided. "I felt as if my imagination was playing a trick on me. Thunderstruck. You had shaken my world to its core, thus, the reason I refused to dance with you. I did not know whether you were real or not."

Her smile increased in size. "What a lovely explanation, although I am not yet certain you do not fool yourself in this matter." Nevertheless, she went on tiptoes to kiss his cheek. "And the second thing I should know?"

"Miss Bennet will be asking you questions, likely in private, which will go beyond the proof of our marriage. When I came searching for you, she reluctantly admitted to me that she had observed our leaving the Netherfield library on the evening we conceived Elizabeth Anne."

CHAPTER SEVENTEEN

THEY SPENT A FORTNIGHT with her family. Darcy remained constantly aware he must be in Dry Drayton, Cambridgeshire, to assume his position at the inn before Mr. Ruffe was to leave. He sent a message ahead to reserve a like room for Elizabeth and Lizzy. They would exchange their vows in the small town before heading to Derbyshire.

Although Mr. Bennet was not happy to have Darcy and Elizabeth sharing rooms, the gentleman swallowed his objections in order to maintain the ruse he had assisted in putting into place. Both Darcy and Elizabeth provided her father the assurances they meant to marry once they departed for Derbyshire. Darcy explained his plan for a quiet ceremony and how he had established his residency in Dry Drayton.

Each day, Mr. and Mrs. Bennet spent hours upon end with their granddaughter, taking the child into the village and telling anyone who would listen how he and Elizabeth had been married all along. Carrying their tale to Mrs. Phillips easily spread the story, not only to those in the village, but to the neighborhood, as well. While he and Sheffield spent much of their time in Mr. Bennet's library, Elizabeth proved the consummate hostess as visitors appeared often upon the Bennet's threshold to behold both a quick glance at the marriage certificate, but also to hear Elizabeth repeat how she should have spoken the truth when their botched wedding occurred, but she was too distraught at the possibility of someone bringing harm to him that she responded inappropriately. She claimed to have been embarrassed from foisting a sham upon her parents' friends and neighbors.

"I have not noted any of the Lucases among those making social calls," Darcy said well into their second week at Longbourn.

Elizabeth leaned closer to explain, "Mr. Bennet made a private call upon Sir William to explain Mr. Collins's part in Lizzy Anne's kidnapping and to offer his gratitude to Charlotte for convincing her husband to act with honor. Upset by the turn of events, Sir William and Lady Lucas set out immediately for Kent. I believe they mean to fetch Charlotte home for her lying-in, especially with the chaos going on at Rosings Park and Mr. Collins's questionable future." She drew her legs up beneath her to curl closer into the curve of his body and to steal his warmth. "Will the colonel replace Mr. Bennet's cousin?" she asked when she was settled.

Darcy shrugged. "I left that decision to Fitzwilliam."

"Has your aunt departed Rosings?" she asked tentatively.

"Fitzwilliam saw her off. Ironically, she left England at Queenborough Harbor rather than from London's docks," he shared.

"Do you know her destination?"

He admitted, "I do not. As long as I am never asked to be in her company again, I am satisfied." Although he knew his measures necessary, it still bothered Darcy to lose so many family members with one swipe of his hand. "I am certain Fitzwilliam and Anne have been made aware of her ladyship's plans."

"When will the Fitzwilliams settle in at Rosings?"

"He will oversee the payment of the quarter day taxes, but my cousin assumes it will be November before he and Georgiana move into the estate. Anne remains with them at Darcy House, and Fitzwilliam reports she is adapting quite nicely to London's social life."

Elizabeth glanced across the room to where Mr. Sheffield and Miss Bennet had their heads together, discussing a book of poetry the gentleman had purchased for Miss Bennet in the village when they had all walked into Meryton earlier in the day. Ironically, he and Elizabeth, as the assumed married couple, were to be serving as chaperones for the pair. "Will he propose?" she asked. "I would not wish for Jane to know heartbreak again."

"I plan to speak to him tomorrow regarding the London bookstore. I have had confirmation from my man of business, who says I should have the deed in my hands by early tomorrow. He has also located a Town home in Picadilly that could prove a viable home for Sheffield and your sister, a house that would allow them to entertain and raise a family. I thought the house might be a wedding present from Mr. Bennet, that is, if your father is willing to assist us in another pretense."

She kissed his cheek. "You are very attractive when you are forceful, sir." They looked deeply into each other's eyes, finding satisfaction. "Shall you turn against me if I can bear you no more children?" she asked tentatively. "Shall Lizzy and I be enough to keep you happy?"

"I love you, Elizabeth," he proclaimed. "Even if we had no children, I would still choose you. I could never be content with another."

"You wished to speak to me, sir?"

Darcy sat in the corner of Mr. Bennet's study, pretending to be addressing his daily correspondence to those in London.

"Yes," Mr. Bennet said casually. Darcy had found Bennet a cooperative co-conspirator, making a few changes and involving Elizabeth's uncle, Mr. Gardiner. "Please join me."

Sheffield shot a questioning glance to Darcy, but he did as Mr. Bennet suggested.

Once all were settled, Bennet began without preamble. "I have taken notice of your attentions to Miss Bennet. Do you mean to speak to my daughter of a future before you depart Longbourn this week?"

Darcy smiled. He had rarely viewed Sheffield flustered, but today was the exception. "I—I would hope to do so, but all I have to offer your daughter is a few rooms over my shop in

Brighton. I believe she deserves more than a simple man. Miss Bennet is everything a man could look for in a wife, and I am not of her social class."

Bennet frowned. "Miss Bennet deserves to be happy, and I think you could provide her that happiness. And as to the other matter, are you not a gentleman's son? I was led to believe you began your career in Darcy's service as his tutor—that you held a gentleman's education."

"I do, sir," Sheffield was quick to say. "Marrying your eldest daughter would be my fondest wish, but I will never own an estate for Miss Bennet to manage."

"Yet, you are capable of purchasing a home, are you not?" Bennet charged.

Sheffield tugged nervously on his sleeve. "Yes, but—"

Bennet interrupted. "I thought you were a wealthy man. Is that not what you told me when we sat in this very office four years prior?"

Darcy cleared his voice. He had permitted Mr. Bennet his fun with Sheffield; now, it was time for him to lead them all to the same conclusion. "I believe Mr. Sheffield's expenses were more than he expected when he made his bargain with you then. Not that he has ever complained about the role he played in rescuing Elizabeth when I could not."

"Knowing Elizabeth and the child have been the most spectacular moments in my life," Sheffield said with emotion.

"Would you not wish to have those moments again?" Bennet demanded. "With your own children? My Jane is six and twenty, certainly still young enough to bear you children of your own. Would that not be your wish, sir?"

Mr. Sheffield blushed thoroughly, but he said, "I can think of nothing grander, sir."

Bennet nodded his head in Darcy's direction. "Then, you and I, Darcy, should discover a means to assist Sheffield and Jane to a better understanding." He turned to ask Sheffield, "Do you wish to remain in Brighton?"

Sheffield shrugged. "I possess few choices. One of my

reasons for not proposing to your daughter is I would not wish to expose Miss Bennet to the gossip that likely awaits my return to the town. Elizabeth and I left abruptly. The magistrate knew we searched for the child, and Elizabeth's 'supposed' husband had returned and was not a Dartmore, but a Darcy. Moreover, how do I marry Miss Bennet when she is Elizabeth's sister, and, in Brighton, everyone thought Elizabeth was my niece? We have told too many lies there to take them back. Miss Bennet should not be exposed to the gossip. In fact, it is likely to affect my business there."

Darcy abandoned his pretense and moved his chair closer. "Elizabeth told me how you had thought to purchase Brooke's before you took up her cause."

"I do not regret my decision, sir. Having Elizabeth and Lizzy with me proved what I have always known: I want a family of my own."

"Then, perhaps, this will provide you the means to know your happiness. It is a gift from Elizabeth and me—a symbol of our gratitude." He placed papers before his former servant, a man who had always been his friend.

Sheffield's eyes scanned the papers. "This appears to be the deed to Fowler's on Park Lane." The man's hands shook as he turned the pages, attempting to take it all in.

"It is not Brooke's," Darcy said with a smile of satisfaction.

"It is larger than Brooke's." Tears misted Sheffield's eyes. "I could not accept this, sir. It is too much."

"You could and you will," Darcy said in serious tones. "Consider it a repayment for your care of the two people most important in my life. Without you, Elizabeth Anne would not be alive. This was the one gift Elizabeth asked of me when she agreed to be my wife again."

"I do not know what to say, sir." Sheffield's eyes again looked over the deed.

"You have time to read the papers a thousand times if you like. Fowler has asked to remain with the business until the next quarter day, which is Christmas so you will have time to decide what you will do with the shop in Brighton. Sell it. Let it out to another."

"My nephew requires an occupation after his service in the war. He wishes to marry," Sheffield said. "Perhaps he—"

"Again, you have time to consider what is best for you," Darcy said with a pat on his friend's back.

Mr. Bennet cleared his throat then. He reached into the drawer, took out a paper with a drawing of a house upon it. "I hope you do not mind, when Darcy informed me of his gift to you, I sent an express to London to my wife's brother, Mr. Gardiner. The man knows London like the back of his hand." Bennet tapped the drawing. "This is a sketch of a house in Town that is available to let with an option to purchase. Gardiner says it is in Picadilly, not many streets removed from the shop of which Darcy spoke. If you are sincere in your wish to marry our Jane, I would have no qualms in investing a portion of her allowance, the rest to be paid, naturally, upon my death, as a down payment on this house. Moreover, her Uncle Gardiner is willing to pay the first three months of the mortgage as a wedding present for you two."

"You would trust me with Miss Bennet's future?" Sheffield said in awe.

"I trusted you with the future of my second daughter, and you proved most resourceful," Mr. Bennet declared. "Miss Bennet is as precious to me as is Elizabeth. She deserves a man who would put her interests above his own—a trait sadly missing from others who wished to claim her hand. Make her happy, Sheffield. Make certain she never regrets giving her heart to you. That is all I ask."

"I will do my best, sir," Sheffield said in reverence.

Bennet laughed easily. "I, personally, despise London, but if both Jane and Elizabeth are in residence in the City, I might allow Mrs. Bennet to drag me there more often."

"How am I to express my gratitude?" Sheffield said in dismay.

"Treat my Jane well. I do not wish to view her ever again

discounting her worth as a woman," Bennet said in warning.

"I will do my best, sir." Sheffield stood suddenly, looking around as if he did not know where he was. He clutched the deed and the drawing within his grasp.

Darcy said in amusement, "I believe Miss Bennet and Elizabeth were in the morning room when I joined Mr. Bennet earlier. If I were you, I would start my search for the lady there."

They had traveled to Cambridge on Wednesday, 25 September 1816, so Darcy might call upon the Bishop of Ely's—Bowyer Sparke—office to apply for the appropriate jurisdiction and submit an allegation, presented under oath, that there were no impediments to a marriage between Elizabeth and him. The allegation required him to supply their names, ages, birthdates, and make a declaration of no need for her father's permission to marry. Although his doing such was more public than either of them liked, the procedure of purchasing an ordinary license was infinitely better than the public calling of the banns. With the license in hand, on Friday they made their way to Dry Drayton, where he paid Mr. Ruffe a nominal fee and replaced the man in the let room, purchasing a like room for Elizabeth and their child. There they would wait until the day of their wedding.

On Saturday, he called upon the vicar at the Church of St Peter and St Paul and presented his license and explained his month-long occupation of a room at *The Black Bells*, claiming to have been in residence for three Sundays, the number of Sundays required for a calling of the banns. Arrangements were made for their service on Wednesday, with the vicar insisting upon Darcy meeting the full residency requirement by staying through Monday, as "he" did not register at the inn until late on Sunday, 8 September 1816. Although Darcy did not approve of the delay, he kept his mouth closed, for the vicar had the right to insist they wait another week, if he so chose. Even if Darcy wished to complain, he would not draw more attention to his marriage to Elizabeth than was necessary.

They married on 2 October 1816, only six weeks short of

their original wedding day. It was a very simple ceremony with only the vicar and the cleric's wife and son who stood as witnesses. Darcy had paid the innkeeper's wife to entertain Elizabeth Anne at the inn during the service, fearing his daughter, as intelligent as ever, would say something to someone at Pemberley that might cause people to question their story of secretly marrying years prior.

"Might we celebrate both days?" Elizabeth asked as she snuggled into his embrace as they crossed Leicestershire and made their way toward Derbyshire and Pemberley. Lizzy Anne was asleep on the opposing bench. "I know it is necessary to maintain the pretense of our August wedding, but I do not want to pretend this one never occurred."

"I agree." He trailed a line of kisses from her ear to the indentation of her neck. "One will be the public celebration required to keep Elizabeth Anne safe," he murmured against her skin. "And the other celebration specifically designed for just us two."

Elizabeth snaked her arms about his neck. "I fear," she said, her lips hovering over his, "we may find it difficult until we reach Pemberley for too much to happen between us." She glanced to their daughter. "Little eyes see it all."

Darcy smiled easily. "That is why we must steal away our moments when we are granted them. Therefore, do not be offended when I instruct you to cease the chatter and kiss your husband with all the love in your heart."

Her lips lingered over his. "And will you kiss me with all the love in your heart?"

"Absolutely." His mouth covered hers. He had returned to all that was important in his life.

It was Friday, the first week of October when Darcy and his new family arrived at Pemberley. Darcy's mind was too full for conversation as they approached his home. As Elizabeth had shown her enthusiasm for Longbourn, his heart leapt with happiness as their carriage made its way to the top of an eminence for one's first view of the house. Here, at this point, the wood ceased, and his eyes were immediately filled with the pure splendor of Pemberley House. The windows gleamed in the autumn sun, giving the exterior the look of a magical light.

Elizabeth Anne, who sat upon her mother's lap, whispered in awe, "It is truly a castle, Papa."

"No, my darling girl, it is simply your home—for as long as you wish to dwell here, Pemberley is yours to enjoy."

1 August 1836, Pemberley House

"I ask you to raise your glasses to celebrate the betrothal of my daughter, Miss Elizabeth Anne Darcy, to Hendrix Beckton, 8th Earl Elmhurst. To the future Lord and Lady Elmhurst."

"To the future Lord and Lady Elmhurst," all in attendance called in response. His guests then sipped their champagne or their punch, depending upon what propriety permitted, and then turned back to their conversations and greeting old friends.

It was the evening of their annual ball, the one that marked the "supposed" years of their marriage. They were the Darcys, and it had seemed to all involved only appropriate to use their public celebration of their marriage to announce the upcoming joining of their daughter, Elizabeth Anne, to an earl. "Who would have thought the Darcys would align themselves with another earldom?" Elizabeth had said over breakfast on this very day.

After all these years, their public faces remained in place because doing so benefited their family, and family remained their first priority. Traditionally, they celebrated their actual wedding date in a more private manner, which suited Darcy more so than this public display; yet, he would not spoil the moment for his lovely Elizabeth Anne.

It had taken close to eight years of hard work and manipulations for Pemberley to recover from 1816, the "Year Without Summer," as it had been called in the newsprints. Unfortunately, 1816 had been followed by a series of wet summers and snow remaining as late as July in parts of the Lake District, countered by dry growing seasons the following year. If he had been at Pemberley when the severe weather had set its sights on England, he might have been better prepared for the eventual downfall of agriculture, as he once knew it. In those early years of saving his family's future, there were days both he and Elizabeth worked the fields around the clock to prove his methods of cultivation viable. He had never heard of another woman like her, and, from all accounts, she was quite "infamous" in that manner, but not for her real "sin" of anticipating her vows.

Fitzwilliam and Georgiana had remained at Rosings for nearly ten years. The Southern shires, in many ways, had had worse weather than Derbyshire, likely because of the extremes from a dry and hot summer in 1818 to frost standing on the ground well into May the following year and snow in October. His sister had borne her husband another son and a daughter, and, from all reports of their life in Oxfordshire, they were quite happy. As Darcy had predicted, while they were still at Rosings Park, Fitzwilliam had served Kent well in the House of Commons, and he now served not only in the Commons for Oxfordshire but also served in the Prime Minister William Lamb, Lord Melbourne's inner circle.

Elizabeth's sister Kitty had married John Lucas and was the mistress of Lucas Lodge. She and Lucas had five children. Meanwhile, Miss Mary Bennet had married the son of one of Sheffield's brothers. Darcy had been pleased to offer Mr. Anthony Sheffield the living at Kympton when it came available. It seemed only fair to keep it in the family. The Sheffields had four children, making Darcy and Elizabeth's extended family quite large. They both adored the idea.

Unfortunately, for Mrs. Lydia Wickham, after five years of marriage and two more illegitimate children, in addition to those of which she had been made cognizant after her marriage to Lieutenant Wickham, claiming the lady's husband as father, George Wickham unceremoniously boarded a ship to America, with a promise he would send for his wife once he was settled there. Some nineteen years later, Mrs. Wickham had yet to hear from him. She now resided with her elderly mother in a cottage near Meryton, for which Mrs. Bennet's sons-in-marriage paid the upkeep. Darcy supposed he and the others would continue to maintain the cottage even after Mrs. Bennet's passing, for Mrs. Lydia Wickham had few prospects available. Although Mr. Wickham had more children than he should have, Mrs. Wickham was not to know such happiness, and as no one had been able to prove whether the gentleman was dead or alive, Lydia Bennet Wickham was not permitted, by law, to remarry. She had paid a high price for her impetuousness.

Elizabeth's father had had his ultimate revenge on Mr. Collins. He had outlived the man by nearly five years and had permitted a more deserving branch of the family tree to inherit Longbourn. Mrs. Collins had born her husband three children in the fifteen years they were together: all daughters. Currently, Mrs. Collins served as governess to his Cousin Anne's children at Rosings Park and was permitted Hunsford Cottage as her residence. He did not know what would happen with Anne's children no longer required a governess, but that decision was not his to make.

Anne had married the minor son of a marquess, who was happy to permit Fitzwilliam and Georgiana to remain at Rosings while he and Anne enjoyed life on the Continent. From what Darcy had learned from his sister Georgiana, Anne was with her mother in Italy when Lady Catherine took her last breath. Her ladyship's remains had been returned to England, and Fitzwilliam had them placed in the family cemetery on the estate.

His Aunt and Uncle Matlock had died together in a carriage accident nine years after Darcy had banished them from his life. At Georgiana and Fitzwilliam's request, Darcy had paid a duty call upon Roland Fitzwilliam, who, according to all who spoke of the new earl, had yet to change his ways. It was the last time he acknowledged his connection to his late mother's brother.

As to Charles Bingley, Darcy's former friend had married the Society miss his sisters had insisted upon him taking to wife. From what Darcy had learned in passing, Bingley had run through the fortune his father had left him, bailing out first one sister and then another, not to mention his wife's family. Moreover, without Darcy's steady hand on Bingley's shoulder, the man had made a series of poor investments which had left him near bankruptcy.

Elizabeth slid her hand into his as he watched Elmhurst lead Elizabeth Anne to the dance floor for a waltz. "Who shall be your partner for this dance, Mr. Darcy?" she asked with a tease.

He looked down upon her lovingly. "I promised our daughter Emilia I would partner her for a waltz. She is too young for another to stand up with her, but she should have the practice before she makes her Come Out in the spring."

"She is seventeen, sir," his wife protested. "Many girls are married by the time they are sixteen. Moreover, the rules you quote are antiquated. Young girls have been dancing the waltz from the time you were on *The Lost Sparrow*."

"My ignorance then," he said with a twitch of his lips. "Yet, you know I do not wish to part with another daughter so soon. Therefore, at Pemberley, as always, our house ..."

"Your rules," she said with an easy laugh. "You, sir, are akin to a dinosaur."

"You are fascinated with dinosaurs," he countered.

"I am," she admitted. "Like you, if I had my way, they would each remain at Pemberley forever."

"And your partner for the first waltz?" he asked, although he knew the answer.

"Bennet means to have his duty done early to his mother and sisters," she said with a smile. She had born him three more children: Two more daughters and a son.

"You shall save me the supper waltz?" she asked. "I do not wish to dine with another. After all, this is *our wedding anniversary*." She presented him a knowing look.

Darcy smiled down upon her. "I cannot forget the day I threw caution to the wind and raced to Scotland to marry the woman I love. Moreover, you are aware of how fond of dancing I am." He lifted his brows in a challenge.

"I know," she said with an answering smile, realizing his lie was meant to tease her. "You love to dance when you find the woman tolerable enough to tempt you." She went on her toes to kiss him briefly.

"You two require more decorum," a very masculine voice warned.

"Where is your wife?" Elizabeth said with a smile.

"Jane is speaking to your Rebecca and our Chloe, reminding them that fourteen-year-old young ladies are not allowed to waltz."

"I just said the same thing of Emilia," Darcy commiserated.

Albert Sheffield not only owned the bookstore on Park Lane and the one in Brighton, but he had opened three others, nearly as large in Staffordshire, Northumberland, and his home shire of Cumbria. He had purchased a small estate in Richmond for his bride, a gift on their tenth wedding anniversary. They were accepted in all the finer houses and were often-sought-after guests at a variety of house parties.

"I believe I shall join Jane," Elizabeth said. She squeezed Darcy's hand and brushed a quick kiss across Sheffield's cheek.

"Elizabeth Anne is stunning," Sheffield remarked in pride as they both turned to view their "Lizzy" on the arm of another man.

"So is your Grace," Darcy admitted.

"I cannot take credit for the look of any of my children," Sheffield declared. "Charles looks the most like me, but Philip, Rebecca, and Grace favor their mother." Darcy's brother-in-marriage chuckled. "Not that I am complaining. Jane's countenance is still the most compelling face I have ever beheld."

"We are fortunate men, Albert Sheffield," Darcy announced.

Sheffield smiled indulgently. "We are just that, sir. We each know the love of a strong-willed woman who crafted both our future and our happiness. We are blessed among men."

Darcy nodded his agreement. "The only true problem either of us possesses at this moment is losing Lizzy again."

"Neither of us will ever lose her, Darcy. She carries us in her heart. We were the men by which she judged all her suitors. Elmhurst is the only one who came close to what our girl was searching for in a husband. She will skillfully mend his deficiencies. Just you mark my words. Soon our Lizzy will be sharing tales of her 'papa' and her 'Uncle Albert' with the next generation."

"I enjoy your version of the future, Sheffield, better than the one I designed with a gaping hole in my life," Darcy admitted.

"Just think, old man," Sheffield said with a pat on Darcy's back. "Soon you will have grandchildren to spoil. Do you not recall the look on Mr. Bennet's countenance when he first met our Lizzy Anne?"

"Perfectly so."

Sheffield smiled. "Soon that look will be upon your countenance. The Darcy legacy will continue because you loved a remarkable woman, and she loved you dearly in return."

~ Finis ~

Meet Regina Jeffers

Regina Jeffers, an award-winning author of historical cozy mysteries, Austenesque sequels and retellings, as well as Regency era romances, has worn many hats over her lifetime: daughter, student, military brat, wife, mother, grandmother, teacher, tax preparer, journalist, choreographer, Broadway dancer, theatre director, history buff, grant writer, media literacy consultant, and author. Living outside of Charlotte, NC, Jeffers writes novels that take the ordinary and adds a bit of mayhem, while mastering tension in her own life with a bit of gardening and the exuberance of her "grand joys."

Blogs: Every Woman Dreams and Austen Authors
Regina Jeffers's Website

Also Discover Regina on…

Facebook, Pinterest, Twitter, LinkedIn, Goodreads, Bookbub, and Amazon Author Central

Other Novels by Regina Jeffers

Jane Austen-Inspired Novels:

Darcy's Passions: Pride and Prejudice Retold Through His Eyes
Darcy's Temptation: A Pride and Prejudice Sequel
Captain Frederick Wentworth's Persuasion: Jane Austen's Classic Retold Through His Eyes
Vampire Darcy's Desire: A Pride and Prejudice Paranormal Adventure
The Phantom of Pemberley: A Pride and Prejudice Mystery
Christmas at Pemberley: A Pride and Prejudice Holiday Sequel
The Disappearance of Georgiana Darcy: A Pride and Prejudice Mystery
The Mysterious Death of Mr. Darcy: A Pride and Prejudice Mystery
The Prosecution of Mr. Darcy's Cousin: A Pride and Prejudice Mystery
Mr. Darcy's Fault: A Pride and Prejudice Vagary
Mr. Darcy's Present: A Pride and Prejudice Holiday Vagary
Mr. Darcy's Bargain: A Pride and Prejudice Vagary
Mr. Darcy's Brides: A Pride and Prejudice Vagary
Mr. Darcy's Bet: A Pride and Prejudice Vagary
Elizabeth Bennet's Deception: A Pride and Prejudice Vagary
Elizabeth Bennet's Excellent Adventure: A Pride and Prejudice Vagary
The Pemberley Ball: A Pride and Prejudice Vagary
A Dance with Mr. Darcy: A Pride and Prejudice Vagary
The Road to Understanding: A Pride and Prejudice Vagary
Pride and Prejudice and a Shakespearean Scholar: A Pride and Prejudice Vagary
Where There's a FitzWILLiam Darcy, There's a Way: A Pride and Prejudice Vagary
In Want of a Wife: A Pride and Prejudice Vagary
Honor and Hope: A Contemporary Pride and Prejudice

Regency and Contemporary Romances:

The Scandal of Lady Eleanor, Book 1 of the Realm Series (aka A Touch of Scandal)
A Touch of Velvet, Book 2 of the Realm Series
A Touch of Cashémere, Book 3 of the Realm Series
A Touch of Grace, Book 4 of the Realm Series
A Touch of Mercy, Book 5 of the Realm Series
A Touch of Love, Book 6 of the Realm Series
A Touch of Honor, Book 7 of the Realm Series
A Touch of Emerald, The Conclusion of the Realm Series
His American Heartsong: A Companion Novel to the Realm Series
His Irish Eve
Angel Comes to the Devil's Keep, Book 1 of the "Twins" Trilogy
The Earl Claims His Comfort, Book 2 of the "Twins" Trilogy
Lady Chandler's Sister, Book 3 of the "Twins" Trilogy
The Heartless Earl: A Common Elements Romance Project Novel
Lady Joy and the Earl: A Regency Christmas Romance
Letters from Home: A Regency Christmas Romance
Beautified by Love
Christmas Ever After: A Clean Regency Romance Anthology
Regency Summer Escape Anthology
A Regency Christmas Proposal Anthology
Second Chances: The Courtship Wars
One Minute Past Christmas, A Holiday Short Story

Coming Soon...

Indentured Love: A Persuasion Vagary
Losing Lizzy: A Pride and Prejudice Vagary (May 2020)
The Courtship of Lord Blackhurst (June 2020)
Obsession
I Shot the Sheriff: A Tragic Heroes in Classic Literature Series Novel (Winter 2020)

Excerpt from Chapter 2
I Shot the Sheriff: A Tragic Characters in Classic Lit Series

Patience was one of less than a dozen female agents, specifically recruited for "special" interventions where only a relatively attractive woman could be more effective than their male counterparts. Last evening, her orders had been to distract Dylan Monroe, a former Realm clerk and agent-in-training long enough for Pennington to take the man into custody and to learn more of the others involved in the ongoing Woodstone-Ransing investigation. And if she could not distract the man or if Monroe did not act as prescribed, then she was to assume a position above the dance floor to guard the Prince Regent from attack.

Unfortunately, she had to improvise, purposely altering her orders when she lost sight of Monroe, who posed as a footman in service to the Prince. When the evening began, she was dressed as one of a dozen maids scattered about the room ready to clean up any spill or assist any of the females with a torn piece of lace or other repair to a dress. She and the real Carleton House maids were, as always, invisible to those in attendance until required. "From my place along the wall, I spotted Monroe fairly quickly and hoped to engage him in conversation or some other sort of distraction until the Royal Guards could swoop in and arrest the man, but Monroe did not remain long in the room, making a quick exit toward the terrace," she began her explanation.

"Having been given a thorough tour of all the passages surrounding the ballroom, I knew immediately where Monroe was headed. Making my decision, I quickly exited the ballroom and took the narrow set of stairs on the other side of the balcony, the one leading to where my overlook point, hidden behind a draped door, had been previously set to protect the Prince."

Evidently, Pennington's plans had shifted, and, although she knew her godfather was well aware of the alteration, she did not know how that affected her role in the matter. "You were likely aware of my retreat from the ballroom," she said quietly.

"I was, although I was not certain what you planned until the Earl of Carleton reported his niece, Mrs. Warren, had also spotted Monroe in the ballroom."

That information explained much of what Patience suspected. "When I noted Monroe's exit to the terrace, I realized he planned his attack from above, and so I raced to the balcony. I originally thought I might pretend to be a maid hoping for a glimpse of the goings on below and delay him somehow or have him abandon his attempt because I would be standing as witness," she confided.

"Despite being proud of your bravery, I never wish you to place yourself in such danger again. It that understood?" Pennington reprimanded. "You are too precious to me."

She nodded her acceptance of his words. This man had been the stabilizing influence in her life since she was a child. When her father had faltered, it had been Aristotle Pennington who had swooped in to save her and her family. "Should I continue?" she asked softly.

He squeezed her fingers in support. "Certainly. Tell me all. No more interruptions," he promised.

She swallowed the tears his kind words had engendered. She was the "odd bird" in her family and often felt unappreciated, but with her godfather's guidance she knew moments such as this one where she experienced being cherished.

"Not knowing what to expect, I did as you instructed. I retreated to my hiding place behind the draped door. Even though I knew Monroe would likely come through the opposing door, the one leading down the narrow stairs to the terrace, it took me by surprise when he actually made his appearance." In truth, she had jumped, her heart slamming in her chest, for, at the time, she did not know whether Monroe's plans included others, nor did she relish the idea of shooting a man up close and personal. Patience was a sure shot, but she had never killed a man before.

"Monroe paused for a few brief seconds, leaving the opposing door open, exposing the passage meant as an escape in case of a fire, before he set the door ajar, likely thinking to use it to make his retreat. He was dressed in the Royal livery, and sweat marked his brow," she said softly.

"He appeared to be in a fervent rush to complete his task. As I looked on, deciding whether to make an appearance or not and still thinking he would have difficulty shooting the Prince with a handgun from his position above, he lifted the lid of the storage compartment, the one designed to keep the supply of candles ready-at-hand and removed a rifle before I had time to act. I paused long enough to catch my breath and my nerves, deciding I must reach Monroe before he could execute his plan. I had my small pistol with me and intended to confront him. However, before I could do so, a woman opened the door and stepped into the area." She would not mention the intense danger nearly choking her as she looked on.

"My first thought was Monroe meant a tryst, but I quickly shoved that idea from my mind. He was there to kill Prince George. What I did not know at the time was whether the woman was friend or foe. An accomplice? But the woman did not approach, and Monroe did not take notice of her. Even so, I had noted her entrance, and I knew if she were part of Monroe's plan, my Queen Anne pistol would not suffice for both, and, if she were an innocent, I could not take the chance she would be injured. Although I know most members of the *ton* by sight, I did not recognize her."

"Mrs. Warren," her godfather said softly. "Sir Carter's love interest."

"Ah," she said. "The lady thought Sir Carter was in

danger?"

"Something to that effect. Mrs. Warren had encountered Dylan Monroe previously. It was she who alerted her uncle to Monroe's presence in the ballroom."

Another piece of the puzzle fell into place. "Should I continue?" she asked.

"Please. I want to know everything you saw and heard," he assured.

She stroked the back of Pennington's ungloved hand as she spoke. "Albeit keeping an eye on Monroe and the lady, attempting to determine if she meant to charge him or not, the chaos below caught my attention. I noted another man in Royal livery standing close, too close, behind Prince George. The Prince had his arm draped about Sir Carter's shoulders, while Lords Swenton, Worthing, and de Wendenal approached cautiously on three sides. Realizing the situation below had taken a turn for the worse, I caught up my rifle to do what was necessary. I also had previously loaded the musket, but its lack of accuracy at a distance would have been too much to risk. I had planned to use it against Monroe, if it were just he and I, but I turned to the rifle instead."

"Did you leave both weapons at the scene, as you were instructed?" Pennington asked.

"Most assuredly," she declared. "Is something amiss?"

"Only the rifle was retrieved. The musket was not located."

"That is odd," she reasoned.

"It will all prove in the end. For now, continued your story," he instructed.

Patience sucked in a quick breath. She had a thousand questions, but her godfather was not likely to answer any of them until she finished her report. "I knew something of the players below, that is, all except Lord de Wendenal." She was vaguely familiar with the baronet and Lords Swenton and Worthing, for they each had served under her godfather as part of the Home Office. "Although I recognized him, I have never taken the acquaintance of Lord de Wendenal." She would not confess to

Excerpt from Chapter 2 - I Shot the Sheriff: A Tragic Characters in Classic Lit Series

her godfather that while she sighted the rifle, using the seam of the barrel as her point of reference and preparing to take action, as was necessary to assure the Prince's security, her eyes had landed upon the man, whose reputation as being both cold and unmoving preceded him. He concentrated on the situation, while she concentrated on him. His evening clothes accented his broad shoulders—the type of shoulders that could easily carry a sea of troubles—the type upon which any woman would wish to rest her head. In spite of the shadows hiding much of his forehead, except for his piercing blue eyes, she recognized the ruthless determination upon his features as he crept closer to what was surely another assailant and danger. In that instant, she thought truly to know such a man would be spectacular.

Her musings had been interrupted by the turning of all heads below, except that of de Wendenal's, to Dylan Monroe upon the balcony. She had been so captivated by Lord de Wendenal, she had not noted the entrance of Lord Godown upon the balcony, who had caught the woman to him and silenced her screams before they occurred. The marquis stood tall, like some sort of Greek god, the man's reputation, as Adonis come to Earth, well deserved.

"As you know," she continued, after bringing her wayward thoughts into order, "Lord Godown appeared on the balcony. Monroe was unaware of the man's presence until it was too late. Lord Godown called Monroe's name and your former agent turned. You know what occurred at that point."

It had all played out as if the seconds crawled by. Monroe turned. Lord Godown threw a knife with expert precision. The knife flipped end-over-end, striking Monroe in the soft part of the man's throat. Monroe emitted a gurgling sound and reached for the knife, his grip on the gun falling away as it exploded—the bullet hitting the plastered ceiling and sending shards of an ornate carvings on those gathered below.

"Realizing my attention had been drawn away from the scene below, I made myself concentrate on what was playing out in the ballroom. Lord Lexford took aim at Monroe, hitting the man between the eyes and sending the body tumbling over the balcony, slamming into the floor with a sickening thud that resonated in my very soul; yet, I did not look away from where Monroe's accomplice jerked his hand up higher, exposing a gun. Screams filled the air, but I lined up the shot to eliminate Monroe's partner." She had never killed a man—never known the grief of taking another's life, but she had sworn a duty to protect Prince George from harm. Her country, and she prayed her God, would forgive her.

"However, once again, my attention was pulled from my target. Another man stood along the edge of the ballroom," she explained, her memory filled with the images of all that had occurred.

"Did you observe his face? Did you recognize him?" Pennington demanded.

"No. He was under the overhang of the balcony. But he seemed familiar. His movements. The slant of his shoulders. But I could not name him." She sat straighter and did not look at her godfather. "I know my responsibility was to protect the Prince—my orders from you had been specific, and you will not approve, but I chose to protect Lord de Wendenal instead. If you mean to arrest me for denying my duties, I shall understand."

A long silence held between them. "You must have fired at the same time as did the senior Monroe and Lord de Wendenal's assailant. All who observed the encounter claimed there were only three shots in total: Dylan Monroe's, Lexford's, and when the elder Monroe attempt to shoot Prince George. Monroe's bullet struck Sir Carter as the baronet knocked the Prince from the way."

"I imagine the uproar could have disguised the sounds," she offered lamely, "making them appear as one, when, in reality, they were fractions of a second apart."

Pennington appeared lost in his thoughts. "Perhaps." Another long pause followed. "Might you explain why you chose Lord de Wendenal over our country's future king? My supervisors will wish to know your reasons."

Excerpt from Chapter 2 - I Shot the Sheriff: A Tragic Characters in Classic Lit Series

Tears misted Patience eyes. She had failed the one man who had never failed her, and she had spent many a sleepless hour last evening, attempting to make sense of her decision. She had known when their conversation began, the answer to this question was the reason for their meeting. Her godfather would not question her decisions, for he permitted his agents much latitude in the execution of their duties, but Lord Liverpool would not be so forgiving. In her three years with the Home Office, she had developed somewhat of a reputation for being impulsive. Her brothers had often declared, *"Father named you 'Patience' because he thought doing so would be a fine plague upon society."*

"I have no reason," she admitted softly. "I do not even know Lord de Wendenal." She shrugged, feeling quite incompetent. "It was necessary, that is all I can say. Lords Swenton and Worthing approached the senior Mr. Monroe."

"As did Lord de Wendenal," her godfather observed.

"Yes, of all the Prince's supposed friends and protectors, it was Lord de Wendenal, a man many of those in attendance last evening openly despise, who acted without thought for his own safety."

Pennington groused, "I wish I could be so certain de Wendenal did not act with an ulterior motive."

"Even if he did wish the Prince's favor, Lord de Wendenal did act when others looked on in shock or in hopes of a different outcome." She laid her head against the shoulder of a man who had always accepted her foibles. "I did not reason it out at the time. Four men protected Prince George, but only one had his own attacker. It all did not appear fair in the scheme of things."

He sighed heavily. "Very much as I suspected." He lifted her chin with two fingers so he might place a kiss upon her cheek. "You were always the first to right a wrong."

"It grieves me you must answer to Lord Liverpool because of my error in judgement," she said obediently.

"Shan't be the first time," he grumbled. "Likely won't be the last. And who knows? Perhaps your choice was not a mistake, after all."

"What may I do to atone for the trouble I have caused you?" she asked.

He grinned at her. "The answer approaches."

Patience looked up to view the slow, but steady advance of Lord de Wendenal. Despite her best efforts to remain calm, she was immediately on her feet, pressing her damp palms deeper into her gloves.

Printed in Great Britain
by Amazon